CW01455007

Carnations
in
Lisbon

C. A. Wilson

Bisham
Books

BISHAM BOOKS
128, City Road, London EC1V 2NX
www.bishambooks.com

First published in the UK by Bisham Books in 2025
Cover Design by Peter Long
Copyright © C. A. Wilson, 2025

ISBN: 978-1-0682375-8-4

For Peter

In memory of Celeste Martins Caeiro
"Celeste dos Cravos"

CARNATIONS IN LISBON

Table of Contents

Doesn't everything die at last, and too soon?

Tell me, what is it you plan to do

with your one wild and precious life?

Mary Oliver

CARNATIONS IN LISBON

PROLOGUE

I slipped into the water and swam to the opposite bank and back again, my strokes barely breaking the surface. The jacaranda tree spread gracefully behind me. For years in the harsh English climate it had refused to flower, but now the first fragile blossoms had appeared, a washed-out blue against bare brown branches – like a symbol of hope. I walked back up the lawn to the house, drops of moisture glistening on my skin. The arched glass doors that used to remind my mother of her home in Lisbon stood open to the August heat.

Joaquim's words came back to me. "Life... love... death." He had taken me to the crypt, a little mausoleum of the kind that Catholics build to bury their dead. A stone angel stood over it, gazing into eternity.

"What was he like, my father?" I asked him.

"He was brave. He was stupid. He was fragile."

I showered and dressed. The memory of that foreign cemetery drove me out into the relentless sunshine of an English heatwave towards a different kind of graveyard, where new mounds garlanded with fresh flowers were laid among crumbling, illegible headstones. Two sets of ashes lay here, with a plaque above:

Douglas Matthews 1942-2011; Elena Matthews 1952-2016.

On the first page of her book, my mother had quoted Oscar Wilde:

"The truth is rarely pure and never simple."

The words seemed like a message to me from the other side of death. Only now did I understand all that she had never said...

1

LAPA, LISBON

2019

The man stopped talking and motioned me to sit down. "Welcome, please," he said.

All the heads around the table turned. I sat. He continued his speech in Portuguese. I didn't know why I was there and didn't understand a word.

My flight that morning had been delayed. I had managed to book a window seat on the plane, so had a great view of the Atlantic Ocean as we swooped out over it and then turned back to the runway at Lisbon airport. The River Tagus appeared below, and a giant aqueduct snaked across the land beyond. But a voice inside my head kept repeating *"Trust no-one."* The voice was my mother's, and her words the mantra on which I had been raised: *"Trust no-one."*

She had died three years earlier, but two weeks ago I had received a letter addressed to her. Entirely in Portuguese, it invited me to the reading of a will to take place in Lisbon. I had never heard of any of the people mentioned and assumed it must be a mistake. Then a smart-looking lawyer called Laurinda Esteves da Fonseca had set up a video call and persuaded me to come.

Because the plane was late, I had missed the briefing meeting she promised with her boss, the notary and head of the firm, Cristóvão Teixeira do Nascimento. So I sat, and wondered what was the point of being here at all if the proceedings were to be conducted entirely in a language I didn't understand, and I was convinced that the whole thing would turn out to be an embarrassing case of mistaken identity anyway.

Then Laurinda spoke in English and I started to pay attention.

"The last Will and Testament of Duarte Barros de Almeida", she said, presumably translating the words of the man I assumed to be the notary, Cristóvão, for my benefit.

"I, Duarte Inácio Barros de Almeida, of Quinta das Magnólias, Rua de São Domingos, Lapa, Lisbon, born on the seventh day of February 1935, being of sound mind and in good health, hereby declare this document to be my last will and testament, revoking all prior wills and codicils."

Her English accent was near perfect and delivered in a voice that was business-like and crisp. Duarte Inácio Barros de Almeida was one of the names mentioned in my mystery letter, but not one that I knew.

The notary continued in Portuguese. Not being able to understand what he said, I studied his appearance. His silvery grey hair waved back over a finely lined forehead that sloped down towards an aquiline nose. His mouth was firm and small over a clean-cut chin. He emanated an air of calmness and competence.

Next to him sat Laurinda, looking as stylish and confident as she had on my screen. She came across as someone who worked not only efficiently but with flair, her manner at once brisk and obliging. I also had a sense that her boundaries were well in place in terms of how much help she was prepared to give, and where lines might be drawn. To put it bluntly, I imagined her to be a great ally to have on your side, but you wouldn't want to fall out with her.

"Artigo número um," said Cristóvão: *"Declaração. Declaro que sou legalmente capaz de fazer este testamento e faço isso por minha livre vontade, sem qualquer influência indevida."*

"Article number one: Declaration," translated Laurinda. "I declare that I am legally capable of making this will, and I do this of my own free volition without any undue influence."

Her statement told me nothing new, so as Cristóvão started speaking in Portuguese again, I studied two men who sat opposite me.

One had a thatch of grey hair that sprang from a low forehead over a craggy face, with two deep lines between eyebrows that almost met in the middle. More furrows carved dual pathways from his bulbous nose down to a wide mouth. His shoulders may once have been broad but now sagged like the flesh around his jowly jawline. It was an ugly and yet fascinating face, with a hint of power that might have been dynamic but was now in decline.

I could see from the notes I had brought and placed on the table in front of me that this must be either Marco Aurélio Barros de Almeida or Joaquim Afonso Mendonça Gonçalves.

The other man was younger, about my own age, with brown hair. He caught my eye and smiled politely. His eyes were an unusual colour, like amber, almost the same shade as his lightly tanned skin.

The two lawyers continued to alternate between them until Cristóvão started a sentence that didn't get as far as interpretation, because the older man stood up so suddenly that he knocked over his chair. As it crashed to the floor, he let out a torrent of words in a guttural-sounding voice that contrasted with the sibilant pronunciation I had heard so far.

Then he turned fierce eyes on me. He spat out a string of words, and as he did so the jowls shook with rage and the shaggy brows plunged into a tormented frown.

I didn't understand what he said, but went rigid in my chair.

No one else reacted at all. Cristóvão sat impassively a few feet away, until the old man lurched across the table and crashed his fist onto it directly in front of him. The lawyer flinched but his steady eyes barely fluttered. Then the man stormed out of the room and tried to slam the door behind him. However, it had a slow-closing mechanism that denied him his dramatic exit.

Everyone was silent. Nobody looked at each other. Then the younger man smiled at me again, and gave a little shrug. It defused the menace of the scene, as if it were nothing out of the ordinary. I realised my fists were clenched on the table, and relaxed them into my lap.

Laurinda stood up, her chair making a slight scraping sound in contrast to the crash of the other one as it had hit the floor. She set the upended seat methodically back in its place, sat down on her own, and resumed the translation, unruffled, in her decisive voice.

"In accordance with the provisions of Portuguese law, specifically those governing the reserved share, I expressly exclude my brother Joaquim Afonso Mendonça Gonçalves from inheriting any part of my assets except the house in which he resides at forty-two, *Beco Barbadela, Mouraria, Lisbon*. This decision is based on the grounds permitted by law including his incarceration in prison and his actions against our family."

The angry old man was clearly Joaquim, whom I now understood was to be cut off from his brother Duarte's estate except for a house which he already occupied. I gauged from this that Duarte must have been worth a substantial amount, otherwise why would his brother be so enraged about inheriting a property?

I wished I was one of his heirs, and not a complete

stranger present only because of a clerical error. I wasn't looking forward to the moment when that became clear, even though it was not my fault. Any kind of inheritance would have been welcome to me at this point in time. I lived in a lovely house on the Thames, a mansion in fact, inherited from my parents. All of my possessions, my books, and my childhood memories were there. The problem was that they hadn't owned the freehold, and in three years' time the lease would expire. The bright side was that the house was worth so little on account of its short tenure that there had been no death duties to pay.

Cristóvão took over again in the lilting intonation which was much easier on my ears than Joaquim's harsh accent:

"Todos os meus bens patrimoniais, incluindo investimentos e outros ativos, deverão ser divididos de forma igual entre o meu tutelado Marco Aurélio Barros de Almeida e a minha sobrinha, Elena Correia Guterres mas se algum deles falecer antes de mim, então este legado passará para o outro."

This time I heard my mother's name, Elena Correia Guterres. I listened hard, but again the complexity of the language defeated me. My heart seemed to lurch as I realised that the moment might have arrived when I would be unmasked as a fraud. I wondered whether there were any tourist sights nearby that I could visit to fill up the hours between the end of my part in this business, which was surely imminent, and my scheduled departure time.

Laurinda began her translation. "All my estate

including investments and other assets shall be divided equally between my ward Marco Aurélio Barros de Almeida and my niece Elena Correia Guterres but if either of them dies before me, then this bequest shall pass to the other."

I tried to work out what had just been said. Was my mother Duarte's niece? But didn't Laurinda just say that if she died the bequest would pass to Marco, whom I now knew to be the man with amber eyes sitting opposite me?

I thought back over the years and could remember only one trip to Portugal. It was all we could afford in terms of foreign travel. I was twelve years old and recalled beaches and cafes, with both parents present. I couldn't bring to mind anything useful at all, and certainly not having been introduced to any Portuguese uncles.

But why was her past never discussed in our family? Did she and my father live together in Portugal, or had they moved to England soon after meeting? Was it a whirlwind romance? Who were her family? I found it hard to believe that I knew virtually nothing about them at all prior to their lives in the Oxfordshire village where I grew up, and that I had never asked these questions while they were still alive to answer them.

I was also wishing I had flown in last night and arrived in time for my briefing with the notary. Then I might have some idea of why I was here.

2

MOURARIA, LISBON

2019

Joaquim sat in his customary place outside the bar. The free tapas that habitually constituted his lunch were eaten and the wine drunk – more than half a bottle when he had intended to have only a glass. The euphoria of that first drink was not something that could be recaptured by the second, nor the third, and definitely not a fourth. But after the scene at the lawyer's office, he needed another.

He signalled to Filipe, the owner of this bar that was like his second home. "Bring me a *Beirão*. Without..."

"Without lemon," said Filipe. "I know. What did your doctor say?"

"Never mind that, I need a *digestivo*. For my heartburn."

"Exactly," said Filipe. "And what did *Doutor* Henrique say about your heartburn and your drinking?"

Joaquim grunted. The sooner this conversation was over, the sooner he would get his drink. "I will have a pain-wracked old age or no old age at all."

"Let me get you a nice glass of milk."

"I have my heartburn and you your profits to worry about. You're supposed to sell me as many drinks as I will take. The drunker drunks get, the more they buy, don't you know that?"

Filipe sighed and went inside. Joaquim felt dazed and depressed. The honeyed tang of *Licor Beirão* would do him good after the stress of the morning he had just spent at the law offices of *Teixeira do Nascimento & Devillet*. He also felt slightly ashamed that he had lost his temper – again – but on the other hand, considering the wrong that had been done to him, they were fortunate he hadn't smashed the place up before walking out.

Two weeks had passed since he received their letter. At first, he assumed it was from debt collectors, and almost threw it away. But although he had no intention of paying any debts, and indeed no means of doing so, in the end he opened it to find out how big a threat this one might be.

At first, it was baffling. He saw the word *irmão* – brother, whose brother? One of Joaquim's brothers wanted nothing more to do with him and the other was dead (but these were thoughts that must be suppressed). It talked of a will of which he was apparently a beneficiary. He was being invited to the reading. Surely only those who inherit are asked to attend such an event, he had thought. And then he had seen another name: *Duarte Barros de Almeida.*

The letter had dropped from his hands. Duarte was dead. It was written there in black and white, but Joaquim had not been able to accept it at the time. Attending the reading of the will this morning had confirmed the news he dreaded. All chance of reconciliation was over now; he would never get his brother back. Joaquim realised he had not lost hope in nearly fifty years, always nursing the possibility that his hero and guide through their childhood, and the one who had tried to teach him right from wrong (though on that count he had failed), would one day welcome him back into the family. Now that prospect was gone.

He found himself reliving a time in the hills where there were horses and dogs, when he had raised a new hunting rifle to claim his first wild boar. Duarte had praised him then, and the recollection of the way it had felt to earn the approval of this hero-figure half a lifetime ago untied all the knots in his gut, leaving only sadness in their place.

As he dwelt on the past, his attention was yanked back to the present by the sight of a face. It peered at him briefly from behind a cork oak tree on the other side of the street, and was gone before recognition sank in. Had it been Lourenço?

He could have got up, walked across the road, and looked behind the tree, but the stone walls of a jail cell from years ago seemed to close around him and took the energy out of his limbs. It was always cold there, except in summer, when the prisoners fried, and the stink of unwashed bodies mixed with drying blood and excrement tainted the air. Sometimes sudden noises penetrated the gloom, like the jeer of a guard or the cries of other prisoners. Once it was Lourenço who screamed, and Joaquim would never forget that sound. As the memory permeated through the mental barriers he had built to repress it, guilt engulfed him.

But who would blame him for what he had done? In prison it had to be every man for himself, surely that was the rule to live by. Should he have accepted the blame instead of denouncing the boy? Lourenço had been no more than a teenager then, thirty years ago, and Joaquim a man who should have been living his life in its prime instead of languishing in jail. He was not that person anymore. Now he mostly sat in bars waiting for time to pass between one drink and the next.

His thoughts scattered in shafts of sunlight that speared through the branches of a jacaranda tree above. Why was Lourenço here? Was it indeed his old cellmate he had seen, or his own decaying mind playing tricks on him?

The face didn't show itself again. For a moment, it had made him forget, but now the shock hit him again, with full force: Duarte was dead. Duarte was rich, therefore Joaquim should be rich. This will that left everything to people he had never heard of was all wrong; Duarte's legacy should have come to him. His mind wandered towards paying off debts – and there was land, where he could build a holiday village, swimming pools, tennis courts, maybe even an equestrian centre. Was he to get nothing at all?

And then he remembered that he had not been forgotten: Duarte had left him the house where he was allowed to live only by courtesy of that unyielding brother. Is that what the old lawyer had said? He was to have that place and not be turned out of it by the Englishwoman and the man with yellow eyes? His mind turned this way and that – rich, poor, a little bit better off, homeless, which would it be?

3

LAPA, LISBON
2019

The reading of the will was finished and despite Laurinda's English translation, I was none the wiser. As everyone else left the room, Cristóvão the notary asked me to stay. I turned my chair to face him, hoping to find out at last who all these people were and whether, as I suspected, I should not have been invited at all.

"Your father," he began, "Álvaro Tomás Aguiar de Almeida."

I stopped him there. "I think there's some mistake. My father was Douglas Matthews. He was English. It's my mother who was Portuguese."

He stared at me. His mild expression never seemed to change. It had probably been developed over years to soothe recalcitrant clients. I knew the feeling; I had clients of my own to manage.

"I'm sorry to have put you to the trouble." As I said

it, I thought of the amount I had spent to get here; the plane ride, the taxis at either end. "Obviously I'm not the person you're looking for."

"You are Elena Correia Guterres?"

"No," I said. "That was my mother. I'm Helen Matthews."

He looked down and sifted through some papers.

"I see. They change your name."

I shook my head. How could I make him understand? His English wasn't great. "I'm Elena's daughter. My name is Helen."

"Perhaps when your English father adopt you?"

Now it was my turn to stare. Me, adopted?

"You have sisters?" he asked.

"No. I'm an only child."

"Then you are Elena. The daughter she have is Elena. They take you to England and change your name."

I stared at the woodgrain in the table. It swirled into a finely polished knot. I couldn't even begin to formulate questions. I was still waiting for the flaw which would tell me this was all a mistake.

He continued in his broken English and I tried to understand. "You not know? About Álvaro? She not tell you?"

"I've never heard of anyone called Álvaro."

"I can tell you some history?"

I wasn't sure I was ready to hear more but I nodded. Listening to him would give me time to think.

"Your father Álvaro is a hero," he went on. "He die for his country, fighting the *Estado Novo*."

"The Revolution," I said. I knew all about the *Estado Novo*. It was a fascist regime here in Portugal, overthrown in 1974. My mother was a journalist and had written a novel about it. Although it was a long time since I had read her book, I remembered the setting.

"Your father he give his life. In 1971. Three years after, the fight is won. But for Álvaro... is too late. But Elena have his baby. You. Elena." He looked down at his papers. "Helen." He put the emphasis on the last syllable and didn't pronounce the 'H', making it sound the same as 'Elena' but without the 'a'. "Laurinda, she tell me you have a new name. I excuse myself, I forget. We have an address for Elena, her house where she lived. My letter find you. You live there also?"

"Yes. But you're saying I was called Elena?" This was crazy.

He spoke in a matter-of-fact way, as if he were providing me with a change of address, not a whole new identity. "Yes. This *advocacia* – this business of lawyers – it was of my father. He was the notary for the family of Almeida and now is me. He tell me the history. So, Elena... Helen. It sound the same, no?"

It did, the way he said it. Hearing her name coupled with mine suddenly reminded me of the times we were together, that were gone forever now. For a moment, my throat swelled and I was unable to speak. Then I forced the emotion down. There were so many questions. "Who is the Elena in the will? Is it my mother? Why am I here?"

"Is you, Elena," he said. She call you Elena, she not

17

marry Álvaro before he die, so you have the name the same: Elena Correia Guterres."

The walls of the room were fading to grey as the sun turned to shade outside. I felt cold, but whether from shock or the lowering afternoon temperature I wasn't sure.

"I really think you have the wrong person," I insisted. "I'm Helen Matthews."

He smiled back at me. It was a polite and professional smile but I thought I detected genuine sympathy there too.

" There was danger," he said. "Portugal was er... finished for your mother. She desire the new life in England. With you. And Douglas. The English."

This was the first piece of information that I knew to be true. I had always assumed she met my father in Lisbon when he worked at the Embassy there, and he had brought her back to England with him. Wives tended to follow their husbands in their day.

The notary was talking again. I tried to follow.

"They are brothers, Duarte, Álvaro, and Joaquim. The one who leave in a rage. Two brothers dead, and Joaquim out of the will. No inheritance for him."

"If Álvaro was my father," I said slowly piecing it together in my mind, "which I don't accept, and if he was the brother of Duarte, then Joaquim would be... my uncle." It was a preposterous and objectionable thought.

"Is correct," he said.

"That's impossible!" I studied the shiny swirl in the wooden table again. Tentacles of doubt were creeping through me.

"Is correct," he repeated.

"But they all have different surnames."

"In England you take only the father name, yes? Here we take father, mother, *avó* – the mother of the parents..."

"Grandmother," I said mechanically.

"Or grandfather. For the honour of any *parente*. Relative?"

I nodded. He looked relieved, perhaps glad to be back in the realm of things that could be easily explained.

"So the children have family names different. Is normal."

It was too confusing for me to follow closely but I could grasp the concept. I made what I thought was a more relevant point. "Joaquim looks nothing like me. How could we possibly be related?"

"Joaquim he is adopted also. Like you. No relation of the blood, only legal. I am sorry. Is complicated for you. The Almeidas, they make him like a son, very good to him. But Joaquim, always different, a bad boy. He come in the war, a *refugiado*."

"A refugee?"

"Yes, a refugee."

One outlandish fact followed another. I felt as if I was drowning. "How do I know all this is true? About me, I mean, and this man Álvaro?"

"If you need *evidência*... I don't know. Is what my father say."

He looked tired. It must have been a strain to tell

me all this, and not the type of conversation he was used to having with clients. On my part, I felt exhausted. Who could I trust? I felt an irrational flash of resentment towards both parents for no longer being alive to answer my questions.

He tried again. "Your father Álvaro is brother of Duarte Barros de Almeida. He leave half to you and half to Marco."

"The other man who was here. The younger one."

He nodded.

"Is he a relation?"

"Like a son to Duarte. No relation. You as niece, you share all his..." He searched for the right word. "All his things. Money, Properties. A boat I think. With Marco. Duarte a rich man."

"What evidence do you have of all this?"

He shrugged. "You not pay, the family Almeida pay you. Why you need *evidência*? You take the money. Is yours."

4

COIMBRA UNIVERSITY

1971

The great hall was dark. Someone had placed candles on the stage. Their glow shimmered across the face of the poet, and shadows played across the woman's hair as she spoke. Her soft voice belied cutting words.

Suddenly overhead lights blazed. There was noise and turbulence. Some people blinked in the glare while others backed away from two uniformed figures who had flicked the switches. The blue and grey of their garments identified them as the riot police, the most violent of all the forces. The poet held her place onstage, staring at them coolly. This was not the first time for her, Elena thought. She looked around for Álvaro.

Gabriela, her roommate, was being enveloped in the arms of her protective boyfriend, Luís. His shoulders were broad and he was taller than most of the students in the room. He seemed never to be afraid, and always ready for action.

"*Nome e documentos!*" The guards moved around the room, taking the names of everyone present and checking their papers. One was stocky, his protruding belly straining against a thick leather belt from which hung a truncheon and a holster for his gun. His profile was shaped like a quarter-moon, with a hooked nose describing an arc that rounded over a double chin. His eyes were small and expressionless.

Luís stood in front of him, his legs planted uncompromisingly apart. He pushed Gabriela behind him. When asked for his papers, he stared defiantly.

The guard raised his cosh, and Luís, moving just a little bit more quickly, grabbed the man's wrist. The boy was strong. The guard lost all his bullishness and looked frightened.

Then Álvaro was there. "Come on, Luís," he said, persuasively, with a smile. The tension eased slightly. "Let the man see your ID. Why not?"

Luís wavered and let the guard go, first forcibly lowering the hand that held the weapon. He handed over his identity document.

It was only then that Elena noticed the other man. He wore a dark suit, meant to blend inconspicuously, but out of place in this room full of denim-clad students. After looking at the identity card, he took a notebook from his pocket and wrote a line. The hook-nosed guard in the blue uniform handed the paper back and then turned to Elena.

She felt an urge to be brave and audacious, like Luís. At the same time, a primitive instinct to run kicked in.

Álvaro nodded at her and she pulled out her document and handed it to the guard. She watched Álvaro as he held out his own. He took her hand and squeezed it.

"No holding hands!" barked the guard. "You – over there." He motioned to Álvaro. "Her – there!" He pointed to a bench by the wall.

Elena stood firm. This was her first encounter with these officials and, like Luís, she would not be bullied. It was her test. Then Álvaro gave her a gentle push. "Go," he said, nodding in the direction indicated by the guard. He turned and walked away to his own designated spot. Momentarily unsettled, she moved to where they had sent her and sat down.

Then, under the dazzle of the lights, she saw a tall, stooped figure swathed in black, hovering under the archway of the open doors. Gomes, the monitor. Why was he here? The man in the dark suit had moved to stand next to him. Gomes's eyes surveyed the room methodically. They rested on her for a moment and she saw a flicker of recognition. She looked away.

Three months ago, on her first day at the university, she had explored the ancient college buildings, winding through corridors and reading plaques on old stone statues. She saw a youth place some leaflets on a bench. She now knew him to be Álvaro de Almeida, but that day he had walked quickly off when he saw her. She had picked up one of the fliers. The paper was cheap and flimsy, and the print small and pale. The headline read: *'Paz, Liberdade, Democracia.'* It was signed *Resistência Acadêmica.*

Who were they, this Academic Resistance? At home

in Chiado, her father had reluctantly agreed to receive the *República* along with his other daily newspapers. It was too political for his tastes. Sometimes it hinted at the existence of an underground group formed by academics across the country's universities and colleges. She had come to Coimbra University determined to find them, and this was the first clue.

Before she could read what the leaflet had to say about peace, liberty, and democracy, a gaunt individual stopped in front of her. He had narrow eyes and an aquiline nose set into a sneer, giving the impression of sniffing something bad. He snatched the paper out of her hand and took the others from the table. He stood too close to her.

"I am sorry you have been troubled by this filth," he said. His manner was obsequious, but somehow menacing at the same time. "You are?"

"Elena Guterres," she said. Something about him made her want to give away as little information as possible.

He repeated her name, making it sound like an affliction. "I am Lázaro Menezes Gomes," he added. "Faculty Director. And Monitor."

She nodded politely and so did he. The monitors were appointed to look out for the safety and wellbeing of the students. Did that mean spying on them too?

"I wish you well with your studies, *Senhorita* Guterres," he said, and walked stiffly away down the corridor, his black garments swishing around him like the wings of a giant bat.

Now he was here at a student event. She had not

seen him attend one before. Was he part of the raid? It was only then that she realised that the suited man standing next to him must belong to the secret police force known as the PIDE, which relied on informers like Gomes to betray people like herself and Álvaro.

On the stage, the other guard was challenging the poet. Taller than Hook-nose, his body suggesting sinewy muscle under the blue serge of his uniform. He grasped the woman's slim arm and pulled her roughly to her feet. Then Álvaro mounted the steps and spoke to him. Elena couldn't hear what was said, but after a moment the guard let go and walked away. He called to his associate and they both left. Gomes and the man from the PIDE had disappeared.

Then Álvaro was back at Elena's side. The second memorable event on that first day at Coimbra had been meeting him again at a performance like this one, and they had talked for an hour. He was in the year above hers. Eventually, when he began to feel he could trust her, he revealed he was the leader of the *Resistência Acadêmica* here at the university. Over the following months he had become her friend.

He said nothing, but stared at her, his face inches away, and in that moment their relationship changed. It had been an easy friendship for both so far, and they trusted each other to the point where they could share their most inadmissible thoughts, like how to bring down the government. They shared a rebellious spirit and she liked everything about him: his manner, his way of thinking, and most of all his pale eyes, where light seemed to fluctuate as his emotions changed.

She was also aware that she found him physically attractive but was determined to ignore it. It seemed to Elena that if her own family were anything to go by, married women must be subsumed into the service of their husbands and offspring. She wanted none of it, and had decided never to marry at all. Therefore she could not take the risk of getting involved in a romantic relationship.

"What did you say to them?" she asked, looking up at him. "You got them to leave, didn't you?"

He didn't reply. She had the sense that in spite of their closeness, there were areas of his life that he chose not to share with her. Then, as he held her gaze, something new happened. In that moment, she became half of a pair and no longer alone. There was a sense of certainty that the space they inhabited together was different from anything she had known before. It was not what she had planned, and not welcome in the context of the life she had imagined for herself, but there was no question that somehow it would have to be managed.

They were suspended in time, and then the spell dissolved as people interrupted. Álvaro let go of her but didn't move away. It seemed inevitable that she would go with him to his room that night instead of returning to her own. That first time, she was smuggled past the concierge in the men's quarters with his scarf over her head, pretending to be a boy. Later they would devise an easier route which went between their windows, around the back of the campus and over a wall in the darkness. Until then, she had believed that Coimbra University and the *Resistência Acadêmica* gave her all the meaning and purpose that she could ever want, but that night she learned that meaning and purpose were nothing without this.

We may struggle to identify at what point our actions take us away from our original plans and ambitions. Was it their love for each other that mapped their fate, or the poet's words, or the risks they took in the months that followed? Later Elena would brood over these things, wondering if just one action had not been taken, or one idea left unconceived, might Álvaro's life have ended differently and lasted longer?

But tonight was for adventure and discovery, and they gave no thought to the future at all.

5

MOURARIA, LISBON

2019

Today they sat inside the bar instead of at his usual table on the terrace. The sun danced through the branches of the jacaranda overhead, something that he usually enjoyed, but this time Joaquim didn't want to be seen. His house would have offered a safer option but he was ashamed to let a visitor witness the decaying mess where he lived, especially this one with her coiffed hair and smart clothes. Laurinda da Fonseca had contacted him only hours after he stormed out of the will-reading. Then they all knew, she told him, that brother Duarte had left everything to the Englishwoman and the man Marco, whoever he was, except for the house that Joaquim was embarrassed to show to visitors.

By the time Laurinda called, he had done little more than drink since leaving the offices of *Teixeira do*

Nascimento & Devillet, and had not even begun to think through the implications of the will. She had ended their conversation quickly after fixing a time to meet, and he sensed that there was something irregular about it. Why were they not at her office? So they had agreed on a table inside Filipe's bar as the place where they were least likely to see anyone she knew.

Now, in the dim light that filtered through the windows, and with a clearer head (he had taken only one drink today, the hair of the dog to sharpen his mind), they each sat over a coffee, hers long and watery with a little bit of skimmed milk, and his an intense black brew. He looked at her from time to time as she talked but mostly stared down at the dregs in his cup.

"The rules here are strict," she explained, speaking quickly in her precise voice. "Some of the relatives are guaranteed a portion of the estate whatever the deceased expressed in the will. It's called the *'legítima'*. I'm sorry for your loss." She added the last sentence peremptorily as if remembering that they were talking about a family bereavement here, not just an interesting legal challenge.

I'm not sorry, thought Joaquim silently, although he didn't mean it; something had torn in him the day Duarte sent him away and the pain would never heal. It was then that he had really lost his big brother, more than now he was dead. Years ago, when he had left the prison, he had asked for Duarte's help in rebuilding his life. He had been rejected. *Mamã* would have helped, he had protested to Duarte, but she was dead. At the invocation of her name, the rich son relented only enough to allow the poor one to occupy a house the family owned in the rundown Moorish Quarter, the *Mouraria*, a place where they had once lodged their servants.

He became aware that Laurinda was continuing the stiff legal narrative that he struggled to follow. "In the case where a deceased person has no surviving spouse, descendants, or ascendants, the inheritance will pass to other relatives in accordance with the hierarchy established by Portuguese law. The first to inherit would be the siblings. And that would be the whole estate, not just a reserved portion."

He looked up. He had not managed to grasp all of the formal terminology, but one thing seemed clear. "*Eu sou o irmão!*" he interrupted. "I am the brother! There was one other, but he died." His voice trailed off. They were touching on events that required more than one drink before being allowed access to his mind. There was a stain on the table in front of him in the shape of a glass. He wondered if it had contained *Beirão* and wished he had some in front of him.

"If there were a wife, children, or parents, they would get a share before you. According to the will there is only a niece, Helen. The Englishwoman."

"The one at the reading," he grunted, looking away. "I had a sister once, Ana Belinha, but she died. Helen is her child maybe."

As he said the words, he reflected that it is a sad man who does not know whether his own sister had a child nor was present at her death. The niece didn't look like the dark-eyed Ana Belinha but perhaps his sister had married a man who was pale, like Álvaro, and then moved to England. There were so many things he didn't know, and so much that he never would. His shoulders, which had lifted at the possibility of winning a part of the inheritance, returned to their customary slump.

"Then you might be entitled to half the estate. Half would be hers."

He sat up straight again. "What about the other man, Marco?"

"He was not adopted by Duarte. He is not entitled to anything except what Duarte bequeathed him in the will, and that would be reduced by the *legítima*."

Joaquim was distracted for a moment from her grindingly technical monologue. So, he was thinking, while the Almeida parents had adopted Joaquim, brother Duarte had not done the same for this Marco, who was about to inherit an estate that should by rights pass to Joaquim. Why? Did that mean they cared for him more or less? Then he realised what the clever lawyer appeared to be telling him and said defiantly, "So I get the *legítima*!"

Now it was she who looked into her coffee. "By law there are certain grounds for setting the *legítima* aside. One is '*Exclusão por Deserdação*': an heir might be disqualified if he has failed in his duties to the deceased, like neglect or abuse. It has to be determined by a court, and the process would involve legal proceedings to prove the allegations."

Neglect? But it was Duarte who had neglected him,

surely, not the other way round. He had been on the receiving end of plenty of abuse in his life and had given as good as he got, and more – but never towards brother Duarte. He took a breath to speak but she went on quickly without looking at him.

"It might also apply in situations where an heir has committed a serious offence against the deceased; physical violence or a public insult, for instance." She glanced up and her impenetrable eyes rested on him intimidatingly. "Are there any such offences?"

He paused, nodded, and then sighed.

"If I am to help you, then you have to tell me," she persisted, always the lawyer in her tone and demeanour.

He wrestled with himself. What could he admit to having done? Where might it lead? He tried to form words, but what came out was, "Do you like *Beirão*?" His insides were starting to burn and what he really needed was a shot of that comforting herbal remedy.

She shook her head impatiently and said, "*Senhor* Gonçalves, I'm here to see if we can find some grounds to overturn your disinheritance. I can be on your side. You have to trust me."

The word 'trust' stung, dragging up decades of betrayal: the duplicity of others, his own vile treachery, and his self-destructive behaviour through it all. He couldn't look at her.

"Now tell me what led to this problem," she persisted, "and we will see if there are any grounds to reverse it."

He tried to haul his mind out of the calamity that

was his miserable life, and selected his words carefully. "I did time. Prison."

"I know. It was mentioned in the will. What for?"

"Stealing." He shrugged and added. "Violence, a bit. Well I had to."

"Did you steal from your brother?"

"No!" he cried defensively. "Of course not."

"Were you violent towards him?"

"Never!"

"Did it damage him in any way, your prison sentence?"

He shook his head.

"Then that may not be an impediment. Is there anything else?"

"There is one more thing."

She waited. He said nothing. She raised her brows in a way that commanded him to speak.

"I am not his brother."

"What?"

"I was adopted. A refugee. I don't even know who my real parents were. Does that mean I can't inherit?"

"It makes no difference," she continued, brushing the issue aside. "The law treats adopted children the same as biological ones. Now is there anything else you have to tell me? I must know all the grounds that might be raised."

All that was left to say were the things that could not be said, so he shook his head. Only one question remained in his mind. "Why would you do this?" he asked. Suspicion had become a habit with him.

"I don't want to be an assistant lawyer in a small

firm all my life. I will start this outside of my job and if we are successful, it will set me up in my own practice. Not immediately," she backtracked. "First, I will undertake some private investigation, and no-one will know. Once I am sure we have grounds, I will leave the offices of *Teixeira do Nascimento & Devillet*. I will form *Esteves da Fonseca Advogadas* – in my own name – and you will be my first case."

He watched her face carefully as she spoke. The explanation seemed to be a reasonable one. She reached into a shiny grey laptop case on the table beside her, and pulled out a card. It showed her name, the name of her law firm, just as she had described, and the phone number she had called him from. Why would she lie? There was one further issue though. "I don't have money to pay you."

"I will take a share. *Honorários condicionados ao sucesso*: no win, no fee."

She was energetic, young, qualified, and wanted to get him his rightful inheritance. He wouldn't have to pay. What was there to lose? He held out his wrinkled hand with its ungroomed nails and shook her immaculately manicured one.

6

REUTERS, LISBON

1971

The sun rose from a moonless night as they left Coimbra behind. A mauve glow spread from the east, shifting colours until the whole sky flushed pink and gold like a sunset. The air was fresh and warm and would not become oppressive even in the heat of the day; October was a kind month in Portugal.

At moments like this, Álvaro found it hard to steel himself for the battles he had to fight. The soul-soothing quality of this special light seemed to enter him, and was far removed from the sheer grit of his daily struggle against the *Estado Novo* regime.

Téo, a medical student in the same year, sat next to him at the wheel of a smart Mercedes that he had received on his eighteenth birthday.

"Your *papai* must think a lot of you, buying you a car like this," Álvaro said.

Téo laughed. "Not if he knew what I use it for."

"I told Duarte about it. I thought he might feel some pressure to do the same for me."

"And will he?"

"It appears not."

Sixteen years Álvaro's senior, Duarte had become head of the family after his father died in the flu epidemic of 1957. Aged five at the time, Álvaro remembered little of that father and nothing of the mother who had died giving birth to him. Apart from the attention of some female servants, he and his sister, Ana Belinha, had been raised without any parental care except for the benign supervision of their elder brother Duarte.

"What would you want if he gave you one?" Téo asked, moving the gear stick up into top gear as they left the confines of Coimbra.

"I'd have the Citroën DS. The way it sweeps down at the back. It's a work of art. Did you know it's designed by an Italian sculptor?"

"No."

"And it has hydropneumatics and disc brakes." Álvaro liked to talk about cars, especially during times of stress. It calmed him.

Another avenue of escape was Elena, who sat in the seat behind. Until he met her, his life had been consumed with attaining his ambition to lead the *Resistência Acadêmica*, and formulating plans to bring down the *Estado Novo*. While thrilling at the time, that existence seemed sterile compared to the life they now shared. Alongside the radical direction of their political activities, their relationship was growing and bringing about fundamental changes in both of them. The two pathways fed into each other: she grew bolder and more confident every day, while he drew strength from her support and belief in him. Tenderness and trust knitted them together. It felt as if their two separate souls were combining not exactly into one, but to create a third entity that was the best of both. They were already committed to spending the rest of their lives together; it had hardly needed saying.

"Heard any more from Gomes?" said Téo over his shoulder to Elena.

"Lucky for him I haven't," she retorted. "I'll be ready for him next time."

Téo laughed but Álvaro sat still, looking straight ahead so that she wouldn't see the anxiety on his face. The evening before, some members of the *Resistência* had assembled in her room to listen to a shortwave radio that her father had provided to help with her language studies at school. No doubt *papai* had imagined her listening to English-spoken cultural programmes, but just as Téo's father had probably not envisaged the uses to which his son would put his car, he was sure that Elena's had not intended her to tune in to news bulletins from London about student unrest, like the one being broadcast that night. As she was translating the reports for the group, there was a sharp rap on the door. Luís stood up to open it. Álvaro switched off the radio.

"What is happening here?" The monitor, Lázaro Menezes Gomes, stood in the open doorway, his face bony in the lamplight.

Luís towered over him. "Just a language lesson, *Senhor Diretor,*" he replied in a convincingly friendly tone.

"And to whom does the radio set belong?"

Álvaro stayed quiet. It was best to say as little as possible and not draw attention to oneself. But Gomes had singled out Elena. He was looking at her. He knew this to be her room and her radio. She had no choice.

"It is mine, *Senhor Diretor,*" she said. Her voice was steady. "I hope we did not disturb you."

Álvaro knew what it cost her to be deferential to this objectionable man. He was relieved at her show of self-control. Luís tended to act on impulse, fired up by his sense of injustice, and Álvaro sometimes feared that Elena might do the same.

"Switch it back on," said Gomes. The hint of a smile warped his long face. "I would like to hear the language lesson also."

"The reception is bad," responded Elena. "We can't get any stations. *Senhor Diretor.*"

Álvaro's satisfaction at her quick thinking was replaced by anxiety at the director's reply.

"I will let the *Reitor* know that, *Senhorita* Correia Guterres." He enunciated her name slowly and stared at her. She didn't look away. "When I submit my report," he concluded.

Gomes worked directly under the newly appointed Rector of the University. No-one could be sure how serious a danger this might be, as the political leanings of the latest *Reitor* were not yet known. Most of the professors were sympathetic to the resistance but wary of admitting it. They wanted to keep their jobs.

The scene had brought home to Álvaro the risks they ran, and when Gomes and the rest had departed, he had tried to warn her.

"You know he could send us all to prison," he began.

"For listening to a radio?" she laughed. "You take him too seriously, *meu amor*."

"They make things up. Once he decides we're traitors, he can tell them whatever will get us charged. He probably has enough evidence already to make them believe any report he sends in. That's how these people work. He's been watching you." His shoulders were as tense as his heart was soft for her.

She put her arms around him, smiling. "Don't worry. I'll be careful."

He didn't want her reassurances. He felt that her sheltered upbringing blinded her to real danger. He, on the contrary, knew tragedy at first hand through the loss of both parents, Joaquim's traumatic history as a child refugee, and the spectacle of that brother's misdemeanours and resulting misery. Duarte too lived a dangerous life, sustaining a complex web of subterfuge that disguised his real allegiances from the powers that ruled, secretly defending victims of the regime while maintaining influential relationships with its leaders. As Álvaro matured, Duarte had gradually entrusted him with this knowledge of his double life, although their other brother Joaquim knew nothing of it at all. Through these things, Álvaro had gained a profound understanding that bad things do happen, even to innocents like Elena.

Listening to her laughing about Gomes with Téo, he felt both fear for her safety and guilt that he was partly responsible. Although it was true that she had been intent on joining the *Resistência Acadêmica*, without his help that might not have happened, and she would not now be here with him on this dangerous undertaking.

The muted colours of dawn had given way to the white glare of the mid-morning sun, and Téo turned off the road into a small village. "Shall we take a break?" he asked.

They stopped at Leiria, at a small bar outside the chapel of *Nossa Senhora da Encarnação*. The sun warmed their limbs while they drank coffee and ate free *petisco* snacks. A woman stared at the Mercedes as she crossed in front of it, balancing a stack of kindling on her head that was a third of her height and probably bore the same proportion to her weight. The old and the new, thought Álvaro; change is happening.

"Perhaps if we ask nicely, Our Lady will overthrow the regime," Téo said, looking up at the rows of stone arches at the front of the chapel. The sun cast the shadow of a cross against its white walls. There were times when Álvaro was not beyond wishing for divine intervention, atheist though he was along with the other two. He sighed, accepting that they would have to do the job themselves without the help of supernatural beings.

"I'll bet that when it happens half the population will credit God, no matter how many of us have risked our lives for it," Elena said wryly.

They laughed. Álvaro relaxed a little. He stretched out his arms and turned his face to the sun.

They were quiet for a moment, and then Téo said, "We can still turn back." He looked at Álvaro. "You don't have to do this."

Álvaro shook his head. Afraid, he certainly was, but determined even more so. "We can't miss this chance," he said. If the film can be made and got out of the country, whatever happens to me will have been worth it."

Through the machinations of passed messages, papers, and translations, word had reached them that a British journalist from the London School of Economics wanted to film a member of the *Resistência Acadêmica* speaking about atrocities witnessed at first hand. The interview would be filmed in Lisbon, and later included in a documentary to be shown in independent cinemas and universities across Britain. The greatest danger was the chance that it might reach the authorities in Lisbon.

Álvaro had taken up the challenge. He exposed Elena to the risk reluctantly, partly because he needed her skills as an interpreter and partly because she insisted. As always, Téo was commandeered willingly as their driver. Álvaro had become fond of the young doctor-in-training. While never pushing himself forward, the boy was always ready to help, especially with his treasured Mercedes.

"You must stay in the car," Álvaro continued. "If we're not back within an hour then leave without us. If anyone who looks like a PIDE approaches you, get away as fast as you can."

"Don't worry about me," swaggered Téo, but Álvaro saw him flinch at the name of the secret police force that terrorised the nation. The boy nodded and swallowed. Hoping that he was hiding his own fear more efficiently, Álvaro gripped his friend by the shoulder and smiled as reassuringly as he could.

The midday sun rode high in the sky by the time the huddled buildings of Lisbon came into view. Téo parked the car in a back street near the broad sweep of the *Avenida da Liberdade*, where the Reuters studio in which the interview would be filmed was located. Álvaro knew exactly where it was, but as he and Elena approached, they saw a pair of uniformed men standing outside. They hid among the Linden trees that proliferated along the central reservation, and watched. Had there been a tip-off?

One of the guards threw a cigarette butt onto the cobbles and ground it under his foot. The other looked up and down the avenue. Álvaro waited. Then a car horn blared and the men turned towards the sound. As they disappeared round a corner, Álvaro and Elena ran towards the building, ignoring for the moment the risk of attracting attention, and slipped through its doors. Álvaro's heart was leaping both from fear of the police and nerves about the interview ahead. He was not yet twenty-two and despite his bold attitude, he had never performed in front of a camera before.

Patrick, the journalist, was waiting in the reception hall and led them through a maze of corridors to a small, dark, room, equipped solely with a table, several chairs, and a large camera on a stand. Álvaro sat where instructed while the journalist adjusted spotlights so that his face would be in shadow. Patrick had assured him that he would appear as no more than a silhouette on the screen, to avoid identification if the film were ever to find its way to the PIDE, and Elena was placed out of sight of the camera altogether; Álvaro made sure of that. But her voice was still audible. That was a worry but unavoidable. The windowless room smelled stale, in spite of its air conditioning, and an unemptied ashtray had spilt its contents onto the table. Álvaro became aware that his hands were wet. He told himself to be calm, and glanced at Elena. She looked nervous too.

"Today I'm interviewing a student in Portugal," Patrick said to the camera. "He lives under an oppressive *Estado Novo* regime established by dictator António Salazar, and upheld after his death by President Marcelo Caetano. If our guest were to be identified, he might face a prison sentence for speaking to me today, so I won't share his name." He turned towards Álvaro. "Thank you for your bravery in joining us today."

Álvaro nodded and spoke, while Elena translated his words. "It would not be a prison sentence like in England, Patrick," he said. As soon as he opened his mouth, any vestige of nerves was eclipsed by all that he wanted to say. "They would beat me up, torture me. I might be killed, and no-one would be held to account for that. The guards can do what they want."

Patrick asked probing questions about the regime's brutality and oppression, and Álvaro laid bare their underground struggle towards freedom. When the interview was over, they slipped through a service entrance to rejoin Téo and get away as fast as possible.

The road where they had left him was short and narrow, lined by shuttered houses. It now lay silent in the heat of the afternoon sun and the car had gone. They felt conspicuous standing in the open and looked for somewhere to hide. Then the quietness was broken by the purr of an engine. The Mercedes rounded the corner and stopped in front of them.

"I followed to check you were okay," said Téo as they climbed inside. "Did you see the police? I came back and sounded my horn, then drove off before they could catch me. Did it work? Did they leave?"

Álvaro laughed. "Yes, my friend. I don't know what we would have done without you today."

They drove back to Coimbra chattering and laughing, with a sense of accomplishment in the air. It was a good feeling: a challenge faced and won. As they entered the city, the light faded to orange and purple on the opposite side of the sky to the morning's tints.

Much later that evening, Álvaro's excitement ebbed as he wondered whether anyone in the government's network of spies and despots would ever see the film, and whether they might find a way to identify him. Or Elena.

7

CHILTERN GRANGE, MEDMENHAM
2019

I sat in my study and looked out of the window. A pair of swans with their cygnets were making their way up the river. My neighbours and I referred to them as 'our' swans because these two nested each spring on a disused jetty nearby. Every year, colonies of the birds divided the Thames into territories and fought to defend their patch and their offspring from usurpers. This year, our swans had held their ground and produced a bumper harvest of seven grey bundles of fluffy feathers.

Thinking about their struggles brought back memories of a certain Englishman and his Portuguese wife who had raised their child on this stretch of the Thames. What battles must Elena and Douglas have fought to win our piece of this territory? For the moment, it looked as if the short lease would see me evicted from it before long.

A reminder popped up on my laptop. Cristóvão the notary had requested a meeting with Marco de Almeida and me. I wondered why. We had already been informed that the estate which we were to inherit from my supposed uncle, Duarte de Almeida, included a substantial amount of assets. According to the paperwork sent by the lawyers, there appeared to be two properties: a mansion in Lapa, which they told me was a prime area of Lisbon, and a lot of land in Sintra which came with a luxury villa. The bequest also included some classic cars, a large sum in cash and investments, and even a boat of some kind. In fact the only possession he had not left us was the house occupied by his otherwise disinherited brother Joaquim.

I had realised that if the estate was as large as it appeared to be, and if the other legatee, Marco, was willing to buy me out, and if I really was entitled to inherit, then I might be able to buy the freehold on my childhood home. Financial security at last? My shoulders relaxed a little. But I was still not convinced that I could be the daughter of a Portuguese activist or the niece of a rich man called Duarte. Douglas was my father. We were alike both in our fair complexions and our shared approach to life.

As Cristóvão's image flickered onto the screen, I wondered what new surprises this meeting would bring. Another yacht perhaps? Marco joined us, we greeted one another, and then the notary got straight down to business.

"I must tell you, Laurinda she has left this firm," he said in his clearly enunciated but imperfect English.

Had he set up the meeting just to tell us this? She seemed to do little more than translate for him.

"She make her own lawyer business," he went on. "She has the client. Joaquim Afonso Mendonça Gonçalves."

Marco and I both shifted our heads to one side, enquiringly and in unison. Presumably this involved us in some way, otherwise Cristóvão would not have addressed it.

"They desire to annul the, er, *deserdação*."

"The disinheritance," Marco said. His English seemed to be fluent, and he spoke it with hardly any accent at all.

"Thank you, Marco. The disinheritance. On the grounds of the *legítima*. That is the portion the family must inherit." He held up his hand reassuringly. "The action will fail. No problems. It is simple stage now. First, we make the *impugnação*. The protest..."

"The contestation," said Marco.

"The contestation. Next we tell them and they must reply. If they protest, then we get evidence, make our claim strong. We ask experts for the opinions. If they protest more, then a judge listen."

"A hearing," supplied Marco.

"Yes, a hearing." The notary looked straight ahead at us through the screen.

And so the landscape of my life changed again. My inheritance might be cancelled. I would not be able to buy the freehold and would lose my home. I stared at some abstract artworks on the walls behind Cristóvão and noted absently that he was in a different office this time.

"What are their grounds?" asked Marco in English, then repeated his question in Portuguese.

"Weak," said Cristóvão, "Very weak. They negate the, er, rupture in the family. The break. The case is nothing. It go away."

Over the years I had experienced dealings with various lawyers, and however helpful they appeared to be, one characteristic they seemed to share was a curious type of optimism: the conviction that their client's success was assured and would be quickly won. The trouble was that the legal team on the opposing side would be telling their own clients the same thing. Now, it was not possible that both could be right, and I had come to the conclusion that the lawyers were more interested in being hired than in winning their cases. I wondered to what extent this applied to Portuguese *advogados*, and to this one in particular.

"How long will it take, and what will the costs be?" I asked bluntly.

"It is some months each step," replied Cristóvão. "I give you details by writing and estimate of the cost. And then you decide how you desire to proceed. Do you have questions this moment?"

"Can we review it and come back to you?" asked Marco.

I nodded and said noncommittally, "That's fine with me".

The notary ended the meeting and I sat staring out

of the window without seeing the river beyond, or the swans that cruised along it. Whatever the weather outside, it all seemed grey to me now. Of course, this had all been too good to be true. Why did I ever think I had a chance of buying this beautiful, dilapidated, monument of a house, and living here until the end of my days? I would end up in a one-bedroom flat somewhere, overlooking a supermarket car park.

Then an email from Marco dropped onto my screen, asking if I'd like to join him online now. We were soon facing each other again. Behind him, I could see pale walls arching into a high ceiling, a giant seascape, an oriental rug. His eyes really were amber, and flecked with gold.

"What are you thinking?" I asked.

He shrugged. "Portuguese law has a mind of its own."

"Like English law," I said.

"When the *legítima* is challenged – the 'reserved portion' – the ruling almost always goes in favour of the family."

"So Joaquim can make a claim?"

"Possibly. But there are grounds to set it aside: where someone has committed a criminal offence, or hurt the family, that sort of thing. It's not clear. So a judge must decide what behaviour crosses the line."

"After a long and expensive legal action," I added. Cost, as always, was a prime consideration for me. I didn't want to end up any worse off than I already was.

"Any area of doubt can be played like a game between the lawyers," I said. "That's what happens here, anyway." I quickly added, "You're not a lawyer are you?"

He shook his head. "No, I'm an architect. I find bricks easier to deal with than people."

"I know what you mean. I'm a business consultant. Clients can be tricky sometimes."

We laughed together.

"So we have to think about how to handle this," he said. "Shall I start by telling you some family history?"

He turned away for a moment, apparently distracted by something to one side, and I wondered who might be there with him.

"Do you have any plans to return to Portugal?" he asked, looking back at me.

"No, why?"

"It would be easier to explain in person. The context of how our family was broken. Fifty years ago."

"Broken?"

"It's a complicated story," he added. "The three brothers. Duarte the patriarch, Álvaro the rebel, and Joaquim. Here we would call him the *ovelha negra* – the black sheep."

"Yes, we say the same. May I ask how you are related to Duarte?"

"Duarte Barros de Almeida." His voice softened as he said the words and a slight smile crossed his face, combined with sadness. "He was like a father to me." He looked away from me as he spoke. "But we weren't related. Duarte knew my parents. They died when I was nine and he took me in. Cristóvão told you Duarte was your uncle?"

"So he says. But then why haven't I heard of him before? I don't know what to believe." I realised I was being insensitive and added, "I'm so sorry. You've lost someone you were close to."

He hesitated and said, "If you could spare the time to come over, I have family photos and newspaper cuttings. I'll show you everything."

I was still deflated by the blow of Cristóvão's news. I needed the inheritance but simply couldn't afford a legal battle. I glanced out of the window. The swans had gone.

"I'm not sure," I said. "Could you come to England?"

"Of course, if you prefer. But there are a lot of photos to bring. And I'd like to show you where your mother grew up."

That settled it. Since her death, I had longed to find out more about my mother's past life. "I'm working until Friday," I said. "What about the weekend? Would that be inconvenient? Your family?"

"I'm divorced," he said. "My weekends are my own. And this is my family." He swung the laptop round and I saw that the earlier distraction was caused by a pair of large brown dogs. They lay in a shady corner of a sunny terrace and lazily wagged their tails as Marco turned towards them. He shifted the laptop up and a wide expanse of water appeared, glistening in the sun.

"This is the River Tagus," he said. "You're welcome to stay here, if you don't mind dogs."

Dogs, yes, I loved them, but staying in a stranger's house seemed a step too far, even though we had been introduced through a notary, and shared an inheritance, and he seemed like a nice, decent person, and surely must be to have dogs like these. Nevertheless, I replied, "Perhaps you could recommend a hotel?"

"Of course," he said. "I'll send you a list."

And so it was agreed. In two days' time I would be boarding a plane to Lisbon again.

8

COIMBRA UNIVERSITY
1971

"No entry here, boy," the guard said, blocking his way. "Go home to play with your toys. No school today!" There were six of them, standing in a line, all wearing the blue uniforms of the riot police, and they laughed.

Luís was early for his lecture at the Faculty of Law and had taken his time to stroll under the shade of the plane trees, admiring the three-hundred-year-old architecture that lined the square. Law was his passion. He was studying at one of the most ancient and revered universities in Europe, and he was in love with a beautiful girl called Gabriela. Life could not have been better. He didn't see the guards until he was almost upon them.

The *Polícia de Segurança Pública* was known as the most ruthless force of the regime. In his head he heard Álvaro telling him to leave now and get as far away from these men as he could, but another voice inside, the bold one, sent him forward. Six of them blocked his way, their hands on pistols strapped around their hips, and two large dogs stood ready to attack.

"Let me through. I have a lecture to attend," he said, curtly. He had once been bullied at a new school, and suffered terribly until his elder brothers convinced him that he must fight back, and had taught him how. The bullies turned out to be cowards when faced with a beating from the brothers Coelho, and Luís had promised himself then that he would never be intimidated again. That year his height shot up and he had started training with weights. No-one would dare challenge him now. But the guards were six, and he was alone.

"Run home to your *mamã*, little boy," one said. They all laughed and another swore at him, but Luís stood firm. The clock set into a high tower next to the entrance chimed out the hour. He would be late for the lecture.

Then one yelped, slapped his hand to his face, and stared at blood that stained his fingers. Students were throwing broken glass from the upper windows. Some of the men stepped backwards and took out their guns while the rest ran into the building.

Luís took advantage of the distraction and slipped through the open doors into the atrium. He could hear screams, crashes, and harsh voices that echoed in the vaulted ceilings. He headed towards a maze of corridors that led to lecture halls and faculty offices. Looking back, he saw that the police were not only refusing admission but denying anyone the chance to leave. One youth tried to break through and they set a dog on him. He limped away, leaving a red trail on the floor.

Luís headed down a hallway. Papers, books, and other debris lay in his path. Glass grated under his feet and the disorder on the floor seemed to reflect his own confusion. On reaching the first lecture hall, he saw that the doors were open. Inside, the police were beating anyone who tried to escape through the windows. His first instinct was help, but there were too many to fight on his own. He moved on, vowing that one day these men would pay.

Further along lay the offices of the Rector and some of the professors. The *Reitor* himself was not there – no doubt warned in advance, Luís thought – but two of his assistants were begging the intruders to bring their accomplices under control. They were knocked to the ground and then handcuffed. Again Luís could see it was pointless to intervene: there were three of them and they had pistols strapped to their belts. But aggression was rising inside him and he wanted to fight, so he continued down the corridor looking for a confrontation that offered better odds.

The next door led into a small classroom that sat in the middle of the faculty offices. About a dozen students were huddled in the corner, taunted by two guards. Heavy wooden desks had been splintered like matchwood. The men were tall, fat, and muscular. Both had coshes dangling from their hands, but Luís estimated that it was their intimidating attitude that frightened the students the most. If challenged, he thought, there was a good chance they would withdraw, then some of the youths might stop cringing against the walls and stand with him to fight them. He saw a chance to reveal these bullies as the cowards that they surely were.

He stepped forward and glanced at the boys. Unseen by the police, he made a fist with one hand and signalled to two of the tallest.

"What the hell are you doing?" he demanded, addressing a guard. He wished his brothers were there with him, but was confident he could handle the situation. "Leave them alone!" He said it as a command. Men like these crumbled when on the receiving end of their own treatment.

For a moment the outcome hung in the balance. The aggressors looked less certain, the two tall students stepped forward, then two more, and a girl joined them as well. The most useful lesson that Luís had learned from his brothers was the art of timing: fast sleight of hand took people by surprise. With a movement so quick that no-one had time to react, he snatched a cosh and lashed it across the face of its owner.

The events that followed happened quickly, and no amount of swift reactions could have saved him. There was a commotion at the door, and he swung round as four more guards pushed their way into the room. A short, blinding pain shot through his head, and Luís knew nothing more.

9

MOURARIA, LISBON

2019

It was three in the afternoon and the blue flowers of the jacaranda were silhouetted black against rays of sunshine that filtered through them. It would soon be time for a sleep. Joaquim had drunk little today. He was entirely confident that Laurinda's action would win him a fortune, and had spent most of the morning planning how the money might be spent.

His mind dwelt on the land in Sintra, where the yellow towers of Duarte's villa overlooked a turquoise-tiled pool, seven acres of fields and hills, and a natural lake: the landscape of his boyhood. He pictured a holiday centre or even a theme park, driven by an imagination which had grown suddenly fertile. They could put a zipline across the lake, enlarge the pool, add a big water slide perhaps – one of those circular ones that children liked – and some high-pressure thermal massage showers for the adults. There would be hot tubs, of course, and the horses in the stables could be rented out for rides through the mountains, for hunting trips even. He would hire one of the best chefs in the country and eat gourmet food every day.

And then there was the wine cellar – Duarte must still have one, surely – there would be liqueurs and whiskies, verbena gin from Alentejo, and he could make his own fruit brandy from the berries of the *medronho* tree. It could be sold – there could be a shop – he could launch a whole new business. That took him off on another train of thought that continued to eclipse the gritty reality of his surroundings.

It was important to plan ahead because in the event that he had to share the estate with Marco and the Englishwoman, he would need to have all his strategies in place to convince the pair of them to agree to his schemes. On the other hand, his share might be big enough to buy them out.

He finished lunch with just one *Licor Beirão* today, feeling positive and optimistic for the first time in a long while, and his indigestion barely troubled him at all.

Then he saw Lourenço. It was unmistakable: the glimpses he thought he had imagined all the other times were real. Why was he here? Was it for revenge?

The sun seemed to go behind a cloud even as its rays lit the face of the man walking towards him. There was no escape: this was not the skinny nineteen-year-old he once knew, but a herculean figure who would have dwarfed him had he stood up, which he did not.

His mouth became dry, and his hands wet, as he steeled himself for whatever was in store; he might be growing old but could still put up a good fight. Nevertheless, confronted with the sinewy giant that the boy had become, in contrast with his own rheumatic frame, he didn't rate highly his chances of winning. He reassured himself that as long as he stayed in the bar he would be safe. Lourenço would surely not attack in such a public place, and if he did, then Filipe the owner might step in – he hoped.

The visitor loomed above him, his face as impassive as Joaquim was trying to arrange his own.

"*O quê*?" Joaquim asked. "So what are you doing here? What do you want?"

"Just passing," replied Lourenço, his casual words belying an aggressive glare. "You could invite me to an *escarchado*."

Joaquim remembered that this anis was a special favourite of Lourenço, who used to hanker after it in the prison cells. It was too sugary for his own taste. He said nothing, but Lourenço sat down anyway and called out his request to Filipe. "Um *escarchado*. "

They eyed each other.

"*O quê*?" asked Joaquim again.

Filipe brought the drink and Lourenço downed it in one swallow. "Let's talk privately," he said. "At your place. There's a lot to say."

Joaquim had no intention of leaving the safety of the bar, particularly not for his house where the neighbours were unlikely to pay any attention to an old man's screams. His hunting rifle sat just inside the door, but Lourenço looked agile; there would not be time to load it.

"You're looking well," Joaquim said. He was lying. He saw tired eyes and shabby clothing. But if he could establish a friendly tone, then that might lessen any violent intentions Lourenço might be harbouring. He twisted his mouth into what he hoped was more of a smile than a grimace.

"And that's no thanks to you," came the curt reply, drawing them closer to a place and time that Joaquim was trying to avoid. But here they were, and the reason behind the visitor's appearance was becoming unpromisingly clear.

Joaquim shrugged and held out his hand. "I didn't mean for you to get hurt," he began. "We all had to protect ourselves, yes?"

Lourenço ignored the gesture. "I was the price you paid to save your lousy skin."

The accusation was undeniable. A prison inspection had uncovered Joaquim's hidden supply of *aguardente,* the illegal liqueur that prisoners brewed to keep themselves sane, and that got his wardens into a lot of trouble because they had been bribed to look the other way. The one thing you did not want to do in that place, even more than getting caught yourself, was to shop your guards. They would retaliate in ways you couldn't begin to imagine.

So in the panic of the moment, he had blamed his cellmate for hiding the firewater and landing them all in a mess: Lourenço the innocent, imprisoned for the first time in his life over a minor robbery, just a boy who knew nothing about how to play the rules and who had been unlucky enough to end up in a cell with someone who was a master at it.

After the revolution, some of the secret police guards had resurfaced in the prison service, where they had continued to indulge their sadistic appetites. Lourenço had been badly hurt by the beating he received that day, and it was a long time before he recovered physically. The real damage was mental and might never heal.

"So what are you doing now, Lou?" Joaquim asked, trying to distract him from the bad memories by using what could have been an affectionate diminutive of his name in any other circumstances.

Lourenço stared back at him dourly. He sat still while Joaquim braced himself not to give away his nerves by fidgeting. He held Lourenço's eyes without blinking, an old technique that had proved intimidating in the past.

But this time it was Joaquim who looked away first. "You want money?" he asked. "Work? Advice?" He left out 'revenge'.

Lourenço continued his menacing glare, and an idea came to Joaquim. At that time, most of his income arose by pilfering from the growing numbers of tourists in the area. *Mouraria,* the working-class district where his shabby house was located, still accommodated a lot of the city's poorest communities but had become popular with holidaymakers who regarded its dilapidation as having character. A short stroll away stood the fancy riverside apartments that were the visitors' preferred rentals.

One day he had seen a family leave their holiday flat with a window slightly open. He slid it up, took the laptop they had left in full view, and slammed it shut again. This had grown into a thriving racket, but he never again entered the properties himself. Instead, a quick text would summon a member of the workshy crew he had assembled over the years, some of whom he had taught to pick locks. It was a lucrative business and low in risk, to Joaquim at least.

So while he sat inwardly cowering at Lourenço's intentions, the thought occurred to him that his former cellmate, with his frayed collar and down-at-heel shoes, might be in need of money as well as, or perhaps instead of, the opportunity to avenge his old nemesis, and so could possibly make a useful addition to the team. *Uma mão lava a outra,* he said to himself: one hand washes the other. He launched into a proposal.

"I have some business you might be interested in."

Lourenço immediately looked engaged. "What sort of business?"

He saw need in the man's eyes and weighed up the level of risk incurred between gaining a new accomplice as opposed to receiving a retaliatory beating at home, because they really should not be discussing these matters in public. Bars have ears.

"Not here," he muttered, standing and throwing some euros onto the table.

He led the way back to his house, over uneven cobblestones, across a set of tramlines, and up a steep flight of steps, to an alleyway banked by tenement homes whose upper windows overflowed with drying laundry. Here in the Moorish Quarter, the buildings had been constructed closely around narrow passages to protect them from the sun, from storms, and from bandits who centuries ago were looking for coins, not laptops. A few decades earlier only the poorest immigrants had occupied the maze of streets, and that was when Joaquim had, by the grace of Duarte, ended up occupying this narrow building with paint peeling from its walls. He had witnessed the population change as artists moved into the cheap properties, then galleries and clubs devoted to culture instead of kebabs sprang up, and finally wealthy tourists came to admire the faded exotica of it all.

Like its neighbours, Joaquim's home had three narrow storeys and was attached on either side to a string of others that may once have been identical. Its windows flanked a squat door through which Lourenço had to stoop, and were framed by a shade of brown that contrasted with a paler colour on the walls.

It was a long way from the palatial mansions of his early years but at least he didn't have to pay rent, and according to the terms of the will, he would inherit and own it outright, whatever the result of the court case. That made him better off than some of the unfortunate tenants in the *Mouraria* who were being ousted by a rising population of expatriate digital nomads.

It felt strange to bring someone through the low front door. Joaquim received few visitors and his cupboards contained little in the way of food – the daily sojourns to Filipe's bar and snacks while shadowing tourists catered for all of his alimentary needs – but he could always lay his hands on a bottle, and found a few beers. There was some stale bread and a tin of sardines as well. He placed them on his unsteady wooden table, accompanied by a plate and a knife.

Lourenço looked at the food, and then back at him. One fist clenched around the knife.

For a moment, Joaquim thought he had made what might turn out to be a painful error of judgement. Then his potential adversary cut the bread and devoured it before even touching the beer. Joaquim's fighting muscles relaxed and he dropped into a chair.

While Lourenço ate, Joaquim sketched out the details of his heists. His visitor's attention seemed now to be fully captured, both by the food and the prospect of earning money through means that required less effort than honest work.

As they talked, he was reminded of the time when this man had first appeared as a youth in his cell, new to prison and trying to hide his fear with an unconvincing swagger. When asked what his crime had been, Lourenço boasted that he had stolen money and hit a man who had lost an eye through the blow. But after the lights went out, Joaquim could hear smothered sobs coming from the other bunk.

The memory blurred with recollections of his own son, Joaquinho, eight years old and shaking with fear when he had last seen the child. It might have been a memory to treasure, had the boy's terror not been instilled by his own father, and had the tears been not for that father who was abandoning his family, but for the mistreated mother who remained behind.

Joaquim's attention snapped back to the present, but something of the protector had crept into his mood; a desire to make up for the ways he had failed both vulnerable boys who had each needed his help years ago. He refilled Lourenço's glass and found another tin of sardines.

"Do you need an advance?" he heard himself say.

Lourenço nodded through a mouthful of fish, while Joaquim searched through his pockets and drew out two crumpled twenty-euro notes. He must be mad, he thought, as he pushed them across the table. He would probably never see the man or the euros again.

After several more glasses of beer, the light was fading outside and Joaquim switched on a glaring overhead lamp. The room now resembled the cell they had shared. It was time to wrap up the deal.

"When I send a message, you answer immediately, *sim,* you are going to do the job or *não,* you can't. If it's *não* too often, then you're dropped from the team."

Lourenço nodded like an animal tamed.

"You take the stuff to my fence and tell me what you gave him. He sells it, he takes his twenty per cent, and he gives you half of what's left."

Lourenço nodded again.

"Don't think you can keep anything back for yourself. I have more spies than Salazar. No-one steals from me twice."

Lourenço's eyes were fixed on the plate that was now cleaned to a shine with the last of the bread. They shook hands and the deal was done. Joaquim had a feeling that Lourenço would stick around now, and that he might even get his money back.

10

COIMBRA UNIVERSITY

1971

Elena woke suddenly. Her clock showed four-thirty. Had she heard a crash, or was it a dream? Then a shuffling noise outside her door told her the sounds were real. She got out of bed and edged through the darkness. The chill of night air intensified the prickle of fear on her skin. Already unnerved by the news that Luís had not been seen since the raid on the law school two days ago, she flinched at her own reflection in a wall mirror. She reached the door and listened. There was a voice without words. A groan.

Álvaro was in his own room in the men's quarters. He couldn't help her. Gabriela was asleep in the next bed. Should she wake her friend? If what was outside might incriminate them, then Gabriela was safer sleeping. But if it were someone come to harm them, she should be given the chance to prepare. Elena felt sick. She wanted to crawl back under her sheets to hide like a child but the moans continued. Whoever was outside needed help and didn't sound capable of hurting them. She opened the door.

A body fell into the room, crying out with pain. It was Luís. His face was torn and swollen. She had never seen so much blood. But he was alive.

"The PIDE," he whispered and swore.

So this is what the PIDE could do. She half-dragged him and he half-crawled into the room. Gabriela woke up and ran to him. Blood matted his hair and stained his shirt, freshly red in places and dried brown in others. The stench from him was overwhelming. Elena turned to the sink pinned to the wall behind a curtain in their room, and retched, then returned to his side. She felt only pity, and guilt at her relief that it was not Álvaro lying broken on the floor. She must fetch him.

She climbed through the window and over the usual wall, then waited while he fetched Téo the medical student. As they slipped back along the same illicit route, a moon almost full emerged from behind clouds and they pulled their clothes around them to hide the gleam of their faces from any eyes that might be spying in the night.

"Is it a warning?" Elena asked Álvaro as they watched Téo examine Luís. "Is it Gomes? Do they know about us?"

Álvaro looked tense. "He knew we were lying about the radio. We must be more careful."

Between them, Téo and Álvaro carried Luís back to his room, where Téo would stay to monitor his condition. Climbing through windows was beyond the pain-racked Luís, so they had to smuggle him past the concierge downstairs. The light was bright there and gave no chance of hiding. Elena and Gabriela planned to distract the old lady while the men manoeuvred Luís between them, but when they approached her, she went to the back of her cubicle and ignored them. Frightened too, Elena thought; she must have seen the guards bring him in.

When all was done, they stumbled out into daylight to face the day ahead, leaving Luís in his room with Téo and Gabriela.

"I can't go to lectures today," she said.

"Do you want to sleep?"

She shook her head. "I don't think I'll ever sleep again."

They went to a street bar outside the campus, and Álvaro drank gin that smelled of juniper berries. It made her feel sick again. The sun burned some strength into their tired limbs. They felt safer there, in full view of passersby, than inside the university walls.

Then a shadow fell across the table. "Good day, dear students."

Narrowing her eyes against the sun, Elena saw the dark figure of Gomes looming above. It was all too much. *Let him denounce us,* she thought. *I can't resist any more.*

"I trust you won't miss your lectures today," the monitor said. "You – and your friends." A smirk played around his mouth, the closest she had ever seen to a smile on that haggard face. Then he moved off without

C. A. Wilson

waiting for an answer.

"Was he listening?" she asked. Her body, relaxed by the sun, tensed again.

"He knows," Álvaro said. "The way he looked at us. You must go away. He has you marked. This was a warning." His voice was urgent, but the defeat on his face told her that he knew what her answer would be.

"I'm not going anywhere." As she said it, a picture of her room in Chiado floated through her mind, that world where everything was predictable, and she could sleep safely for hours or days on end. But she was still ruled by the fantasy of becoming a heroine of the resistance. "I won't leave you or this fight," she declared, her voice thin with fatigue. She was too tired to know whether she meant it or not, but it seemed like the appropriate thing to say. Of one thing she was sure: she didn't want to be parted from him.

He looked desperate. "I shouldn't have let you get so involved. If anything happens to you..."

"I got myself involved. Once I found out you ran the *Resistência,* you didn't have a chance."

She laughed and he smiled, though she could see he was trying not to.

"It's not so bad," she said. "What have we done? Helped a friend, listened to a radio."

"Made a film," he added. "Condemning the *Estado Novo.*"

She couldn't argue with him. That was a serious crime. They didn't speak while the waiter brought coffee, black and strong, with free food. She could not face any of it.

70

"Please." He reached across the table. His hand was dry and warm against hers. "Go home to your family. One day when it's safe we'll be together."

She raised his hand and pressed it against her face. Despite her fear, which was real, the bone-aching tiredness that weighed down her limbs, and all that had been done to poor Luís, she couldn't leave. "You're not getting rid of me now."

The next morning everything changed. Still feeling ill, Elena went to the university medical centre. Álvaro had gone to see Luís's family, so she was alone when the doctor on duty, a dour-faced woman, examined her. She asked some questions that Elena didn't dare answer truthfully, and then announced without a smile, "You're pregnant. About ten weeks."

11

ALFAMA, LISBON

2019

Flying into Lisbon had been quite different this time. As the ocean came into view, and the estuary, and the aqueduct, I knew why I was here. From Marco's list of hotels, I had chosen a small pousada in Alfama, the oldest part of the Moorish quarter. It was a simple place that suited both my budget and my liking for antiquity. My room had carved wooden furniture, sketches of cobbled streets and coloured houses on the walls, and I could see a balcony through a pair of glass doors.

I turned a handle fixed to an iron bar that stretched from the top to the bottom, and a heavy mechanism clicked into place, releasing the bolts. I stepped outside. The cathedral towered in one direction and the River Tagus glinted in the other. It was late spring and the afternoon sun seeped deliciously into me after the chill of winter that lingered back home.

I went back inside and got ready to meet Marco. From the few pieces of clothing squashed into my hand luggage, I selected some white linen trousers and a silk top, and swapped my travelling shoes for a pair of pale leather sandals.

It was Friday evening and I would be here until Sunday. I didn't know whether Marco planned to take me to his house this evening to look at photographs, or what he had in mind for us over the weekend, if anything at all. He might have other commitments, or perhaps we wouldn't get on or want to spend the following day together. I just hoped that tonight would find me sitting in the warm evening air, eating Portuguese food.

He was standing in the hotel reception, on cue at seven, when I walked down the stairs. We shook hands and I noticed his unusual eyes again. In that light they looked darker, like burnt umber.

"What would you like to do?" he asked politely. "Have you eaten?"

"No. I only just arrived."

"We could walk to somewhere local? There's plenty to choose from."

"That would be nice."

"What sort of food do you like?"

"What do you recommend?"

"You could sit outside or inside with air conditioning..."

"Would outside be okay? It's too cold for that in England."

There was a slight hesitancy between us, naturally for two strangers who had just met, but I liked his manner. It was helpful but not intrusive.

"OK. Then grand or simple? Local or international? Spanish, Italian, Asian? We have all the food of the world here."

"Simple, please. And local of course. When in Lisbon... is there anywhere we could go that overlooks the river?"

"Yes of course, you must have a water view. We can walk to a place I know that serves simple Portuguese food, outside, on a terrace over the river."

"That sounds perfect."

And then we walked. It was no great distance, but we went slowly because the route was interesting. The streets of the old town were narrow with steep steps and alleyways. The cobblestones were picturesque but perilously uneven to walk on. Some of the houses were dilapidated and others had been gentrified in the new touristic economy.

I knew that the old man Joaquim lived somewhere in this area and hoped we wouldn't run into him. In the wider avenues stood baroque churches with gothic towers, and grand mansions graced with eerie stone carvings of mermaids and sea monsters – a legacy of Portugal's seafaring history, Marco explained. And almost everywhere, tall trees spread a canopy of lavender-blue blossoms.

"They're jacarandas," he said when I admired them.

"There's one in my garden! Now I understand why my mother planted it. But it never flowered."

He smiled. "It's nice to think that Elena had that little piece of Portugal with her. But I don't think it would like the cold."

I wondered what memories had surfaced whenever she looked at the flowerless tree which was now mine. When the time came for me to leave, I would have to say goodbye to that symbol she must have planted to remind her of home.

He stopped then, in front of a museum and pointed out an inscription on the walls. It was only later that I understood why he was showing it to me. He translated the text as he read it out:

Aqui – Here
do silencio das 'gavetas' – from the silence of the 'drawers'
da patria amordacada – in this gagged homeland
dos peitos desfeitos pelas torturas da PIDE – from breasts torn apart by the torture of the PIDE
subiu o clamor da Liberdade – the cry for freedom rose
floriu Abril – April flowered.

"The Carnation Revolution," I said.

"You've heard of it?"

"My mother wrote a book: 'Lisbon Flowered'. It's years since I read it, so I don't remember much detail, but I know there was a dictator called Salazar and a revolution where soldiers put carnations in their rifles. That's what the book was about."

He looked at me, surprised. "Your mother wrote

'Lisbon Flowered'? I read it in translation, *'Floriu Lisboa'*. I loved that book. And the film too. I never knew it was written by our Elena."

"She used her married name, E. A. Matthews."

"That's amazing. I wish Duarte could have known."

He looked astonished and impressed. I felt irrationally pleased. "But that inscription," I asked, "what are the 'drawers'?"

"This building was the headquarters of the PIDE and the Aljube prison. It was for political prisoners. The cells were narrow; the guards called them drawers. People were tortured here. It was horrible."

I felt sick. I hadn't given much thought to this part of my mother's life before. How involved had she been? I had thought her a spectator, but did she really have a child with a man murdered by the regime? Was I that child?

We walked away from the horrors of the past through a multi-coloured huddle of houses that looked like the pictures on the walls of my hotel room. I wondered idly whether my tiny budget would stretch to one of these when I lost my home, now that the inheritance was in doubt. Perhaps I should start a new life here. Was there a market for English management consultants? Then we turned a corner, and the river stretched out ahead of us, glowing under the late-day sun.

Marco led the way into a small restaurant and up onto a terrace which overlooked the water as promised. Mismatched old furniture filled the floor and there were plants everywhere: little pots of herbs on the tables and tubs of giant tropical leaves in the corners. We positioned ourselves with a good view of the river, agreed on a bottle of rosé wine, and he told me his story.

"My father died when I was eight. He was a friend of Duarte's family. He was fond of me, for some reason, and when my mother died a year later, he took me in. He even gave me his name, Barros de Almeida. He paid for my schooling and training as an architect. It was only as I grew older that I understood how kind he had been. Nothing was ever refused – it was extraordinary really."

"You were lucky. But it's sad that you lost your parents so young. Do you remember them?"

"I have a sense of my mother – warm, kind. Like most mothers I suppose. But my father? I don't even know his name. No-one ever talked about him. He must have been bad." He seemed pained for a moment and then recovered. "Anyway, we're here to talk about your family history, not mine. Duarte had another brother, Álvaro. Your father." He looked at me uncertainly.

"I know that's what Cristóvão said, but my father was Douglas. I have his grey eyes and brown hair."

He studied me. "You have Álvaro's grey eyes and Álvaro's brown hair."

My breath stopped for a second. This was new information, and the most convincing yet that their version of my parentage might be true.

"His colouring was light for a Portuguese," Marco went on. "There was a British ancestor in the family

77

two hundred years ago, Duarte told me."

I found my voice. "A throwback?"

"Yes, a throwback. Each generation has someone who is paler. Like you and your father Álvaro." He stopped as if he had said too much. "I'm sorry. This must be hard for you."

The waiter laid plates of sardines before us. We picked at them slowly as we talked. "I don't know what to believe," I said. "Anyway, it's only biology. No-one could have been more of a father to me than Douglas."

Suddenly I felt the need to defend him. "Did he know? That he wasn't my father? If it's true?"

He nodded. "You were a baby when he met your mother."

I stopped breathing again. The whole of my family history was being rewritten. Somehow, the story seemed more credible now, coming from Marco, than it had when Cristóvão told me.

"It was a scandal at the time because she wasn't married," Marco said. "I think the family wanted to arrange an adoption, but she refused. She kept her baby and then Douglas came along. She was going to be arrested, so he took her to England. Then they married, and I suppose no-one knew they were different from any other family."

I blinked. "Arrested?"

"She was plotting against the regime. She was a freedom fighter with Álvaro. They both risked their lives."

I had vague memories of similar events taking place in the book, but had read it as an adventure story, not an autobiography. My hands felt cold in spite of the warm evening. If I was not who I had thought, then who was I?

"Álvaro..." Mark went on. He shook his head. "They killed him. She had to escape."

The waiter cleared our plates and refilled our glasses. A pink sun was setting over the Tagus and reflecting its rays through the pale *vinho rosé*. It was a romantic setting but I wasn't feeling sentimental.

"Why didn't she tell me?" I drank some water to clear my head.

He looked at me sympathetically.

Had she sat here by the river? Perhaps in this very restaurant? With Douglas or with Álvaro? I started on a dish of cod that had been placed in front of me. It was herbal and creamy but I barely registered the taste.

"What about her parents?" I asked. It was like a giant jigsaw whose pieces I had to fit together.

"They never got over it, Duarte said. She was their only child. But it must have been a relief to know she was safe."

"Did she ever see them again?"

"I don't know."

"England and Portugal aren't that far apart. We were poor at first, but later we could have visited them."

"There was a lot of unrest after the revolution. People were afraid the regime would come back. There was another revolution the following year – a violent one. The communists tried to take over, but they failed. The people wanted democracy, but it wasn't easy. I don't think she would have dared to come back at that time. Then your grandparents didn't live long after that. Alexandra had cancer, and Rodrigo fell from a horse, in the early eighties, I think.

"The collapse of the regime was bad for them. They lost all their money. Their investments were in the colonies, so when Portugal granted independence, they were ruined. Duarte was luckier. His wealth was here, in farming and property."

I tried to order all the questions that were crowding my mind. "So, what happened to Álvaro? The man you believe was my father?"

His hands rested on the table, playing with his empty glass. The waiter came over and filled it, and then mine. "There were terrible things then. People were imprisoned, tortured, killed. Álvaro was one of those. He was in that prison we saw. I'm sorry to tell you this. He was brave, your father, very brave. So was your mother."

I felt a chill, whether from the night air or the shadows of history, I didn't know. I slipped my jacket over my shoulders and took a sip of wine. Scenes I vaguely remembered from the book returned to me, of betrayals and atrocities, and a father I never knew. "Is there anything else?" I asked him.

He shook his head. "Duarte didn't talk much about the past. It was too painful, I think. He never got over Álvaro's death. There were things that Joaquim did that he found unforgivable, too. And then his wife died. Duarte taught me to look to the future and enjoy the present. The past is gone, we can't change it."

"I was raised with that philosophy too. Do you have any photos? Of Álvaro? Or my mother with him?"

"There are boxes of pictures in my house in Santos-o-Velho. Some of them were given to me after Duarte's death and I haven't even opened them yet. You must come there tomorrow, and we'll go through them together, if you'd like that?"

"I would," I said, feeling grateful. I felt he was on my side. "You're very kind."

"I like to help. And we'll talk more about the legal mess. It's complicated. You must be tired."

Suddenly I realised I was shattered. It was not just the wine, or the travel, or being in strange surroundings; I felt as if tectonic plates under my world were shifting.

I don't remember our walk back to the hotel or wishing Marco good night. I went up to my room and slept without dreaming until dawn edged through the curtains the next day.

12

PIDE HQ, LISBON
1971

Inspector Vitório Soares sat at his desk on the upper floors of the DGS building. Most people still called the secret police force by its old name, the PIDE, but Soares was meticulous in using the new one. Nevertheless, the organisation behaved just as brutally as it had when named the PIDE. Soares regarded such matters as outside his mandate.

A dim glow penetrated the room from a window blind that was always drawn, to shield it from the block across the street. The DGS had enemies among the people of Lisbon, and Soares worried that the building opposite offered a vantage point for snipers. The main light in his office came from a stark fluorescent tube overhead, illuminating the desk he had acquired on his promotion to this floor nine years ago. He had joined the PIDE ten years before that.

The worksurface was made of scuffed polished wood, fastidiously arranged, with a coaster precisely placed for the coffee he took twice a day. A cleaner in the building once told him that his was the only desk without cup stains on its surface. He was proud of that. On one side lay a tray labelled 'IN' which contained a pile of brown envelopes from the agents he supervised. He reached for the top one and opened it.

Inside was an innocuous report about a man who appeared to be acting suspiciously but was found to be innocent. Soares reached for his 'No Action' stamp, which sat next to an ink pad beside the IN tray. It gave a satisfying clunk. He took the trouble to ensure that the pad was always filled, unlike some of his colleagues whose imprints were near-illegible smudges.

He replaced the paper into its envelope, readdressed it, and slid it into a tray marked 'OUT' on the other side of the desk. Eventually a clerk would sort the report into one of the grey metal cabinets that lined the walls of his office, and there the note would lie until one day the suspect might go too far, and then all the history contained here could be used against him – or occasionally her.

The handwriting on the next envelope made him sigh. It was a report from *Agente* Joaquim Mendonça Gonçalves, who sat in a smaller office two floors down. The man had nowhere near enough experience to do his job. He made mistakes. Only recently he had overlooked the mention of a student whose name figured prominently in the list of dissidents maintained by the department: Luís Rafael Coelho. He had hit a guard in an attack which was unprovoked, according to the guard's report. He had already been arrested once. Had Soares's own scrupulous inspections not triggered a second arrest, that boy would be back in Coimbra University causing trouble, instead of behind bars, where he belonged, at Caxias prison.

Soares was fairly certain that strings had been pulled to arrange the appointment of Gonçalves, although he had no idea who had done the pulling, nor why. Such was the way of the PIDE, lately the DGS. Gonçalves himself had made it clear that he would rather be out on the streets hounding the citizens of Lisbon, and Soares would have been glad to be rid of him, but clearly someone with influence wanted him here in this building, filling out forms, whether he was suited to the task or not.

Because they came from Gonçalves, Soares sifted through the papers with extra care. He was not surprised when he found one which the bungling clerk had failed to staple to any of the reports. He grew more interested when he realised that the communication was very incriminating indeed, and might prove useful in his pursuit of promotion.

The shadow of his father, a Chief Firearms Officer overseeing all the gun licensing in the country, remained hanging over Soares a full decade after the old man's death. Parental expectations loomed large alongside his growing sense of failure. He had given his career, and in many ways his life, to the PIDE, and after nineteen years was impatient to move up to the next level. He reached for his telephone and dialled Gonçalves's extension. "Come to my office at once," he said curtly.

When Gonçalves entered, Soares continued to sift through papers while the agent shifted uncomfortably in front of him. When enough time had passed to suitably intimidate the man, he handed the sheet of paper across. "What is this?" he demanded.

Gonçalves took it from him. He shrugged. "I haven't seen it before," he said.

"And yet it was among these reports you sent to me." He waved the brown envelope.

Neither spoke. Gonçalves slouched despondently. Then he started to read the document. Soares could see his body stiffen. Now he looked frightened. And so he should, thought Soares. Posts like his don't come easily in the DGS.

"And what does it say?" he went on, playing on the man's nerves in a manner he had perfected over the decades.

Gonçalves started to read out loud:

"On August 25th 1971 I had the privilege of being invited by the Head of the DGS to view a film and provide my expert advice. I was asked to identify the man and woman appearing in that film. It was in English but the man spoke Portuguese and the woman translated. I am pleased to say that I fulfilled my task. The traitorous pair are students of mine, among the many for whose welfare I am responsible."

He stopped.

"Go on," Soares said.

The agent remained silent. His face paled and the paper started to tremble in his hand. Was he that scared of losing his job, Soares wondered? In that case, why didn't he make more effort to do it properly? He was irritated now. He snatched the report back and read it out himself.

"Álvaro Barros de Almeida and Elena Correia Guterres are their names. Signed: Lázaro Menezes Gomes.

"Do you know how long we have been looking for something to incriminate Almeida?"

"Yes sir," said Gonçalves. His voice was a croak.

"And you didn't see this in your reports."

"No sir," whispered Gonçalves. "I did not." He shook his head. His whole body swayed with the movement.

"I will decide what to do with you later," said Soares. "Now get out of here."

Gonçalves shuffled away and Soares looked at the document in his hands. What a prize. Álvaro de Almeida was a dissident who had been watched by the department for months, years even. So far nothing incriminating had surfaced in the reports from informers that passed through the department. Now here was evidence not only against the activist, but his girlfriend too.

A month earlier, a film had been circulated

throughout the police force and all its agents in the field, including university monitors like Gomes. A collaborative effort between Britain's corrupt educational establishment and a communist newspaper, it had been sent from spies in England and included anti-*Estado Novo* propaganda spouted by two unidentified students. The speaker was shown only in silhouette, and his translator not at all. The agents were asked to identify them by their voices.

So far, the search had drawn a blank, but here, now, was a report which had not been submitted at the time because the idiot Gonçalves had somehow lost it. Until now.

Soares reread the words and sat thinking for a while. This short note provided all the proof required to bring Almeida in for questioning, and then a few days of interrogation would break him. They would get all the details about his accomplices and the Guterres girl, the one with the shortwave radio. She would be next. And then surely Soares would be rewarded with a promotion that would have made his father proud.

13

SANTOS-O-VELHO, LISBON

2019

"That," Marco said, handing me a photograph, "is Elena."

The picture showed a child aged perhaps twelve or thirteen, with the long dark hair I remembered before it turned white, the same delicate features and straight nose, and most of all, the thoughtful expression I knew from the face of my mother.

We were sitting in Marco's townhouse at Santos-o-Velho. It was the day after our dinner on the Tagus. A partly drawn blind screened the intense sunshine that streamed through a wall of glass doors, while beneath it the river glinted and sent up faint noises from an unending traffic of cabin cruisers, tourist barges, and fishing boats.

We had spent the morning strolling around Chiado, where my mother grew up, looking at stately old mansions and wondering which one might have belonged to her family. We were easy with each other now, like old friends. Spread out on a table in front of us were a box of loose photographs and some albums pasted with black-and-white images of the past.

"Who are they?" I asked, pointing to the elegant couple on either side of the child. The woman's square-shouldered suit followed the stark lines of wartime fashion but was topped by an elaborate hat. Beside her stood a tall man with a moustache.

"Rodrigo and Alexandra," he said. "Your grandparents." He turned back to a previous page. A slender bride stood in a sea of swirling lace, her handsome young groom moustachioed beside her. Leafing through the book, I saw her metamorphose into a sophisticated middle-aged woman, next to an increasingly grey-haired husband, and a girl in between them who grew taller in each shot: my mother.

"You have never seen these before?" asked Marco.

I shook my head. "I suppose she left everything behind."

He picked out another picture from the box. "Here she is at university."

I was stunned – again. I was becoming used to life as a series of revelations. The picture showed an elfin girl with long dark curls, quite unlike my own fair, straight hair. Her clothes had the bohemian look I had seen in photographs of students in Britain of the 1970s.

"She never told me she went to uni." That and a few other things, I thought.

"Coimbra. It's the oldest one in Portugal and maybe in the whole of Europe. It was an achievement to get a place there. Especially for a woman in those days."

"Do you know what she read?"

"Law, I believe. She was clever, your mother."

I nodded. As well as her novel, I remembered her churning out serious articles for political papers, always in immaculate English. She must have been smart, but it was not something we talked about at home.

"This one," said Marco, extracting a piece of paper from the box, "Is your father. Álvaro Barros de Almeida."

He handed me a yellowing newspaper cutting. I saw a man whose hair appeared to be fair, but it wasn't possible to make out his features from the blurred monochrome shot. In one corner there was a small header: *Diário de Lisboa 9 Novembro 1971*. From the Portuguese text I could guess the meaning of a few words: *acusado, subversivo, condenado*.

"It says he was accused of subversive activities, and found guilty," said Marco. He drew out another photograph. "This is a better shot."

It had the look of a professional portrait, coloured in the warm tints of the photography of fifty years ago. His grey eyes and light hair were plainly visible now. The eyebrows curved at the same angle as mine did, and both of our noses were small but long and straight. I had always thought I inherited that from my mother. What transfixed me was the jawline. From a normally proportioned chin, it widened out to a slight squareness at the sides. It was a little bit unusual and unmistakably the same as mine. But the strange thing was, he also resembled my father Douglas enough to have been his brother. It was unnerving – my face in his, yet Douglas's too.

Marco studied me. "He looks like you."

"But he looks like my father too. I mean my real father." I stumbled over the words. "I mean Douglas." I picked up my bag and took out a photo that I carried everywhere with me. It showed the three of us together: Elena, Douglas, and me.

Marco looked at each picture and back at me. "He does."

This didn't help to clear up the mystery of whose daughter I was. "I wonder if it matters," I said, unsure where my thoughts were leading as I spoke. "Álvaro couldn't be a father to me because he died, and no-one could have done it better than Douglas. Did he know me? Álvaro?" As I said it, I realised I was coming round to the notion that the story might be true.

Marco shook his head. "You were born just after his death. It must have been a tough time for Elena."

"And then she met Douglas."

I tried to work out the dates in my mind. I had always thought that they married in Portugal, and then had me. I tried to recall what was written on my birth certificate, then realised that it would have been changed when Douglas formally adopted me.

Everything Marco told me might be true, but I resisted. I needed to know for certain. As one secret after another came to light, it was like watching my life story as I knew it going up in flames. What would rise from the ashes?

"I got the papers from Cristóvão," I said, putting the pictures aside. Talking about legalities felt like stepping back onto safe ground. I needed a break from all the mysteries.

"So did I."

"I've translated them online, but I'm not sure how accurate that is. What do you think?"

"I'll give you my understanding. You already know Joaquim's action is based on the *legítima*. That would entitle him to a share. But he's been cut out on the grounds of having harmed the family."

"What did he do?"

Marco seemed to be struggling, and then said, "I don't know how to tell you this. Duarte believed that Joaquim betrayed Álvaro to the secret police. Duarte never forgave him."

It felt as if we were falling back into the fire again. "What happened?"

"I don't know. Sometimes I wondered if it was all a misunderstanding, but Duarte wouldn't ever discuss an alternative."

He sat silently for a moment, his face overcast. "Joaquim spent time in prison as well. Robbery and violence. Cristóvão thinks that alone may be enough to defend the action. If not, there are other avenues."

"Which would take months of due process and cost all parties a fortune," I said drily. "And give everyone a lot of headaches too."

"I agree with you on that," he replied.

We seemed to agree on most things. We both remained quietly with our thoughts for a while. It was an easy silence. On the wall opposite was a giant oil painting of the view outside, streaked gold and pink by a sunset. I thought that was a lovely touch, a view of the view, and started to wonder if I could do something similar at home. Then I remembered that firstly, I had no money, and secondly, it might not be my home for much longer.

Marco spoke and pulled me back to the present. "It's a big estate," he said. "Worth fighting for?"

"I don't know. Is it right to take an old man's inheritance?" This had been bothering me. I needed money badly but not enough to steal from a pensioner. "We're talking about a betrayal which may or may not have happened, in the distant past."

"I've thought about this too," he said, "but Duarte insisted that you should have Álvaro's share, as his daughter. He knew there might be a fight. I promised I would make sure it happened."

"So it's Duarte's way of taking revenge?"

"No. He wasn't that sort of man. But Álvaro's death... it was a terrible loss for him. His will was the last thing he could do for his favourite brother; that's how he saw it. When he sent Joaquim away after Álvaro's death, he gave Joaquim his share, so that he would never have to see him again. So Joaquim has already had his inheritance, and he's getting his house. The rest is yours and mine. If Joaquim has no money, I'll look after him, of course. He's part of the family. But I made Duarte a promise. So I think I have to defend this case."

"I understand. And I'm sorry we have to go through all this now." I felt like touching his hand, in sympathy. But I sat still and kept my hands in my lap. "Duarte meant a lot to you, didn't he?"

He nodded. "It was time. He was old and ill and missing his wife. Everyone has to die."

He spoke simply but it was heartfelt. Some words came into my mind and I said them out loud. *"Doesn't everything die at last, and too soon?"*

He looked uncertain and said, "I suppose it does."

"It's from a poem. The next line is: *Tell me, what will you do with your one wild and precious life?"*

"Beautiful."

"When people I loved have died, these words made me think about what they did with their lives; the choices they made without even realising it, sometimes. It seems my mother made some big ones."

"And your father too."

We were moving back into the land of uncertainty. I was filled with memories and doubts. Through the blinds, I could see a boat chugging past, full of tourists having a party and playing loud music.

Eventually he spoke. "It's a big decision for you. Why don't you go back to England, think it through, and talk it over with people who can advise you? For me, I'd like to take this to the next stage."

If I refused to go ahead, I realised he would fight the claim anyway, and I might end up receiving a share without having paid anything towards it. I looked around the room, vacillating. The furnishings were polished antiques, and a sculpture stood in one corner, an abstract version of the maritime figures we had seen on old buildings yesterday. Most of my own furniture was second-hand by necessity. He was clearly wealthy, unlike me, but still I felt it wouldn't be fair to have him pay, and it would leave me in his debt. I wrestled with the options.

"I'm worried about the cost and the stress of being involved in a lawsuit," I said, "in a language and legal system I don't understand."

"I get that. I could deal with everything and keep you informed. So you'll have all the papers and know everything that happens, but you won't need to talk to any lawyers. And you don't need to contribute anything to the cost until you feel comfortable with that."

"That's incredibly kind, but I must pay my way."

We talked on about the intricacies of the case. By the end of the afternoon, we had considered every possible way to move forward, and all likely outcomes. All that remained was for me to weigh them up and decide, and we agreed I'd best do that from home.

The light was fading, and it felt like time to eat. A cab took us back to the old town. It stopped outside an unimposing door which opened into a flight of stairs leading up to a shaded rooftop terrace. As darkness fell, lights twinkled all over the city. It was magical. I felt tired but calm.

"This is my favourite restaurant," Marco said. "The *Tasca Antiga Lisboa*. Real Portuguese food and more locals than tourists."

I agreed and realised that this was the nicest weekend I had spent in a long time, despite all the unsettling revelations it had brought. Conversation came ever more easily between us as we drifted through discussions about Portugal and England. The evening passed without any more debate about the lawsuit.

When faced with a difficult decision, I seem to be able to access an inner voice, and on the few occasions I haven't listened, I've come to regret it. This time it was telling me to join Marco in fighting the case, but I still couldn't banish my anxiety over the cost. I would have to dip into savings that were needed for the future.

I boarded my plane to London the next morning as confused as ever.

14

CHIADO, LISBON

1971

Duarte stepped back into a doorway as if to avoid the rain that ran over his hat and in rivulets down his neck. But it was not the weather that weighed on his mind; he was here to achieve the impossible.

Sheltered by the lintel above, he wiped his eyes clear of the drizzle and glanced sideways down the street while facing straight ahead. Around the corner stood the headquarters of the secret police, and in that building worked the only man who could help him now: João Constantino de Abreu. So Duarte stood watching through the rain and waited, counting on his old friend to walk this way when he left his office, and not in the opposite direction. Álvaro's freedom, and possibly his life, depended upon it.

The trauma of having lost both parents when barely a grown man himself had hardened in Duarte a vow that neither of his younger brothers would ever face trouble alone; from then on he was not just the head of the family but the fixer, too. He hadn't always succeeded in rescuing Joaquim from his usually self-inflicted predicaments, but Álvaro was different. Whatever the problem, Duarte had usually managed to find a solution, whether the issue was a recalcitrant horse, a struggle with schoolwork, or an adolescent crush. For that boy, he would lay down his life if required.

At last a figure turned into the alleyway. Silhouetted against the rain, the agile gait and set of the shoulders were unmistakable. Hoping that he had also been recognised, Duarte stepped out of his shelter and walked slowly, so that Abreu would have to pass him. When he heard a slight cough close behind, he spoke quietly.

"They have Álvaro," he said briefly.

"He's here in the Aljube," replied Abreu without making any movement that acknowledged contact with the man just ahead of him. "I knew you would come."

They both slowed their pace so that Duarte's next words came before Abreu had even caught up to him. "What can be done, *meu amigo*?"

Now Abreu was alongside, and though looking straight ahead, Duarte could see that he gave an almost imperceptible shake of the head. "I have tried. He has been reckless, your brother. They were waiting for him. Now they have their evidence, on film, God help us. What was he thinking?"

Duarte had wrestled with the same incredulity, but all that mattered now was to save his brother's skin. When Álvaro's involvement with the *Resistência Acadêmica* had escalated, it was Abreu who obtained a position with the PIDE for Joaquim, the adopted brother who was so different from his siblings. It made him a direct channel for names of activists plotting against the *Estado Novo,* able to divert any information about Álvaro or his close associates. It was Duarte's only means of protecting his youngest brother. The flaw in the scheme was that it depended on the undependable Joaquim; that had always been the weak link, and now it had failed.

"All I can ever do is shift a few papers or delay a signature," Abreu said. "They have spies everywhere. One department denounces another."

Duarte and João had become friends at school and remained in touch ever since. Under pressure from his father, Abreu had allowed himself to be recruited into the PIDE straight from university. At first, both boys struggled with a conflict of principles. Their friendship cooled. Abreu reached the brink of resigning from the force more than once, but as he scaled the ranks, he found covert ways to help the victims of Salazar. Over the years, he had saved the lives of a rising number of dissidents and returned them to their families, without any of his colleagues ever knowing what was happening under their noses. No-one except his wife and his old friend Duarte, now close to him again, knew that his sympathies lay not with his employers but with the forces aiming to bring them down.

Abreu's voice sounded hollow as he mouthed the next words: "I have to be seen to condemn Álvaro."

A picture came into Duarte's mind from many years ago, of Abreu rescuing Álvaro after he went missing in the hills as a boy. He had cradled the child as if he were his own. Duarte also recalled his own sense of confidence, then, that Álvaro would be found and all would be well. He wasn't feeling that now.

"I am the only person who could make the film disappear," went on Abreu, "but that is how they would know it was me. They would convict him anyway and me with him. I have done all I can. I had to sign the order to have him interrogated. I had no choice. You know what that means. It killed me to do it, Duarte."

Abreu moved slightly ahead, his hat tipped forward against the rain, and they continued their charade of two unconnected men walking at different speeds. Duarte found himself unable to speak.

"There are no good choices," Abreu said. "He will be in Santiago within days after they have finished with him here. They are torturing your brother. He will give them everything." Abreu glanced towards his friend without turning his head.

Duarte said fiercely, "They will get nothing from Álvaro!" His voice failed on his brother's name. He had to stop himself from screaming. No-one ever returned from Salazar's concentration camp at Santiago.

Abreu was ahead of him now and moving away. The drizzle turned to a deluge and hammered the cobbles at their feet. It smelled fresh and earthy after days of dust and dryness. Duarte could only just catch his friend's reply.

"They will get everything, my friend. No-one resists. Don't believe the hero stories, everyone breaks. I'm sorry."

He dropped his briefcase then, and the act of bending to retrieve it enabled him to turn and add, "Protect the girl! Elena Guterres. That is all you can do." He straightened and his pace picked up as he moved away, his shoulders hunched against a wind that sprang suddenly and pitched needles of water into their faces.

Duarte stopped and swayed, leaning against a lamp post to keep his balance. His legs felt heavy, and tears joined the rivulets of rain running over his skin. He stared after the retreating figure of Abreu until it disappeared. Álvaro was not a hundred metres away at the PIDE. What was happening to him, now, right at this moment? Duarte's brain, normally so sharp, was refusing to think. He could only bring to mind the time that Álvaro had begged for a car, a stylish French Citroën. He wished he had given it. The boy could have ten Citroëns now, if that would only bring him back.

15

MOURARIA, LISBON
2020

Joaquim sat under the awning listening to the sound of raindrops pelting overhead. A cool breeze agitated the February air, and today he was joined at Filipe's bar by only a few smokers on the terrace. Everyone else sheltered inside.

Laurinda seated herself purposefully opposite him, and shrugged off a long black puffer coat that looked wet through. Shiny high boots with her customary spiked heels kept her legs dry. One look at her face made him wish he were somewhere else.

Today, he had already drained a glass of neat whisky instead of his usual wine or *Beirão*, and he signalled through the glass door, untypically closed against the weather, for another. Keeping his eyes on the table, he left his guest to order her own drink.

She remained silent until a weak *espresso carioca*

was placed in front of her.

"Talk!" she said abruptly.

Her mouth was set in a straight red line which he found as unnerving as the scowls of the guards who used to threaten him in prison. He said nothing, wondering how he could translate the horror that had lurked inside him unspoken for nearly fifty years into words that could be said to this android of a woman.

Instead he stared into his glass, already one third empty. It sat among a series of recent wet rings that would create stains to match the others on the table.

When he failed to speak, she did instead, and her voice sometimes rose to a shout.

"When I work for a year WITHOUT ANY PAY, and I spend hours and days sorting through evidence and arguments and precedents, and I put together a BRILLIANT case, and then spend weeks and months submitting defences and papers and contestations, without charging NOT ONE CENT! And then I give my best performance I have ever done in front of a judge – he was impressed with me, I knew – and then we lose the hearing because my client – my pathetic, idiot, WEASEL OF A CLIENT – has not told me the truth about his miserable life..."

Joaquim had never been spoken to like this before without returning a clip around the head, or a broken nose on some occasions, but strangely this time he felt more like beating himself up than the lawyer. It was true that he was a pathetic idiot and a weasel. But he didn't regard himself as someone who hit women. That was a long time ago and in the past.

"We turned down a settlement. A good one. We could have taken it and saved ourselves all the trouble. Saved ME all that work. Talk," she said again.

He stared down.

"TALK!"

The sound of the rain had stopped. Filipe came out to wind back the awning, permitting a pale sun to filter through the jacaranda overhead. Droplets dislodged by an imperceptible breeze shimmered on the table, and the air carried the fresh scent of wet leaves along with a perfume that must be hers.

Joaquim waited until the bar owner had returned inside, and then began to speak. Once started, he found himself unable to stop; the words poured out.

"I was young and I was stupid. More stupid than I had any right to be at thirty years old, thirty-three or something like that.

"There was my big brother Duarte. When I was a kid he taught me how to shoot wild boar in the hills, and then when I got my first crush on our cousin Inês, he taught me how to talk to girls. He was my hero.

"And then there was Álvaro. He was a dreamer, loved his books. I protected him like Duarte did me, and it was I who taught him to shoot the boar and talk to the girls. But he was more interested in reading." He shook his head. "I never understood that.

"Me, I wanted to live, to taste every flavour, travel, explore, break all the rules. But all of that took money, and it was the wicked hand of fate that made me the second son, not the first. Even adopted, as the eldest I would have been the heir. But Duarte got it all when he was just twenty-two years old, when *papai* died. *Mamã* was dead already, when she had Álvaro."

He crossed himself without pausing.

"She died for him, the only woman who ever really loved me.

"So Duarte got our city *palácio* in Lapa, the country estates in Sintra, all the business interests. Me? Nothing. Well, not nothing, he gave me an allowance, a good one to be fair, but I was ambitious. I wanted more.

"There was a young guy I went to school with, Fábio. His father was one of the big fish in the PIDE. So we were all frightened of Fábio, but he didn't need to be afraid of anyone because of his *papai's* job. That's what first got me interested, the power. Why live in terror when you could join them and have other people be scared of *you*?"

He paused. Laurinda didn't answer and he hadn't expected her to. He had almost forgotten she was there.

"No one ever respected me, not the way they did Duarte. So I got a job there, at the PIDE. It was my first money I had ever earned myself, not just given to me by a father or brother.

"I dreamed about being the Director one day – that man was rich, he could afford the best of everything. Of course it was all corrupt, the *Diretor* was stealing money from the state on the one hand and the victims of the state on the other. But who was I to stop that? It would happen whether or not I stuck my snout in the trough; it didn't mean I approved of what they did.

"When I started work there, Álvaro cut off all contact with me. He was at the university in Coimbra, and getting involved with the students who were causing all the trouble. I wondered why he wasted his youth that way, with all those brains of his. It looked like a hopeless cause. The regime had been going for forty years, and nothing ever changed. Well, it seemed that way at the time. Yeah, yeah, I know it was only a few years later and we had the revolution. Álvaro's side won. He would have been a hero then.

"So there we were, Duarte with his money that he didn't know how to spend – he never had any children to pass it on to, so what was the point of hoarding it like that? Álvaro with his principles, too busy agitating to enjoy life. And me, an agent in the secret police."

Filipe walked around the tables clearing plates and glasses. Laurinda signalled for another coffee. Joaquim continued talking, so engrossed in his revelations that he forgot his need for a drink.

"Now the main reason I joined the PIDE to get that money and status was because of my wife Aurélia. Aurélia Ilduara da Luz Branca. "

His eyes softened and looked into the distance as he said her name.

"She had a shine to her hair, burnished streaks, and her eyes glowed. Amber, like a she-wolf. That was why they called her Aurélia, for the gold in her eyes." He paused for a moment. "Anyway, struck by lightning, that was us.

"She was nineteen when we met; an innocent. I was seven years older. I got her pregnant. Her father had to let her marry me, but he didn't like me at all. Nobody did, except my Aurélia. And my *mamã*, but, like I said, she was dead."

He made the sign of the cross again.

Laurinda looked at her watch.

"Can we move this along?" she said coolly. "I have another meeting."

He didn't acknowledge she had spoken.

"So our first years together were bliss, but her whole family looked down on me and that began to grate. I wanted to impress her, and her people. I had my allowance, but I needed some status, and more money to splash around.

"That's when I applied to the PIDE. I think it was Fábio's father who fixed it. I didn't have the right qualifications because I bunked off lessons all the time to go hunting. I blame that on Duarte who taught me how to shoot. But I applied and they turned me down, and I told a few people, and one of them was Fábio, and then I tried again. This time I got hired. It must have been Fábio's father." He nodded to himself.

"The money was even better than I hoped: cash for looking the other way, bribes to win favours from us, no questions asked about expenses, that kind of thing.

"And the women. Some of them liked a powerful man, someone with position and influence in the PIDE. Some had relatives they needed protection for, like to stop them going to prison. They could be very nice to us then."

Laurinda sighed and rolled her eyes without trying to hide it.

He went on. "I was in the section that controlled the informers and collaborators in Lisbon. I felt like a somebody at last. But Aurélia, she wasn't impressed. She wouldn't have chosen to marry a PIDE agent.

"We met at one of Duarte's hunts. She saw my brothers: two good men, one rich, upstanding, and the other a teacher's pet, that was Álvaro at school. She was marrying into that family. Yes, that was it, I think. She didn't know I was not like them."

He shook his head.

"She hated the PIDE. I didn't like the violence either, it kind of stayed with me, some of the things they did. Haunted me. But if I had broken ranks, I would have been the one arrested and tortured. So that wasn't an option, was it, do you see?"

Laurinda sipped her coffee and looked away.

"So, there I am with stress at work and getting no respect at home. She never said it, but I knew. I knew. The love died in my Aurélia, and I started to go with other women. But they meant nothing. She was my queen, and there were times when I hated her for it.

"Before things got really bad and I was permanently locked out of our bedroom, she had our beautiful son.

"We named him Joaquim after me and Aurélio after her, but we always called him Joaquinho. I thought he might grow up to become all the things I had failed to, and we might be like brothers together. But the arguments at home got worse. I would try to make it better afterwards, but he was afraid of me. They both were."

Laurinda's face remained blank. He didn't notice.

"I started drinking. It didn't improve my temper. Then I was hitting my Aurélia, my prize, my angel, frightening my precious boy with my drunken rages. I went to Álvaro and asked him to forgive me, told him I wanted out of the PIDE. I begged him to help me; I would live a decent life, be a good husband and father. Of course, he agreed; he was a good soul.

"But I knew too much, and my bosses made it clear what would happen to me if I tried to leave. I was afraid. So I used my little brother's goodwill to spend time with him and his friends at the university, and with some who were not so much his friends.

"I know, that's shameful. I didn't see it that way back then.

"There was one guy there called Gomes, Lázaro Gomes. He was meant to be looking after the students. But what they didn't know was that he was a plant from the PIDE, paid to keep his eyes on what they were doing. Between us, with me inveigling myself in with my brother's rebels and Gomes spying there, we were able to get hold of a lot of information. The students were up to no good – revolutionaries and Reds. I was always careful not to implicate Álvaro of course. I wasn't a monster.

"We were ordered to make a list of the ringleaders in all the universities. Coimbra was right at the top of it, and I got some kudos at work because of my connections there. There were a lot of bohemians, arty types, you know, hopelessly out of touch with reality. Just like my Álvaro. I didn't tell them at the PIDE he was my brother, of course.

"Anyway, the way it worked was, Gomes would come up with the names of the troublemakers and hand them to me."

Laurinda sat down in front of him once again. She had slipped inside, presumably to the ladies' room, but he hadn't noticed her absence.

"Duarte didn't often talk about my work with the PIDE, and I'm sure he didn't approve of me being there, but just after I joined, he sat me down and we had a serious conversation about it. I was expecting a telling-off for having taken the job, but all he said was that our misguided brother Álvaro was behaving stupidly and might turn up on Gomes's lists. So we agreed I should look out for that and not let those lists go any further.

"There was a girl he was involved with – I can't remember her name – and Duarte said we should do Álvaro the favour of taking her off as well. He mentioned some other friends too, so I said I'd make sure that none of those names ever got past my desk.

"Well of course, Álvaro was my little brother, I'd have done all of that anyway. But it was good to have the conversation, it made me feel part of the family for once, instead of a stain on its name.

"So when notes from the informers arrived, first of all I would check to see that none of the kids Duarte had listed were mentioned. If they were, then I destroyed that paper. It happened occasionally and, thank the saints, I was there to protect all these people. And then I would pass the rest on to my chief.

"Anyway, this all worked fine until two events

collided with each other. One was a drunken spree of mine. Aurélia had celebrated Joaquinho's eighth birthday with a party for his little classmates and she hadn't told me. Of course I was angry, and I had a right to be, but it hurt. It was the pain that drove me out to the bars that night, so really it was her own fault.

"There was a lot of pressure at work; they wanted names and said I was taking too long. I was still drunk from the night before, and I got the notes I had checked mixed up with the ones I hadn't. A report about Álvaro slipped through.

"He'd been in a film. And his girlfriend. They were protesting against the regime. That Gomes, nose into everything, he recognised their voices. I didn't know. I swear. Do you have any idea what I would give to have that time again, to check those reports?"

Laurinda's eyes were glassy with inattention and she was busy ordering another coffee from Filipe, who had come out to unroll the awning against another shower.

"I'd have killed Gomes rather than give Álvaro away. I wish I had."

His voice rose above the pounding of the rain.

"And then it was done. They came for him one night, my little brother. We never saw him again. I thought I had influence, but the doors all closed on me. I had got drunk and offended the wrong people too many times. I was desperate, so I went to Duarte. I was sure he could fix this, through his big fancy friends. But I was wrong.

"They were holding Álvaro in the *Aljube*. You know,

there's a museum there now all about the revolution and prisoners and torture. Well that used to be the PIDE's prison and our headquarters. When you walked past that building you could hear the screams. Right here in the middle of Lisbon. I had to listen to them while I worked.

"The guards had no pity. They dreamed up a whole range of torture, very creative someone was. It wasn't just beatings, though there were plenty of those. They would hit the soles of the feet and then make the prisoner walk; electric shocks, cigarette burns where they would hurt the most; and then the mental torture: keeping them awake, or the 'statue': a man – or a woman, yes, they did these things to women too, and you can imagine what else – would have to stand without any rest for days in their cell. I don't know how those prisoners survived. Sometimes they begged the guards to finish them off."

Laurinda was staring at him, a grimace of distaste on her pretty face. He had her full attention now.

"Well," he continued, "my brother ended up there all because of me. He died and I never knew how. We couldn't save him, not me, not Duarte with all his money, not God in Heaven, though I asked Him enough times.

"I wish I could unknow all of this, but every morning I wake up and there it is again. Duarte looked at me that last day, and I could see in his eyes that his heart was breaking. For Álvaro of course, but maybe a little for me as well, because he was sending me away, so then he would have lost two brothers.

"He handed me a bank draft for a lot of *escudos* and told me never to come back. I avoided the PIDE then, and went back to my Aurélia and my boy, but Duarte had got to her first and she wanted nothing more to do with me.

"A pit opened inside me. It had always been there but now it got bigger. I think it started with all the things that happened in the war before I got to Portugal."

Laurinda closed her eyes, sighed, then opened them to check her phone. There were no new messages.

Joaquim went on. "I don't remember much. There was a woman who seemed in my mind like our *mamã* – Duarte's mother – but of course it wasn't. I think she was my real mother. She was pushing me towards a stranger and saying, *Don't say a word. Never open your mouth. Not to anyone.* Why? What would have happened if they heard me? I can remember the sense of her words, but not the language she spoke."

Laurinda shrugged, uncrossed her legs, and recrossed them on the other side. The aroma of coffee drifted across the table from her third cup, just placed there by Filipe.

"That's all I remember until I got to Duarte's house. His parents took me in, like I was their own son. Once I asked *mamã* if that woman who told me not to speak was her, and she said it wasn't because she would never send me away, not ever, she promised.

"She told me that I didn't say anything at all for a year, and then what came out was Portuguese. But I would never answer questions about what went before, she said. And then I forgot it all. I had dreams, bad dreams. I used to wake up screaming in the night. They still come to me sometimes, those nightmares.

"So now with what I had done to Álvaro, not meaning to at all, like I said, the pit opened up and got bigger. I don't know who I am. Am I a Jew? Am I Russian? Do you know what that's like, not to know who you are?"

Laurinda stared at him coldly. "I'm a lawyer, not a psychiatrist. I already said that being adopted makes no difference, if that's why you're telling me all this. So please get on with the facts."

Joaquim continued. "I couldn't live with myself. I wanted to die but I was too much of a coward to do it. So instead of killing myself, I went home and..."

He stopped. He looked at the table and then up at the sky. Blue patches showed through the branches above.

"It was bad. I left Lisbon. I never saw them again." He sagged, like a clockwork toy unwound.

"I took my new BMW with me and wandered around Europe. It was the 1970s and things were wild in Paris, in Rome; they knew how to live. Back home the revolution happened. What kind of a coup was that, without any fighting? Salazar was dead, Caetano was packed off to Brazil, and Portugal got democracy. I read about it in the papers.

"Every year after that, my money dwindled. So I started to steal and sell the things I stole. I beat some people up, what choice did I have? I got caught and went to jail. Two years. I learned some useful tips there, like how not to get caught again. But I came out with nothing, nowhere to go, so I went back to Duarte. I thought he might help me build a decent life. But he turned his back on me, his own brother.

"And my son died. Duarte said it happened while I was in jail. A hunting accident. I wasn't there to save him, my boy Joaquinho. And then Aurélia died too, Duarte said, of pneumonia. So I had failed everyone. Three of the four people I cared most about were dead, and the other turned his back on me.

"And that is how life is, and why Duarte cut me out of his will, and why we are here today. Can you get me any money?"

16

COIMBRA UNIVERSITY
1971

She sat in her room. She had barely moved for a day and a half since they came for Álvaro. People arrived and left, and perhaps she collapsed into sleep for short periods, but was unaware of it. The sun set and rose, and now it was dark again, and Gabriela was here, holding her hands.

"It's bad news," Gabriela said.

Elena knew what was coming. She tried not to listen; if she didn't hear the words, then it would not have happened. She stared beyond Gabriela's shoulder towards a painting on the wall, an eerie scene of fairies and elves in a wood, which she had owned as a child and brought with her to the university. If she kept looking at the picture, then time surely could not move forward and she would not have to know the truth.

But Gabriela spoke and nothing could change what

she said. "I'm sorry, Lina. He's gone. Álvaro is dead."

More people came into the room. There was screaming and crying. Some of it emanated from her, but she couldn't distinguish which. Coffee was pushed into her hands but she couldn't drink. A reflex in her mind told her she must contact Álvaro; he would know what to do. The thought kept returning like a revolving door, each time leading to the knowledge that she could not, and would not, comprehend.

"We don't know what happened," said Gabriela. "Álvaro's brother Duarte called the Rector."

"We must go to him. To Álvaro," Elena heard a voice say, and then realised it was her own.

No-one spoke. She knew she wasn't making sense. A spasm stabbed inside her but the physical pain hurt less than her mental agony. Gabriela hugged her.

She tried to understand what it meant that she would never see him again. The very concept of 'never' was impossible to grasp. People fussed and the pain came again, and then again, making her double over. It was happening every few minutes now.

Gabriela sat back and stared at her. "Lina, is it the baby?"

The words made no more sense than the news about Álvaro. She was still shaking and Gabriela wrapped a blanket around her.

"I'm going to call your parents," Gabriela said.

That broke through her dazed state. "No, you can't."

Gabriela cupped Elena's face in her hands, and said gently, "There is going to be a baby. You need your *mamã* and *papai* now."

The birth was still two months away. Only days ago it had not seemed to be so pressing that decisions must be made. Time moves slowly when we are young, and it was only on looking back years later that she could see how reckless they had been. No-one but Gabriela and Téo knew about the pregnancy. As her shape changed, she wore looser clothes. Sometimes she and Álvaro had talked about how to tell her parents or his brother Duarte, whether they should marry, or how they would live. No firm conclusions had been reached. The one thing they were sure of was that they would keep their child.

Finally she faced Gabriela. "What will I do now?" she asked. "How will I live without him? Tell me our baby will be alright!"

"Everything will be fine," said Gabriela, hugging her again. "We will look after the baby together. You'll never be alone."

The words hovered in the air, so clearly a lie. For the first time in her life Elena knew she was truly alone. Into the void of the horrifying present tumbled memories: secret nights in his room or hers, facing up to Gomes, nursing Luís. They were always together, she and Álvaro, each one half of the same pair. Now that it was over, time should have stopped, but it moved on relentlessly. Still she could not grasp the finality of death.

A doctor came and then an ambulance. The next clear memory she had was of lying in a bed. *Mamã* was there, with *papai* sitting next to her. The sheets were plain white, not the embroidered ones of her room at home in Chiado.

She moved a hand down to her stomach, soft now where it had been distended and firm. *Mamã* said nothing but nodded towards the other side of the bed. She turned and saw a cot. It was plain and clinical, with white wood and metal bars. Inside lay a miracle. *Mamã* leaned down, lifted the bundle all swathed in white cotton, and gently settled the baby into Elena's arms.

"Your daughter," *mamã* said.

A different kind of love entered her then, not replacing what she felt for Álvaro, but augmenting those feelings with something new.

"You can come home as soon as you're well enough," added *mamã*. "We'll look after you."

She didn't find out until later that her father had wisely dissuaded *mamã* from sharing her plan to have the baby adopted immediately so that Lisbon society would never know. Dizzy and confused from exhaustion, drugs, and grief, she shook her head. "I can't leave Coimbra, *mãe*. There is so much more to do. We must fight!"

The look on their faces reminded her, for the first of many times, that the 'we' she had referred to no longer existed. But her future had been entirely bound to Álvaro's for so long that the idea of giving up their cause felt like losing all that remained of him.

"Who called you?" she said. "Was it Gabriela? The doctor?"

Another look passed between her parents. "A man called Duarte came to see us," *papai* said.

"Álvaro's brother." She wished she knew this man that Álvaro so looked up to, but that was unlikely now.

Papai nodded. "He said we must get you away. Any more anti-government activities and you will be arrested."

Mamã was trying not to cry but a choked sob escaped. Tears spilled down her face as she said to her husband, "We agreed not to tell her now. It's too much. Wait until she's stronger."

Papai's eyes seemed to sink into the dark circles underneath them. There were lines she had never noticed before. His head hung down and then he raised it as if drawing up all his strength.

"Come home," he said. "Please."

A memory came into Elena's mind of her room in Chiado. She was lying in bed on a sick day from school, and the overriding sense was one of safety. She looked at the baby in her arms and adjusted the soft linen around the tiny face.

"You need rest," *papai* said. His voice was firm but his eyes pleaded with her. *Mamã* cried quietly.

Álvaro never gave up. How could she? But she was responsible now for his daughter; all that was left for them. Finally, she nodded and said, looking at the baby, not her parents, "Just until I'm stronger."

The child lay in her arms, unaware of the chaos into which she had been born. She looked serene. Elena let *mamã* take her, as her thoughts dissolved into drowsiness. Her eyes closed and she didn't see them leave.

17

COMPORTA, LISBON
2020

My flight to Lisbon arrived early this time. I wondered whether Marco would be there yet but as I stepped through the doors I saw him immediately, casually dressed in chinos and a faded cotton sweatshirt. We kissed on both cheeks and walked across the terminal, chatting about the flight and the weather. The exit doors swung open and delivered us into warm spring air.

"It's good to be here," I said. "We have freezing March winds at home."

"It's good to have you back," he said.

I glanced at him and we smiled. A year had passed since we first met at the notary's office, and I had returned four times since then. Over the course of these visits, the proportion of time spent planning legal challenges as opposed to enjoying each other's company had gradually reversed. This trip was different to the others because I had accepted his invitation to stay at his beach house in Comporta instead of in a hotel.

The possibility that his interest extended to more than friendship had occurred to me. I wasn't yet sure of how I felt about him. I liked his looks – if I had a 'type' he definitely fitted it – and his easy personality, but I had to ask myself what I wanted at this point in my life?

With one failed marriage behind me, I had no desire for another. I was happy with my friends, my work, and my interests. Apart from the anxiety over my home, and that was a big one, I felt complete. There were times when I was lonely, certainly, and would have liked someone to share life with, but there are risks involved in that. If things go wrong the fallout can be cataclysmic. I had experienced that kind of relationship before and was wary of opening myself up to the possibility again.

I had given up any expectation of finding the perfect partner and regarded the concept of 'soulmate' as a myth. Besides, I reminded myself, perhaps he had someone in his life already? He had shown no more than friendship to me so far, and our meetings were ostensibly to discuss the litigation anyway. I would worry about any further developments when they happened, if ever.

The journey was short. Marco's car soon turned through a pair of wide iron gates and along a stone-covered driveway. The place looked as old as his townhouse was new. A white turret rose through mismatched terracotta tiles on the roof, and bracts of purple bougainvillea arched up the walls.

"It was a fisherman's cottage," Marco said. "I extended it but went to a lot of trouble to match all the original building materials. Not my usual style, but it's a labour of love."

"It looks ancient," I said. He was always surprising me, this man. I was expecting a modern house like the one in Santos-o-Velho. The trend here was to knock down old buildings and replace them with glass boxes, yet he had gone directly against that and created something that appeared to have stood there for centuries.

He turned a long metal key in the lock of a heavy wooden door. It opened to a tumult of barking and tumbling fur. "The family," he said.

There were two of them, large dogs with short curly hair. One was brown and the other a mottled tan colour. They ran in circles around Marco, whimpering with excitement. I stretched out the back of my hand to be sniffed and was rewarded with a lick and wagging tails.

"Brisa", he said pointing to the dark-haired one, "and Marujo. That's 'Breeze' and 'Sailor'. We love the sea, all three of us. If the weather's calm, we could go out this weekend, if you'd like to?"

"I'd love that. Where's your boat?"

"In the marina at Troia, a few minutes away. Sometimes we stay out all day in the sun. We swim, snack, sleep when we feel like it. If it's rough, then we motor behind the peninsula and moor up somewhere for lunch."

I loved sailing but not in rough seas; I loved dogs, and the bigger the better; I also liked houses on water and Marco had two of them. It seemed that we shared the same tastes.

"Now, the important thing is, what would you like to do now?" he asked. "Late lunch? Go for a walk?"

"I think I know what some members of your family would like. Could we take the dogs out? Unless you're hungry?"

"There's nothing I'd like better."

We walked through the house over stone-flagged floors. The furniture and art were like the ones in Santos-o-Velho; Marco had a way of mixing old with new, but always keeping things simple, and it worked well in both settings. The back of the cottage opened out into an extension, a big living room that led to a conservatory.

Outside was a raised terrace where the aquamarine waters of a long pool danced in the sun. Further on, over a white wall, I glimpsed the blue-green panorama of the Atlantic Ocean. Lemons patched the trees with bright yellow, and a fusion of colours thronged in the shrubs and flowers.

He unbolted an ancient wooden door and we emerged onto a long, sandy beach punctured by rocks. The dogs bounded straight ahead and plunged into the water.

"I feel like doing the same," I said.

"You might think twice about that. The sea's

freezing, even in summer. I swim in it sometimes though."

"I swim in the Thames in England."

We smiled at each other, recognising another affinity, and an unexpected one. The dogs shook themselves dry and chased each other along the beach.

"So, tell me more about your life," he said. "You're a management consultant?"

"That's right. My clients are mostly directors of big companies or in prison." I realised how strange that sounded. "I do charity work for prisons. They need skills like mine but wouldn't be able to pay commercial rates. It's the part of my work I love the most."

"It must be satisfying."

I nodded.

"And what do you to with your spare time?" he asked.

So far in all our meetings, the talk had been mostly about the court case or my newly discovered Portuguese relatives. Our personal lives had hardly been mentioned. Now felt like the right time to go deeper.

"I was married but it didn't work out. I don't have children. I live alone in a big old house on the Thames. It belonged to my parents. So I have a lovely view like yours."

It was not to mislead him that I didn't mention the problems with the lease; the day just seemed too beautiful to bring up such a painful subject.

"I'm happy there," I added in case the picture I had painted sounded lonely, and then wondered if I had given the impression of not being open to anything more than a platonic relationship. I wasn't sure about that myself at this point.

"I'm divorced too," he replied. "In this country, when I was young, there was an expectation to marry. Duarte introduced us; Joana was beautiful, from the right family, and he thought she'd make an ideal wife for me. He could be over-protective sometimes. Though for a few years, it seemed he was right. We had a son, I renovated a beautiful house for us in Lapa, and my business was thriving. I thought we had the perfect life.

"I had a business partner, Antonio, and we were planning to move south to the Algarve. It was just starting to be developed for tourists and there were fantastic opportunities for architects. Antonio was single. I used to wonder if he was gay, but didn't want his family to know. It was legal now, but there was still a lot of prejudice. I thought of him as part of the family. He even came on holiday with us. Joana loved the idea of moving down South and so did the boy."

"It sounds idyllic." I wondered what had gone wrong.

"Then I found out they were having an affair."

I stared at him in shock. He looked back at me. His eyes were unshielded. I felt an urge to protect him and make everything right.

"It had been going on for years. Antonio wasn't mine. When he was born, she said she wanted to name him after her father. I remember saying to them both how great it was that our best friend was Antonio, so it was kind of in his honour too. Perhaps they found that funny. I don't know."

"How could anyone do that?"

He shrugged and nodded. "So they went off to the Algarve. I've never seen them again."

"Not even your son?"

"He wasn't my son."

I wasn't Douglas's daughter, except in every other sense of the word but biologically.

"I haven't committed to anyone since." He looked stricken. "I find it hard to trust."

I put a hand on his arm. We walked on in silence. I was glad he was here with me, breathing sea air and warmed by the sun. His mood gradually lightened, and by the time we got back to the wooden door we were both smiling again.

The dogs stood wagging their tails as he opened it. He made coffee for himself and tea for me. For the rest of the day we relaxed in the garden without talking any more about our past lives. The conversation we had shared felt like a step in a new direction for us, and I think we both needed time to adjust without taking it further. Apart from feeling sympathy for him, I felt little curiosity about what had gone before. It just didn't seem relevant any more. I found out later that he felt the same.

We roasted butterflied lamb on the barbecue and drank wine from the Douro Valley. As darkness fell, a red moon rose eerily over the sea. We gazed at the inky water and listened to it splashing gently onto the sand. The dogs lay by our sides, contented, occasionally pricking up their ears at the sounds of the night.

It is not always the obvious things in life that lead to our decisions. I now knew much more about this man than before, had met some of his friends, and understood that we shared a great deal in common. But what made me leave the guest quarters unoccupied, to share his room that night, was the way he behaved with his dogs. To anyone else that might sound crazy, but for me, his great care for them was the reassurance I needed that I would be safe with him.

The next day we started making plans for the rest of the year, and then he drove me to the airport and I caught my flight home.

It was the fifteenth of March 2020. Within a week, the world would go into quarantine and travel would be outlawed altogether.

18

BRITISH EMBASSY, LISBON
1972

She stood in the ballroom uneasily in the velvet, mini-skirted, cocktail dress *mamã* had ordered instead of the plain black column she had requested. Having refused one of the bubbling flutes being circulated by uniformed waiters, she did not now know what to do with her hands. She wanted to be at home with her books and her baby, but deals had been done and parental demands now had to be met.

In return for their support, to which the only alternative was to give up Álvaro's child for adoption, she had agreed to attend social events like this one. The saving grace was that most were now barred to her. She was an unmarried mother, and shunned by the patrician society of Lisbon, who were afraid she might corrupt their own daughters, or worse, that their sons might fall in love with her.

Here at the British Embassy, a different society prevailed. Expatriates from all over the world lived outside their own social norms and adopted a more liberal code than they might have done at home. Blind eyes were turned to extra-marital affairs, and apparently to illegitimate births as well. Her parents had quickly accepted this rare invitation that included their disgraced daughter, in the hope that tonight she might meet a young man who would marry her and 'give her child a name', as *papai* put it.

As the fizzing glasses circulated, extravagantly dressed men and women gossiped, laughed, and networked furiously in the space around her. The louder the babble, the more she withdrew. She fixed her eyes on a giant clock over the main entrance to the hall and watched its second-hand tick forward. The longer she stared, the slower time seemed to pass.

At ten past nine a middle-aged man with receding hair left his wife's side and made his way towards her. She looked around the room for a distraction but there was no escape.

"May I have the pleasure, young lady?" His patronising smile told her that this was the work of *mamã*.

They loped stiffly round the room while a small orchestra played a thirty-year old waltz. She remembered the steps from distant lessons at school. He held her at a polite distance and the smile never changed. She thought of her pretty little daughter, at home with the maids, and envied them.

Then the ordeal was over, and the hands of the clock

showed nine-sixteen. She requested water from a waiter and he returned with a crystal glass of it. Nine-eighteen. Dinner had been eaten and carriages were not until midnight, and there was nothing to rescue her in between. Her whole body was rigid with resentment against society, its expectations, and the monolithic state machine that had murdered Álvaro.

Her parents were now engaged in conversation with a tall, dark man of about her own age. She allowed herself to be introduced.

Her jaw tightened with annoyance as *mamã* said to him, "Please go ahead if you'd like to dance."

His smile broadened. "Elena," he said, "my favourite name! And you look lovely tonight."

She took a slight step backwards.

"And what do you do with your time?"

The parental deal demanded she engage. "I was reading law at Coimbra."

"Not any longer?" he enquired.

"Now I look after my baby."

"Ah," he said, looking disappointed. "You married young!"

How should she continue? A noncommittal smile would have sufficed. Then they could have danced and duty would have been done.

Instead, she said "No," and held out the hand that was bare of a ring. She couldn't stop herself. "I don't have a boyfriend either."

His smile vanished. He walked away. What a relief.

Then she saw her mother's face. There was a time when Alexandra would have sparkled at an event such as this. She had loved the social round: the giving and going to parties, the fashionable clothes that seemed to be constantly in need of renewal (*papai* used to complain), the anticipation, and the dissection of news and events afterwards. Now she looked defeated. A gifted musician, she had complied with family expectations and chosen marriage over a beckoning career as a concert pianist. Instead, she had enjoyed performing solely at the soirées of friends. But with invitations dwindling in the face of social disgrace, these days found her playing alone in the music room of the house in Chiado. Elena would listen to the Scarlatti sonatas and Chopin nocturnes, executed perfectly and without an audience. This, Elena knew, was her own doing. She was entirely responsible.

"I'm sorry *mãe*," she said, looking at that troubled, beautiful, well-loved face. Small lines were starting to mark it in places. *How many did I put there?* Elena wondered.

So when the next possible suitor appeared, she was less reserved towards him. This one had fair hair and grey eyes. Like Álvaro.

"They tell me you speak English very well," he said. "Which is fortunate because my Portuguese is atrocious."

She nodded. "I do."

"I have to tell you, you look..."

Her mood sank as she waited for the usual tedious string of compliments.

"Bored stiff! - I don't like these parties either."

She laughed. It was so unexpected. *Mamã* was

watching and looking happier.

"I'm Douglas. Douglas Matthews. And you are Elena Correia Guterres. I know your parents."

She found herself shaking hands with him. Although his eyes were the same colour as Álvaro's, they danced with a frivolous humour, whereas Álvaro's were always intense, except when he was sad. This man was older too, by maybe ten years.

"You don't look too happy," he said. "Is it because of me? Have I said something to offend you?"

There was no suitable answer. If she told him she was missing her fatherless child, he would leave as quickly as the last one had, and she would have let *mamã* down again. She looked back at him and took a breath to speak, then said nothing.

"Would you like to see the view from the balcony?" he asked. "It's quite spectacular, the lights all over the city."

Did he think she had never seen Lisbon at night, he an *estrangeiro* and she a native of the place? Nevertheless, she would give anything to escape this dancefloor with its stuffy waiters, condescending men, and gossip about money, possessions, and who happened to be sleeping with whom.

She slipped away with him, avoiding the eyes of her parents, but pleased that they were finally seeing her in the company of a man, and one whom they knew and most likely approved of. As she walked across the floor, he took her elbow as if to guide her. It was an old-fashioned gesture and something Álvaro would never have done, but she allowed herself to be guided.

When they reached the terrace doors she stopped. He seemed nice and it wasn't fair to mislead him. "I have a baby but I'm not married," she said abruptly.

He looked at her in surprise.

Here it comes, she thought. Still he said nothing, so she continued. "I thought you should know that."

She turned to leave, but then he laughed.

"This is 1972, for heaven's sake," he said. "Are you planning to join a nunnery or can you come out to the terrace with me?"

She smiled in spite of herself, and they stepped into the fresh night air.

19

MOURARIA, LISBON

2020

Joaquim sat in his kitchen staring through the grimy window at an empty street. He couldn't even get out to the bar because of the 'State of Calamity' that the government had declared the day before. Just when everything was returning to normal, it had all shut down again. This Covid virus was worse than Salazar.

He grunted and frowned at the glass that sat empty in front of him. The bar being closed, Filipe had come to him, carrying a bottle of *Beirão,* but had allowed him only one shot. Filipe said it was for the sake of his health. Joaquim didn't know whether the man cared about that or was just being miserly, but he wasn't asked to pay, so he drank up. They talked mostly about Joaquim's indigestion and Filipe's gout. The light from the overhead bulb bounced off the shiny bits between the grey tufts of the bar-owner's hair.

After Felipe left, he sat staring at the empty glass for an hour, with nowhere to go and nothing to do. Money was tight when there were no tourists to steal from. Eighteen months had passed since the reading of the will. Cheap bars and poverty should have been a thing of the past for him by now, with the plans for his holiday resort submitted to the *Direção Municipal de Urbanismo* at the Town Hall, and meanwhile he would be living the life of luxury that brother Duarte had denied him for so long.

The word 'brother' gave him the same jolt it always did when he heard it, even in his own mind. It dredged up memories of the other dead sibling and the events he tried in vain to forget.

Laurinda let herself in without knocking. Joaquim reflected that had they been at the bar like the old days, Lourenço might have turned up as well. His old cellmate had taken to hanging around more frequently than Joaquim felt he should, although he had to admit that the man's company helped to pass the time, and was even enjoyable sometimes. He had taken Lourenço into his confidence over his plans for investing the inheritance that was coming his way, and liked to meander through ideas with this willing listener. He had even promised the man a job, and it would be real work, not stealing laptops.

He looked warily at Laurinda. As always, her shirt was crisp and her manner even more so. Her skinny bottom was wrapped in a pencil skirt today, not the close-fitting trousers she sometimes wore, and a fine gold chain encircled her neck. She exuded wealth, privilege, and hard-nosed efficiency. She frightened him.

"What the hell is taking so long?" he grunted. "Why don't I have my money?"

"The law never hurries itself," she replied. "How fortunate for you that it is my time which is being expended and that you don't have to pay for it. Of course, telling your lawyer the truth from the start might have speeded things up."

The double reprimand put him in his place. "OK," he said, "What's happening?"

"Everything in the courts is delayed. No-one is at work. They're all paid to stay home. That should mean they work faster, not slower, but we all know what *trabalhar em casa* really means. Except for people like me who work for themselves and get no help from the government at all."

She launched into an account of what had been filed, and the contestations, and hearings, and appeals. When she got to legal precedents, he lost track, and after twenty minutes of this she took herself off, leaving him none the wiser.

No sooner had the door closed than it opened again and Lourenço came in; his third visitor that day, breaking all the Covid rules. He must have been hiding, waiting – and probably listening by the window. Joaquim reminded himself not to fall into the trap of trusting this delinquent, or the sassy *advogada* who had just left, come to that.

"Who's your girlfriend?" asked Lourenço, smiling a little too keenly. "Nice..."

Joaquim interrupted before he could finish. "She's not a girlfriend, she's my lawyer," he snapped.

He looked across the table. Sometimes he forgot that Lourenço was no longer nineteen years old but a middle-aged man in his late forties. Still, the urge to be his protector surfaced again, as it sometimes had in prison, before he had done the opposite and shopped the boy to the guards. That was one slate that might now wipe itself clean if he could only get his hands on his inheritance, and he would feel a hell of a lot better if it did.

The role he had in mind for Lourenço was a sort of second-in-command, someone who understood his ways and could maintain discipline and honesty among the teams of workers that Joaquim planned to employ when his holiday village came into being. The fact that Lourenço was not exactly the embodiment of either discipline or honesty, he pushed aside.

He had shared the idea, and could see a trace of hope flare up in Lourenço's eyes whenever it was mentioned. Joaquim understood that look very well: it was the aspiration, which he shared, to be treated with respect and never to be poor again; to become anything but the person he was today.

"Can't she be a lawyer and a girlfriend?" Lourenço asked insolently.

Before Joaquim could react, he produced a tall bottle from under his jacket. An anise flower stood suspended in the liquid, coated in sugar crystals. He poured a glass for each of them.

"No-one drinks this *merda* any more," said

Joaquim.

"My father drank it, and his father before him."

"And they both spent more time in jail than you."

Joaquim kept complaining even as he raised his glass and drained it. There was no other alcohol in the place and no money to buy any.

"Where did this come from, anyway?" he asked. He knew that Lourenço was as desperate as he was, neither of them being eligible for the furlough payments that the government doled out to people with jobs to stay home from.

"The supermarket," Lourenço replied. "It's so full they don't see anything that happens anymore."

Joaquim laughed. Now that the parks and the beaches and the cafes were closed, food stores were the only entertainment left in town, and the sole place where the sociable could socialise. There was a big store at the end of the street. He had been stealing most of his supplies there since March, undetected by staff who were busy on the tills and keeping their distance from customers.

"What's new?" Lourenço asked.

"Same old," Joaquim replied. "Papers, courts, lawyers, this, that. More time and money."

"Not your money. That was a smart move."

Joaquim shrugged. It was, he had to agree, although it had been Laurinda's idea, not his. He didn't relish the thought of the amount that she would walk away with if they won but as he didn't have any means of paying her, there was no choice. "She can afford it," he said. "Private income. Investment fund from *mamã* and *papai*. It paid for her flat and very nice it is too, in Estrela looking out across the park. Poor little rich girl."

"An investment fund," repeated Lourenço. "Smart, cute, and loaded too. If she loses the case, you could marry her instead." He yelped with laughter.

Joaquim swore. Lourenço laughed too much at his own jokes. He couldn't afford to lose. What else was there for him? "Maybe there's another way," he said, squinting through a beam of sunlight that briefly penetrated the window around this time of day at this time of year. "What if they were gone, those two who will inherit?"

Lourenço looked up at him. "Marco? And the Englishwoman?" Joaquim had shared all the details of the legal battle and Lourenço appeared to enjoy following the story like a soap opera. But he looked wary now.

Joaquim shrugged. "Perhaps if they weren't around, it would all come to me." He stopped there, letting the thought sink in. The drift of this idea was much bigger than anything he had contemplated before. Certainly, there had been violence and murders enough in his life, especially during his days with the secret police. But that was another world and a long time ago.

This was as far as he would take this conversation, for the moment. He just hoped that Laurinda would win the case for him. He drank his anis, grimacing slightly, and poured himself another.

20

HOTEL AVENIDA PALACE, LISBON
1972

"I need your help, Douglas."

She placed the emphasis on the last syllable: "Dugl*uss*", but still came nearer to the English pronunciation than most of his Portuguese acquaintances could manage. That was different, and so was she.

They had been sitting in the lounge of this fashionable hotel for twenty minutes, where he had hoped to entertain her with the very English custom of taking High Tea. But she refused anything more than a coffee, declined the tiers of little sandwiches and cakes that were delivered to the tables around them, and a glass of champagne was apparently out of the question.

Had it been any other woman, their first date might have been an evening in a cocktail bar, but there was something disarmingly old-fashioned about Elena's parents that shaped his approach to their daughter. He shifted in his seat and looked out of the window. Conversation had been sporadic and he was struggling to find a topic that interested her. A request for his help was a welcome development.

"Anything, Elena," he said, leaning forward. "What can I do for you?"

"They won't let me leave the house and they listen to all my telephone calls. I'm never alone."

He looked at her, surprised. "Really? I thought your parents were quite liberal."

"With everyone except me. But I have a history."

"I know," he said. "Do you want to tell me more about it?"

She changed the subject abruptly. "There is a friend I need to contact."

Her hands played nervously in her lap. Then her eyes looked straight into his, and all of his attention was engaged. Although he would happily have remained staring into those dark irises for the rest of the afternoon, he moved the conversation on by trying to help. It was his nature.

"Is it your baby's father you want to get in touch with?" For him, nothing was out of bounds, he was trying to tell her.

She looked shocked. "That's not possible. No, it's my friend, Gabriela. She telephoned but we couldn't talk. There's always someone listening." She looked down.

He felt totally lost now in this conversation that

only a moment ago seemed to be turning his way. "Tell me," he said. "I'll help if I can." Was Gabriela another girl who had got herself 'into trouble', he wondered? Standards were changing in his native England, where couples could live openly together without marrying, but that was a long way from being considered acceptable behaviour in Lisbon. The *Estado Novo* maintained a strict moral code.

"I didn't know what to do. I have no friends here. The ones my parents would allow me to see don't want to know me. So I thought of you."

He sat up straighter. His disappointment that she was here for his help, rather than the pleasure of his company, was tempered by the implication that he might be regarded as a friend. He smiled confidently and waited.

"So I told her to contact you. I had to think in the moment. It was very wrong of me I know."

"But of course," he said. "I'll be happy to help. Tell me what I can do."

He was fascinated. Before reaching the milestone age of thirty that year, he had led a bachelor's life that included affairs, but none of them meaningful. After an upbringing in the narrow confines of the English upper classes, he had followed his ancestors to the University of Oxford. As a tall, white, wealthy male, loosely related to England's nobility (one uncle was a baronet), all doors were open to him in the culture of 1959. To say that his horizons were widened there would be an understatement. Then he had unthinkingly followed his father into the Foreign Office, and the respectable post he now held at the British Embassy in Lisbon might lead to an ambassadorship one day.

"She knows where you are," Elena continued. "She will make contact and give you some papers they want me to translate."

"Who? What do 'they' want you to translate?" he asked. Up until now he had been listening because of his interest in the girl herself; now he grew intrigued by what she was saying.

She looked steadily back at him. "Douglas, if you're going to help me, I must be honest with you. So that you understand it's important to be careful."

Ever the rescuer, he was elated at the idea of being of service to this interesting *Senhorita* with the questionable morals, and what harm could it do, just to put her in touch with a female friend? Why would her parents object to that?

She went on, her eyes holding his. "I was in a group at Coimbra. A resistance group. It works against the *Estado Novo*. You know about Salazar?"

He nodded. Her voice had lowered.

"We were the *Resistência Acadêmica*. It's in all the universities. We organised the protests. I was part of that."

This was not at all what he had expected.

"The father of my baby was a leader of that movement. They killed him."

"What?" His words stumbled out. "I'm sorry. I've heard about atrocities..."

Her eyes widened and her finger touched her lips. He lowered his voice.

"But you're so young. Just students. The baby's father..."

She nodded. "Álvaro. A student."

"Just at the start of your lives. What kind of monsters... ?" He was too shocked to say more. He was angry for her, too.

"I can't bring him back. But I will give everything I have to bring down that sick government. It's all I can do for him now."

He understood it, then – why she wasn't out enjoying life, or studying, or doing whatever would move her forward, with her pretty face and her quick intelligence.

"There's something happening at Coimbra," she said in a whisper. "The *Resistência* are demanding a formal review of censorship. They have names, facts, and evidence. I must translate for them."

How simple his life had been just an hour ago, when all he had to do was persuade this woman to join him for tea and then fall in love with him. Why must it be so complicated? He cared about the repressive conditions in Portugal, of course he did, but had never considered himself to be someone who might get involved in changing them. Such activities could affect his future career advancement; he might even lose his job. Were there criminal implications as well? Deportation? Imprisonment?

"Elena, I'd like to help. There's not much I wouldn't do for you, believe me. But you know I work for the British Embassy here. My position carries a lot of trust. Now, for me, I may not like the *Estado Novo*, but the person I am is the job I do. I'm a Diplomatic Service Officer. That word 'Diplomatic' tells you everything. Do you understand what I'm saying?"

"That you won't help." There was no resentment in her voice, just sadness that sagged her shoulders and pooled in the dark eyes that looked back at him.

"Not won't," he said. "Can't. To plot against the government would go against everything I'm here for. We're here to oil the wheels, not take them apart."

"You live by their rules," she mocked gently. "Don't you have any of your own?"

He liked the way she reacted without tears or tantrums, in that meticulous English with its grammar and syntax perfect to the word. But why must this soft voice speak of danger and death at all? Although he had always been something of a rebel and never fond of rules himself, he wasn't drawn to fighting for causes. Nevertheless, his urge to help her was so overwhelming that he found himself thinking of ways around all the reasons not to do so that he had just listed. Douglas was a man whose heart ruled his head.

"Have you heard of the Treaty of Windsor?" he began, thoughtfully.

She shook her head.

"Eight hundred years ago, England and Portugal vowed to '*give aid and succour*' to each other. That treaty has been re-signed through the centuries. The last time was just before the war. Now I have to ask myself, am I giving my aid and succour to Portugal by complying with the regime or would I be more useful helping to dismantle it?"

What he really had to ask himself was whether his dual English-and-Portuguese patriotic spirit ran that deep, or was he just trying to talk himself into breaking the law? He pushed the question away.

She waited. Her hands were still now, and all her attention gratifyingly upon him.

"So what you're asking is that I pass some papers from this Gabriela to you? And back again? No-one could ever know, of course. I'd lose my job, and I can't bear to think about what might happen to you."

She looked him full in the face and said, "They will know. They always know."

He could see she was struggling inside. He loved her honesty, that she would warn him like this instead of just taking advantage of his wavering resolve. Did she find herself unable to lie because of the connection that he sensed between them? Did she feel it too? He almost took her hand, but there was something about her that made him keep a respectful distance.

"Not this time," he said, surprised to hear himself talking as if he had already agreed to her insanely dangerous request. "I know how to be discreet. And there's one great advantage for me if I do this: you'll have to see me again."

They smiled at each other. We each see what we want to see and interpret events as we would wish them to be. Sitting in the Avenida Palace that day, surrounded by the tinkle of teacups and gossip, Douglas felt certain that the bond he felt growing between them was a romantic one, and not just about the delivery of illegal papers. He touched her hand.

21

CHILTERN GRANGE, MEDMENHAM
2020

I opened my laptop and entered my password. I had begun my working day in this way a hundred times before, but it all felt different now. How strange that someone from another country with its own language, customs, and history, should be the one who made me feel as if I had come home.

After that first stay at Marco's beach house, I had returned for a week, and he came to see me as well, dodging lockdowns, wearing masks on planes, and taking ubiquitous Covid tests. The hassle was worth it for the joy of being together.

I seemed to have found the storybook romance that I had dreamed of as a teenager, before discovering that real relationships were more likely to be perplexing, unsatisfying, and heading for a messy end. Now I found myself waiting for the splinters to appear that would drive us apart. They always showed up eventually, didn't they? But with Marco there was never any doubt or friction, just an illogical sense that we had always been together and always would. The happiness seeped into every area of my life – even the pending catastrophe of losing my home weighed less heavily – and it was hard to remember what my life had been like without him.

Between our visits, there were weeks of enforced isolation. I didn't mind at all. There was a heatwave that year, which made my house the ideal place in which to be incarcerated, and I enjoyed sitting alone by the river, ensconced in my summerhouse, reliving our time together and mulling over the future. I had never experienced this before: the sense that nothing could go wrong. I was even beginning to rethink my cynicism about the existence of soulmates. It had taken me a lifetime to meet mine, but I was daring to hope he was here.

When confined to our separate countries, we spoke every day. We made plans for Christmas in Lisbon, a magical time, he said. As the leaves on my jacaranda fell, and the media filled with forecasts of more Covid gloom, we made a pact: at the first hint of another lockdown I would catch a plane and be marooned with him instead of alone in England. Being shut up in my chilly house through the darkness and rain of winter would be quite different from confinement during the glorious summer weather we had that year. I couldn't bear the thought of it. If our governments imprisoned us again, we would serve our sentences together under

Lisbon's winter sun.

Instead of checking for business mail every morning, I now opened my personal inbox first to see if there were any messages from Marco. Today there was an email, and it was from Portugal, but not from him. Mildly disappointed, I studied the name of the sender before opening the rest: *naosabes@tedigo.pt*. I didn't recall having seen that address before and thought it might be my first taste of Portuguese spam. I read on.

"Something you not know. Marco he is son of Joaquim Mendonça Gonçalves. You no can trust."

I struggled with the inept English. There must be a hitch in the translation, I thought. But I had to abandon it for the moment, because my first appointment of the day was due to begin. I was meeting the trustees of a charity which supported ex-offenders, and even though it wouldn't help my precarious finances, it was important to me. An hour passed before I closed the connection and was able to return to the question of who had sent the message and what it meant. I read it again:

"Marco he is son of Joaquim Mendonça Gonçalves. You no can trust."

It didn't make sense and my finger hovered over 'delete'. Then I remembered how I had been misled about my own parentage all of my life, and that Marco said he remembered nothing of his father, not even his name. Still, this I couldn't believe. Someone was trying to cause trouble. Could it be from Marco's ex-wife? But the marriage ended amicably, he said.

I typed *naosabes* into my browser. A translation came up that separated it into two words, *nao* and *sabes*. They meant 'you don't know'. What was *@tedigo*? I fed the domain into my browser but it generated an error message. *Te digo* meant 'I tell you.' So this email came from 'You don't know' at 'I tell you.' Who tells me? The message was unsigned. Another web search failed to reveal the owner of the domain.

I needed to talk to Marco. I reached for my phone and his affectionate face soon filled my screen. Before I could begin, he spoke first.

"We're going to have some additions to the family." He looked happy and excited.

I smiled questioningly.

"Brisa, she's pregnant. There'll be puppies!"

"How lovely! When?"

"The vet says five or six weeks."

We talked for ages about the puppies – I was longing to see them – and the email seemed insignificant in comparison. It might best be discussed in person, I reasoned, and by the time we met, the issue might have resolved itself. Marco's news called for a celebration, so we raised a glass of champagne to each other on the screen, a regular event for us now. We chatted for an hour; we always had so much to say to each other. Then I went back to work.

That night I turned to Jen, my best friend. We

bought lockdown takeaway from the local pub, and talked a lot about my new life in Portugal. I told her about the email and found myself growing increasingly uneasy as I spoke.

"Should I be suspicious?" I didn't know why I was asking her, for she had never met Marco, but I needed to talk it through with someone I could trust.

"What are the facts?" she asked efficiently. Jen was a great listener and posed all the right questions. "What do you know for sure?"

"Well," I began, examining it all in my mind, "Cristóvão told me about Joaquim's lawsuit. We had a video conference with Marco."

"Have you spoken with Cristóvão since then?"

"No. I agreed Marco would handle everything. I was worried about dealing with the lawyers, the language, the stress. He offered to do it all for me."

"And you trusted him?"

"Of course. If you knew him..." I realised how lame that sounded, and I could see that Jen thought the same.

"And Marco said he'd cover your costs?" she asked.

"Since the first one, yes. I paid that myself. But the rest are charges he would have to pay anyway, he said. I refused at first, but I just couldn't take the financial risk. I will give it back though," I added. "If we win."

"It does beg the question – how do you know that the Portuguese lawyer, Chris..."

"Cristóvão. He's a notary."

"How do you know he's acting for you?"

It was a good question. I hadn't spoken with him

directly since that meeting with Marco, and I wasn't paying him. "Marco tells me what Cristóvão has said and sends me all the papers. He translates them for me."

"Do you see the originals? Or just Marco's translation?"

I felt stupid. "No, I haven't seen the originals." Why had he not sent them? Why hadn't I asked?

"So let's imagine, just for the sake of looking at all angles, what if Marco is the son of that man... ?"

"Joaquim. He couldn't be. He's slim and fair. And nice, and sensitive. Joaquim's a brute. Dark-haired, thickset. They're nothing like each other."

"So let's say Marco's some sort of a throwback."

I froze, remembering how he had explained Álvaro's fair complexion using that very word, 'throwback'. Such things happen.

"Could Marco, Joaquim, and Chris the lawyer, or notary, all be working together? To nudge your share of the inheritance their way?"

It was not impossible. The empty cartons from our meal lay spread across the table. The food had been average, nowhere near Douglas's standards. For months I had felt I might finally be attaining something like the life they had shared, my parents, filled with love and trust. That hope was unravelling now, undermined by doubt.

"Has Marco ever mentioned his father to you?"

"He abandoned them, Marco and his mother. He doesn't even know the man's name."

"Hmm." Jen was silent. That 'hmm' said it all. "Who

might have sent the email?" she asked, taking another tack. "Someone whose first language isn't English."

I sat back in my chair. Breaking everything down step by step in this way helped me to feel calmer. "It sounds like Cristóvão. He doesn't quite know where to put the pronouns. Then again, Laurinda's fluent, but she could be pretending. Disguising her identity."

"Who's Laurinda again?"

"Joaquim's lawyer. She left Cristóvão to set up her own practice."

"Hmm," Jen said again. "What about Joaquim?"

"The only English I've heard from him is swearing."

"So it could have been Chris the notary, Laurinda the lawyer, or Joaquim the old man, if he has any English other than swearwords. Is there anyone else?"

"Well I wondered about Marco's ex-wife. But they split on good terms."

"How do you know?"

My shoulders sank a little. "He told me." I had made assumptions about everything and had no evidence that any of it was true. I couldn't believe I had been so trusting.

We talked around in circles for a while, and although we couldn't come to any real conclusions I felt better for it. Jen left and I fell into a deep sleep full of dreams that reflected my tangled thoughts – there were people I couldn't identify and tasks I had to complete – and then I lay awake in the early hours trying to make sense of it all, but failed.

The next morning, I read the email again.

"Marco he is son of Joaquim Mendonça Gonçalves. You no can trust."

But I was so sure of him, I argued with myself, and he was devoted to his dogs. *Bad men could love their pets too,* the doubting 'me' in my head replied. But his values and beliefs had chimed so strongly with mine, I protested, and we agreed on everything. *A conman might do all of that to win your trust,* I countered.

A dark period of uncertainty followed. I felt like a child told that Christmas is cancelled, as indeed it was as far as our plans in Lisbon were concerned. I began to fear I would lose not only my house but the whole inheritance too. I didn't know if I was more upset about the loss of those things, or the man I'd dared to think might be the love of my life, or the bright future I'd started to build around the idea of that.

Not knowing for certain was the worst of it, and I wavered between confronting Marco or accepting I had been duped. I continued to talk it over with poor Jen, who must have grown sick at the sound of his name, but she persevered and made me look at the situation from all angles. She warned me against him, of course. It was sensible advice but didn't help me at all.

The November lockdowns were announced and I didn't get on a plane. I felt the problem should be discussed in person but couldn't risk being stranded there if my worst fears turned out to be true. Soon travel became impossible, and that bought me some time. I started avoiding Marco's video calls and delaying replies to his messages. He was clearly hurt but didn't press me.

I resumed dealing directly with Cristóvão for the legal case. It was a relief when he confirmed that he was indeed representing me against Joaquim's claim, and he sent me the Portuguese originals of all the documents to date. They matched Marco's translations. Did that put Marco in the clear? I debated it with Jen and came out as doubtful as ever.

Cristóvão assured me that we were in the final stages of litigation, and that it was unlikely any more funds would be required. That was a huge relief. If we were successful, I was determined to pay Marco back everything he had spent on my behalf so far. Then would that be the end of it? I vacillated. I didn't know, and would have to see him again to find out. For now, I resolved to find some comfort in the solitude that the new restrictions imposed, focus on my work, and hopefully rediscover my ability to sleep through the night.

The months of isolation that followed stretched into the bleakest winter I had ever known.

22

RIVER TAGUS, LISBON

1973

Winter gave way to spring and there were more days of sun than rain. A blanket of blue unfurled across the city as all the jacarandas burst into flower, and there were times when Elena found herself forgetting to be unhappy.

The Englishman was always there and seemed to find baby Lina as enchanting as she did. They would wheel her pushchair through blossom-lined streets down to the Tagus, where the child watched the ducks, fascinated, while Douglas sipped his tea and Elena her coffee. She was coming to understand that relationships could be quite different but still worthwhile. "Count Rolim's throwing a spring party," he said. "You won't want to go will you?"

"Please, no," she replied.

"Me neither," he smiled. "I'll say we're busy."

Relieved to be excluded from her parents' social life, she had been exasperated when invitations started to arrive for Douglas and herself as a couple. Fortunately he appeared to be happy to turn down all except essential ones. In the eyes of the world, they led a simple life. What no-one knew was that just as Álvaro had once drawn her into his circle of conspirators, she was now luring Douglas into hers.

He took the invitation out of his briefcase and handed it to her. Underneath, she felt an envelope which she knew would have come from the *Resistência Acadêmica*. They had devised a system where Gabriela would call him at his desk whenever she had new papers for translation. Using a special code, they would arrange a drop-off time and place, and then Téo would drive her to Lisbon and park his flamboyant vehicle as discreetly as possible while she made her delivery. She might leave the package in a bin or on a bench, but only after ensuring that Douglas was watching and no one else. Then he would pass it to Elena, a simple process now that they were so often in each other's company, and after she had completed the translation, the procedure would be reversed to return it.

Gabriela, who added affectionate letters to the dispatches, had told her that she and Téo were now regarded as a couple at the university. It was a cover that suited them both, for she was still committed to Luís, whose incarceration only hardened her determination to fight, while Téo had known for some years that he could only ever fall in love with a man.

Same-sex relationships had been condemned as an 'act against nature' by Salazar and punishable at worst by imprisonment, at best by social stigma, and regularly by violence. Being involved in seditious activities doubled the odds of being caught and the punishment if he were. Elena was afraid for them both.

"Thank you," she said, taking the card from Douglas and pretending to read it, while slipping the concealed package into a shoulder bag carried for the purpose. She felt guilty about putting him in danger, because whereas she had willingly collaborated with Álvaro, she knew that Douglas's involvement arose only out of his desire to please her. Although he was risking only his job and not his life, she liked him too much not to care.

"Lina looks pretty today," he said. "Like her mother."

Elena smiled. Somehow compliments from Douglas didn't land with her as the frivolous flattery that she detested in other men. She never tired of watching her daughter. The child had been named Elena too, but everyone called her Lina.

"Do you think she likes me?"

"She adores you."

"And does her mother?"

She moved her eyes to him and smiled again. He touched a hand to her face and she kissed it briefly. The physical attraction she felt for him had come as a surprise. When Álvaro died she had thought it was the end of such things for her, but had not understood how life goes on whether we want it or not; what is unthinkable one day becomes normal and even welcomed the next. It seemed natural that they should spend occasional nights together. Both of her parents turned a blind eye. She already had a baby in the nursery so had nothing to lose; that was their attitude. They were pragmatic people and relieved that at least she was out of danger. They were also quite unaware that she had found a way back into it through the auspices of this man of whom they so greatly approved.

"We feel like a family," he said.

She nodded, her eyes on Lina.

"We could make it formal. Marry. Get a house."

Sometimes he talked like this. He wanted commitment from her, but her heart still belonged to Álvaro. There were times when his presence was so real she could almost touch him: the feel of his fine hair on her fingers, a smooth skin, a soft mouth. Sometimes she thought she heard his voice just out of reach, and then, turning, would lose the sound. Moving on was a concept she couldn't grasp.

"I could adopt Lina," he continued. "She would be like my own daughter. We could have more Linas, lots more, and some little boys too."

Elena spluttered. "Do you really not know me at all? You think having babies is on my agenda? I'll never forgive them for what they did to Álvaro. The father of my child." She didn't see the sadness that crossed his face and went on with her outburst. "I'll fight them with everything I have!"

Her hands were clenched. She bent down to the pushchair and adjusted a toy.

He switched tack. "In your own house," he said, "you could see whoever you like. Your old friends could come and stay with us."

Blue-tinted blossoms fluttered down as a bird landed in the trees above them. The thought of autonomy transfixed her. Her own house.

"You could study law again." he went on. "Maybe here in Lisbon."

She pictured a room lined with books; Gabriela and Téo planning with her there.

"And I know we don't care about such things, but it might be better for Lina if her mother were married."

He was right about that, she knew. Her daughter deserved the very best start that life could provide. She had brought this child into a world of violence, but Douglas was healing the wounds. And he made her happy, sometimes, she couldn't deny it. Why not be his wife? Not only did she like being with him, but he reminded her of Álvaro: his tall body, the pale eyes, the intuitive nature. Álvaro was gone; Douglas was here.

There was also the loneliness that had engulfed her. Nothing had prepared her for that. She felt more isolated in the company of others than when alone, because they were not Álvaro. Except when that company was Douglas.

A low barge with a tall mast drifted by, its hull a mass of bright colours. Lina had tired of watching the ducks and reached out to be lifted onto the seat between them.

Elena felt the touch of the child's soft, plump arm against her own, and saw that her little hand on the other side was wrapped into Douglas's strong one. She felt at peace now, her emotional storm evaporating in the warmth of affection and sunlight. Álvaro's voice fell silent, and the void he had left grew smaller. That was happening more often these days.

Within two months, she and Douglas were engaged. By all appearances, her life was back on track; the baby would become legitimate and family honour restored. Both of her parents were ecstatic, but would have been less so had they known that not only was she still working for the *Resistência Acadêmica,* the tasks she undertook for them had moved on from simply translating foreign newspaper reports. Her job now was to create tracts in English laying bare specific names, dates, and executions. In the eyes of the regime it would be treason, and punishable by imprisonment or death.

She hadn't told Douglas about this change of direction, and hated herself for hiding it. Was it only his job that hung in the balance – which was bad enough in itself – or did they arrest foreigners too? Would he have diplomatic immunity? She didn't know, but just hoped that neither he nor anyone else would ever open the sealed packet of the papers that were being passed to and from the *Resistência Acadêmica.*

23

CHILTERN GRANGE, MEDMENHAM
2021

I clicked on the link, and Cristóvão's face appeared on the screen, bearing its usual polite expression. Since receiving the anonymous email six months earlier, I had ensured that all my dealings regarding the lawsuit took place directly with him, even though I no longer entirely trusted anyone involved in this business of the will, including the notary himself. The others on that list were Laurinda, Joaquim, and sadly Marco; in fact all of them.

When my visits to Marco had stopped, I first of all pleaded impatience with the rigmarole introduced on travel between our countries because of the pandemic. When he offered to come and see me instead, I didn't invite him. Soon our only contact was in connection with the case, and as we were each dealing directly with Cristóvão, that too eventually ceased. He now belonged to that part of my mind reserved for regret, not just for what we'd had, but for the future I'd imagined us sharing.

These thoughts visited me in the quiet of the night, but during the daytime I suppressed them and got on with living. I reminded myself how lucky I was to have good friends, my own business, and to be spending my lockdowns by a river while millions were shut up indoors. Although there were times when the flow of water, which used to be so exhilarating, seemed only to increase my loneliness, I was mostly able to put such feelings aside and focus on work.

Today Cristóvão was smiling. He looked satisfied almost to the point of smugness. "I have good news, Helen. We win our appeal. We have success."

"Do you mean the case is over?"

"No. But is good for us. We will win."

I had heard this ring of certainty from lawyers before and didn't know how to interpret it. Since withdrawing from Marco I had insisted on paying my way. It was not what I had planned, but what else could I do?

I'd originally embarked upon our defence as a calculated risk, cocooned by his support, and when the costs began to rise I had allowed him to cover them even though it ran against my natural instincts. Whether or not he was prepared to continue with that arrangement – and we hadn't discussed the subject since I received the email – I wanted to distance myself from him and accept no more favours. So I had told Cristóvão to bill me from then on.

I, or more accurately Cristóvão, had been wrong to think that most of the expense was behind us. In the face of every judgement that went against them, our claimants lodged a new appeal. Even if we were ultimately successful, Joaquim had no means of covering our costs. Judging by the size of the inheritance, that wouldn't matter as long as we won, but for the moment, the mounting charges had become such a drain on my finances that I started to assume the worst. I became convinced that the case would be lost and would take the little I had saved towards a deposit on a new home along with it. When I managed to sleep, my dreams saw me struggling with gargantuan tasks. I would wake with a feeling of relief that they weren't real and then remember that reality was not so great either.

Cristóvão remained optimistic. "You will have your inheritance, Helen," he said. Then he listed the assets again. "You must to decide with *Senhor* Almeida who has which things. The villa in Sintra is nice."

I didn't want to own anything in Portugal or ever go there again. I just needed enough to buy the freehold on my house. How complicated would it be to arrange all this with Marco, if indeed we ever actually won?

Looking back over my life, it seemed so simple before all this had happened. Then I had only the one problem, impending eviction, but now there were a mountain of worries to distract me every day. And my heart had been broken. It seemed to suck all my energy away so that tasks which might once have been interesting challenges now felt like insurmountable burdens. Everything took longer and I found myself giving way to uncharacteristic procrastination. I was tired.

"I don't want to keep any of it," I said eventually. "Do you think Marco will agree to sell? Or buy me out? If we win."

Cristóvão had never questioned why I wanted to deal directly with him. He looked back at me steadily, and then his next question crossed an invisible boundary.

"Helen," he began, "I don't know what happen with Marco. You no like him now. I apologise if I say too much, is hard the English for me. He is good man. You can trust. Is not like Joaquim."

Why would he think that Marco might be like Joaquim? Was it because the claim in the email was true? Could Marco be plotting with Joaquim to steal my half of the inheritance? And Cristóvão too?

"Marco is good," he repeated. "I promise. Marco you can trust."

I looked back at his friendly face on the screen and again heard the echo of my mother's voice saying "*Trust no-one*". Sometimes I had wondered what could possibly have made her so fearful, but she never would speak about the past. As I grew up, my own response had solidified into a resolve to do the opposite, and to trust everyone in the hope that they would live up to my faith. Fortunately, they usually did. So perhaps I had nothing to lose by confiding in Cristóvão; at the very least I might be able to gauge from his reaction whether he was telling the truth.

"Cristóvão, can I share something with you?"

He nodded and waited, his finely shaped eyebrows lifting slightly.

I hesitated and then plunged in. "A year ago I received an email from a Portuguese address. It made a crazy claim. It said Marco's father is Joaquim. I got to know Marco... quite well. But he never told me that. If it's true, it's a conflict of interest, isn't it? We were fighting the case together. He should have told me."

I had never seen Cristóvão unnerved before, but he floundered now.

"Surely it's nonsense?" I said.

"Is difficult," he began, and then halted.

"At first I didn't believe it," I went on. "But it made me realise that I knew practically nothing about Marco or this lawsuit. Everything was through him, all the translations. So I began to distrust him."

"You tell Marco this?"

"No." Why hadn't I? There might have been an explanation. I should have given him a chance. Self-doubt ballooned inside me.

And then Cristóvão shocked me. "Is true, Helen. But Marco – he not know."

"What?"

"He no tell you because he not know. It was the secret of Duarte and now Duarte he is dead."

The words hung in the air. Another secret. Outside my window, a pale winter sun played on the bare branches of the jacaranda and the water beyond. The sight left me unmoved. I couldn't think.

"Joaquim is Marco's father?" I repeated slowly.

"Yes. Marco is the son of Joaquim."

I let the words sit in the vortex they had created. Perhaps if I waited long enough I would know if they were true.

"How's that possible?" It came out as more of a protest than a question. "Marco has light eyes, brown hair. Joaquim is dark."

"Marco is like the mother. Aurélia. My father say she have special eyes." He struggled to find the words. "Like gold. I see them in Marco."

The memory of amber eyes, the overwhelm of information, the suspicion; my heart seemed to curl up inside me. If they had been lying to me about Marco's motives for helping me with the lawsuit, then this story of his parentage might be a lie as well – along with everything that they had told me about my own. My neck ached with the tension. I was angry and exhausted. This lawyer was putting me through a mill of uncertainty again.

"You haven't told him?"

He shook his head. "I make promise to Duarte. And is better that way, no? How you feel to know Joaquim is your father? And he is bad man, if he know, he never leave Marco alone. Ask always for money."

"I thought Marco might be plotting with Joaquim. That's why I came to you."

"Joaquim not know. And I not tell him."

I wondered briefly what kind of a legal position that statement put Cristóvão in, but it wasn't my concern.

"Did you send me the email, Cristóvão?"

He shook his head. "Me, no."

"Then who?"

He shrugged. "No-one else know. That is what I thought."

It was a big question but I had other more important ones to deal with. "So, Marco is Joaquim's son but neither of them knows it?"

Cristóvão nodded. "Marco is the son of Joaquim. Joaquim abandons the mother of Marco. Marco's name is Joaquim then. They call him Joaquinho, little Joaquim. Afterwards Aurélia, the mother, she change it to Marco. Then she die. Duarte give him the family name. Years after, Joaquim returns. Duarte say, your son is dead. Is best for Marco."

I tried to follow. "What does that make Marco to me then? We're cousins?"

"No," said Cristóvão, "You no relation. Joaquim he is adopted by the father of Duarte."

As I tried to make sense of this new landscape, there came a sense of relief that I wasn't related to Marco in a way that might have compromised our relationship. Annoyed with myself, I dismissed the thought.

Cristóvão smiled. "If you and Marco together is a problem, I tell you."

I saw my face flush on the screen. Was he reading my mind?

"Are there any more secrets you're hiding?" I said sombrely.

He smiled and shook his head. "Now you know everything, Helen. You decide what you tell Marco. But please, I implore, no tell Joaquim. For Marco."

24

COIMBRA UNIVERSITY

1973

The ambush came one night, as they always knew it would. Téo left Roberto's room at the darkest hour to return to his own. There was no other way, although both knew the risks they ran. To be caught like this was evidence enough if the PIDE wanted a conviction, and Téo knew that the informant who now stood blocking his path would probably add some embellishments of his own. He pulled out of his pocket the bundle of *escudos* that he carried specifically for times like this. He had bought his way out of trouble before.

Gomes took the notes but didn't go away. It was horribly obvious that he wanted something more.

"*O quê?*" Téo asked. "What else?"

Teodoro Leonor Sá Nogueira de Lorena was the only son of Sebastião, the Third Marquis of Lagoaça. His father was rich, and passionately devoted in equal measure to his child and to the *Estado Novo* regime. Although disappointed by the sensitivity of the boy, who chose to study medicine instead of the Marquis's preferred choice of law, he spared his heir nothing. The car Téo received on his eighteenth birthday, the one he employed to ferry dissidents around, was a brand-new Mercedes-Benz SE convertible. Unaware that one day there would be a need for anonymity, Téo had chosen metallic paint which shone pale gold under sunlight and streetlamps. Nothing could have been more identifiable; the authorities already knew to whom it belonged and the purposes to which it was put.

Gomes replied. "You have other friends, not just him." He nodded towards Roberto's door.

Roberto was a fellow student on the medicine course and shared his sensitive nature. Both boys were slim with fine, elegant features and thick wavy hair, which they wore as long as they could get away with, in the style of the psychedelic groups they followed from America and Britain. Their misfortune was to have fallen in love with each other but, like lovers through history, they were ready to risk everything to be together.

'Other friends' – what did Gomes mean? Téo prayed to whatever gods might be listening that it was same-sex liaisons that the Monitor suspected, and not anti-government ones. There was so much in his life he had to hide. He knew he had been watched for some time.

"You were a *companheiro* of Almeida," said Gomes. Taller than Téo, his narrow eyes looked down from either side of his long, flared nose.

A feeling of dread clamped Téo's chest at the sound of his murdered friend's name. His limbs felt too heavy to move, and besides there was nowhere to run.

"His slut Guterres. Elena Guterres. She's plotting with your friend Gabriela de Quintela, yes?" He moved closer.

Téo shrugged shoulders that had started to shake. The shock of hearing the women's names added to his confusion. Though he worked for the *Resistência,* it wasn't out of bravery like the others; they were simply the only society that accepted him and Roberto as a couple. It was a relief not to have to hide the relationship that was illegal in the eyes of the state, but as far as the *Resistência* went, he could never be more than an acolyte.

"You know what they do to your kind in prison, *escroto*?"

Gomes was close enough now that Téo could smell his sour breath and the musty taint of the gown that enveloped him like a black shroud. He shrank back against the door of Roberto's room.

"You won't share a cosy little cell, you know. Different prisons it would be."

Téo went rigid. "What do you want?" he whispered.

"Proof," Gomes said, stepping away. "Not you two, *estúpido*, you can do your disgusting things. I want the papers Quintela gives Guterres to translate. Tell me where they come from and who they go to."

How did he know all this? They were always careful. Gabriela would meet him on the outskirts of the town, where he had imagined they would drive away unnoticed; lately she had even caught a train to the next station, where he would pick her up.

"I can't do that," he said. "I'm only the driver. Gabriela doesn't let me see the papers." He realised agonisingly that he had just confirmed Gomes's suspicions about Gabriela, while distancing his own wretched skin from blame.

"Get them to me," said Gomes shortly. "Unless you prefer the alternative." He made an obscene gesture and walked away, a dark shadow disappearing into the gloom of the night.

Téo sank to the ground. He very much wanted to return to the safety of Roberto's room and be held by him until the terror subsided, but he didn't dare. After a while, he struggled to his feet and slinked back to his own.

There must be a way out of this, he thought. Someone with influence. Duarte. Álvaro's brother. He would know what to do.

25

MOURARIA, LISBON

2021

Filipe's bar stood on a corner of the street. If Lourenço approached from the south side, the cork oak gave him enough cover to see before being seen. Joaquim's preferred position, which almost never varied because he got to the bar earlier than most, was in the middle of a row with his back to the wall, and it provided the best view of anyone who might be looking for him. Unless that person happened to be shielded by a cork oak, Lourenço thought.

Today he maintained his hiding place and studied the girl sitting opposite Joaquim. Her face was turned away, but he recognised her as the pretty lawyer. She had pulled her hair back into a sleek ponytail, and a geometrically cut jacket broadened her little shoulders. On previous occasions when he had watched from behind his tree, she had appeared

174

confident and animated. She tended to use her hands, which looked delicate and slender, when speaking, as much as her voice. But today she sat upright, rigid against the chair. She seemed defensive, or was it aggressive? Joaquim was unnaturally still, his face dark as thunder. He knew she was fighting a case that would deliver both himself and Joaquim from their miserable existence. What had gone wrong?

Lourenço wished he could get closer and hear what they were saying. It had been easier during lockdown, when he was able to hang around Joaquim's kitchen window. As she stood up and left the table he saw that her neat features were frozen like stone, the eyes like black points and mouth set in a crimson-painted line. She was still a treat to look at though, with that body like a triangle that narrowed from the sharp-shouldered jacket over barely-there hips, down to matchstick legs that tapered into pointy-heeled shoes. She reminded him of a doll that his sister used to play with.

As Lourenço reached the bar, Joaquim said testily, "So what did you hear? Hiding behind your tree."

Lourenço opened his mouth to speak and then closed it again.

"She lost the damn appeal," spat Joaquim.

Lourenço could feel the fury but said nothing. To his surprise he found himself feeling sorry for the old man. The one he had regarded for so long as his nemesis was becoming a figure to be pitied and – though this was almost too tragic for Lourenço to admit to himself – his only friend. But whereas Lourenço himself was young enough to entertain hopes for the future, he realised now that the legacy represented Joaquim's last chance. He was old, in failing health, and ran a third-rate pilfering outfit. It would never amount to more than a few *Beirões* and sardines, and one day, inevitably, he would be caught and returned to prison.

"But I have a plan," Joaquim growled, lowering his voice. "*Oleandro!*" he said, brightening as he stared into Lourenço's surprised face.

"Who?" Lourenço asked, searching his mind for a person or place called after the oleander bush.

"You gather up some branches from the *oleandro*. A lot of them, a whole sackful."

Lourenço looked around. They were surrounded by the shrubs. They were everywhere, waving their coloured blossoms in the air. There was a yellow one next to the jacaranda and a pink one over by the oak. "You want me to send flowers to people?"

"You strip off the leaves and boil them up. Then you strain the liquid, and it is poison that you have. Poison kills."

Lourenço had brushed the sap of this plant once. His skin came up in a rash but he doubted it could kill anyone. And who was Joaquim planning to take out? Not the pretty lawyer, he hoped.

"You give it to Marco and the Englishwoman." He made a cut-throat sign across his neck. "Without them, I get my inheritance."

Lourenço stared back at him. Could this be the first sign of dementia? Lourenço's uncle was affected that way, *Tio Tonho*. He had hallucinations and became quite aggressive, talking about bombs and assassinations. Besides, even if the two heirs were dead, what difference would it make? Joaquim had been disinherited anyway.

Then it occurred to Lourenço that now there would be no job in a holiday resort, managing staff and being someone people had to respect, and he realised how much he had been counting on that. He felt the weight of failure inside, familiar like an old anchor. He didn't want to be a petty criminal all his life and end up mouldering in a bar like Joaquim.

"And you my friend will share that inheritance. You will be my business partner. Ten per cent of all my holiday village."

Lourenço said nothing. The scheme was crazy and he was no murderer, but there might be some advantage to be gained from this. He stalled for time. "Why me?" he asked. "Why don't you poison them yourself? And keep all your per cents?"

"I am old, boy," Joaquim said. "I can't go harvesting bushes. My back aches and my knees are gone. How am I going to get to have tea with Marco and Helen? Why would they see me? But you, they don't know."

Lourenço played along, the beginning of an idea coming to him. "OK, I could get the plants. I could boil it up on your stove. Do you have pans?"

Joaquim shook his head.

"We need some. Big ones, and strong too. They're not cheap, my friend."

"How much?" said Joaquim.

Lourenço shrugged. He had no idea what cooking

pots cost. "Two hundred euros."

He was sure Joaquim didn't know the price either, but to Lourenço's surprise he conceded. "OK, you got it."

"How do I know you will give me my ten per cent?" Lourenço added, sensing a chance to get his hands on some real money.

"My word. *Há honra entre ladrões,* honour among thieves, my brother!"

Lourenço knew very well that there was no such thing as honour among any of the thieves he had personally encountered, and particularly not this one, but as the poisoning would never take place, that was irrelevant. The thing was to extract as much cash as possible out of Joaquim while he had the chance. He knew that one of the housebreakers in their crew had just come away with a big haul: four laptops, six phones, and four thousand euros in cash. Because the boy had been openly bragging about it, Lourenço was fairly sure that a full half of the proceeds would have found its way into Joaquim's pocket. The boys in this gang were afraid of their leader. They usually paid up.

"OK, give me a couple of thousand as a show of intention," he said as a starting figure, expecting to be haggled down.

Joaquim grunted acquiescence.

He must be very keen to get started, the surprised Lourenço thought.

"Not here," the old man said. "Back at the house. Come after me, ten minutes."

Half an hour later, a satisfied Lourenço walked

away from the crumbling building with two thousand and two hundred euros in his pocket. He had no intention of killing anyone and spending the rest of his life in jail, nor of picking oleander leaves, but he did have a plan, and he had just acquired the funds to put it into action.

26

BRITISH EMBASSY, LISBON

1973

Douglas's eye was caught by a brief headline on the front page of 'The Times'. The paper was a day old, having arrived by airmail from England with other British newspapers in a regular delivery.

Until this point, the morning had been going well. Outside, the sun had climbed to a perfect angle to light up the orange flame of a trumpet vine that scaled the wall outside his window, and a fresh cup of Earl Grey tea sat steaming on his desk. His thoughts were fixed on Elena and the relationship that felt unlike any he'd known before. She was without guile and yet beguiled him; she was seriously committed to her cause and yet could be as whimsical as any of the socialites he had wasted too much time on in the past; the centre of her world was her daughter, whom he adored as well. He was falling in love. So this was what it felt like. Why did he have to wait for so long?

"Arrest of the Three Marias." The heading was tucked into a corner, under a picture of a trio of women who reminded him of Elena, with tangled hair and the sort of dark, casual clothes she favoured. Turning to the page that ran the story in full, he learned that these women, all named Maria, had been detained in Lisbon for publishing what they claimed to be a feminist book. The *Estado Novo* didn't agree, and had labelled it 'pornography'.

He finished the article and compared the women to his fiancée. The similarities went beyond their hair and style of dress: there was a defiance in their expressions which reminded him of hers; they had written poems and articles that criticised the state. What was Elena actually translating in the documents he handled for her? He had respected her confidence by delivering the packages unread but was beginning to wish he'd been less scrupulous, then he might have had a better idea now of how to protect her.

The phone on his desk rang and he reluctantly put down the paper to answer it. The voice was male and so quiet that he could barely make out the words.

"Perigo! Elena. *Grande perigo!"* it said, speaking quickly. "They take the girl."

"They took Elena?" Fear exploded inside him. "Who is this?"

"No Elena. The *Polícia* take Gabriela. Elena she the next. Duarte say she must go. Help her!"

The line went dead. *Perigo,* the man had said, *grande perigo.* The dictionary on his desk gave him

181

the meaning: 'great danger'. There was no time to think. He was out of the door and into a taxi before he had even formed a plan.

Only minutes later he stood in Elena's pretty private sitting room, where her baby lay in a cot sleeping quietly beside her. She answered his insistent questions, and he hoped she was telling him the truth.

"That must have been Téo. Terrible English? Yes, Téo. He drove Gabriela here and back to Coimbra. No, we weren't writing a book. We don't have anything to do with the *Tres Marias*. But I would if they asked me."

She looked at him, defiance showing in the angle of her chin.

"Do you think this is a game?" His voice was harsh with an anger she had never aroused in him before. It was out of fear for her. "How bad is it? What exactly have you been doing?"

"My work is with arrest logs, witness names, facts, figures, anything that can be used against the *Estado Novo*."

He despaired of her. "You could go to prison!"

"Yes, if the police have them it will be bad. Very bad." She spoke without showing any emotion.

He was terribly afraid. Arrests were rising as the factions in this troubled country lined up against each other. There were tortures and executions. How could she be so calm?

Her face softened into a mix of resignation and affection. "You'll have to find another fiancée my darling!" She laughed as she spoke, but her voice cracked into silence.

A dozen plans ran through his mind, each dismissed as unworkable. It was coming home to him that they had only one real chance: to leave now, and within the hour – leave Lisbon, Portugal, his job, and her family. Leave the baby.

"I'm taking you to England," he said. "We'll marry and you'll be safe."

Her expression was unreadable.

"Your parents will look after Lina. We'll come back for her when it's over."

Adrenalin pulsed through him. All the pieces of his well-ordered life were being thrown up in the air without any clue as to where they might land. He harboured a vague idea that they could return one day, Elena to her daughter and he to his job, but in his heart he knew that his diplomatic career would be finished if he fled the country with a wanted fugitive. What could he do in England? His once-wealthy family had all died poor, and he no longer had any roots there. How would they live? He stared out of the window, blind to the sunshine that had lifted his spirits only hours before.

"You think I would leave my daughter?" Elena said slowly.

"Elena," he said, "My love. They won't let you take her into prison."

She looked stricken. Had she never thought this through?

"We must tell your parents," he said quickly. She watched, looking defeated, as he left the room to find them.

Rounding the curve of the main staircase he heard

raised voices in the hall. Five guards in dark uniforms surrounded the maid who had let him in minutes before. She looked terrified. He heard Elena's name and saw the woman shaking her head.

"*Ela não está aqui,*" she said. "*Eu não sei onde ela está.*"

He understood just enough. She was telling them Elena was out and she didn't know where. Bless her, he thought, creeping quietly back up the stairs before they could see him.

Everything then seemed to happen in slow motion, but in real time they were out of the building and through the back garden in minutes, taking nothing but a quickly packed bag, and the baby without whom she refused to leave.

Disappearing through the orchard, across a boulevard, and into a maze of side streets, they headed on foot towards the sanctuary of the Embassy. From there Douglas would arrange their escape. How that might be done, he had no clear idea.

27

CHILTERN GRANGE, MEDMENHAM
2021

I kept a photograph on my desk of my mother and my father, Douglas that is, standing under an ornate archway in what I had managed to identify as the British Embassy. I had rummaged through boxes of family albums, and this was the only one I could find of them in Lisbon. I had re-read her book, but there were no clues there as to how they met, married, or came to be living in England.

Some things I would never know for sure, including, it seemed, the truth behind Marco's motivations regarding the court case and his relationship with me. I had exhausted all avenues of thought on that one and yet still could not get it out of my mind. My last conversation with Cristóvão, when he shared the secret about Joaquim, had left me wavering. Jen warned me against them, but I was plagued by uncertainty.

Brushing it off, I reminded myself that lockdown had ended only days ago, and we were now free to go almost anywhere in the world. Jen and I talked of taking a holiday. I decided to start planning it instead of sitting around brooding.

I couldn't even get as far as opening a browser; apathy enveloped me. Instead, I looked at the photo again and then through the window above it. Out of the hundreds of memories I carried throughout this house, I could see my parents sitting down by the river, he with his gin and tonic, and she with her white wine. In my mind, they looked much like the picture on my desk, apart from touches of grey that wound through their hair.

I turned back to my laptop and opened my inbox. Every time I did this, I felt a glimmer of expectation; I still looked for Marco's name, even though I knew it wouldn't be there. If it had been, then I'd have to delete the message anyway.

This time, I got a jolt as I saw an email from Portugal. But it wasn't from him. Thankfully it wasn't from *Tedigo,* like the last time, either. Instead, it was fairly innocuous and quite interesting. A Portuguese charity working with prisons wanted to connect with some of the organisations I worked with, to exchange ideas and explore mutual support. It was called *RedePrisão,* which translated as "Prison Network." It was signed *Lourenço Diogo Garcia Lopes.*

I was about to investigate further when the sound of the doorbell chimed into the silence and made me jump. The ancient bell-pull that sat embedded in the wall by the front door had given up functioning years ago, and I had installed a battery-operated contraption that had an extension on every floor, and even one down in the summerhouse. It was loud.

Logic said this must be either a hawker or a canvasser; unexpected callers never happened these days. Texts made arrangements simple now, so people always made contact before visiting. Should I ignore it? I crept to a window at the front of the house and looked down. There was a maroon car parked in my driveway. I wasn't the best at identifying makes of car, but it looked like the one owned by a solicitor who lived two doors down. His wife had health problems; perhaps they needed my help. I ran down the stairs and pulled open the door.

It was not my neighbour. Marco stood right there on my doorstep. He looked uncertain, and then broke into a grin. I smiled too, I couldn't help myself.

"Cristóvão told me," he said.

My first reaction was relief that I was no longer the guardian of the terrible secret about his father's identity. Then I realised he hadn't actually said that. Jen would have urged me to send him away, but she wasn't here, and he was. I tried to stifle a wild excitement that had flared in me, just to be standing here close to him again. I looked at the amber eyes and we stood, for I don't know how long, neither of us speaking.

Only minutes ago I had been telling myself that if he so much as sent me an email, I would delete it. Now

I found myself stepping back and saying, "Come in." It seemed natural for him to be here in my house again. I used to worry that his architect's eye would be picking out all its dilapidations and areas that were begging to be renovated, but he had never mentioned any of them. It didn't matter now.

We sat down by the big glass doors, on chairs that were arranged to capture the best views of the river. I offered him coffee and he refused. I opened a window, aware that the house had a musty aroma of old wood that I had grown used to. It was late May and my jacaranda might not be flowering, but everything else was. Scents wafted in on fresh, cool air.

"Tell me everything," he said. "Whatever you're thinking, I can answer it. I can explain. I can give you whatever proof you need."

I tried to find the words. It was difficult to say anything without mentioning the anonymous email, and then I would have to tell him that he was the son of Joaquim. I couldn't do that. It wasn't my secret to tell. Duarte, the patriarch who seemed to be revered in an almost god-like status by everyone in this family, had decided that Marco should never know. Cristóvão had begged me to keep the secret. Who was I to go against all of that?

I cursed the lockdowns. If only we had been able to meet and talk when the email first arrived, I would have accepted Marco's denial that Joaquim was his father, genuine as far as he knew, I would not have discussed it with Cristóvão, and our separation would never have happened.

"I went into a spiral of doubt." I stumbled on. "It all seems stupid now."

He looked puzzled for a moment, and then said, "What doubts? Let's take them one by one."

The biggest one was whether to share Cristóvão's secret. Everything else seemed dwarfed by that now.

"Can I tell you something?" he said.

I couldn't look away.

"Every day for a year I've asked myself what went wrong. What did I do? Had you met someone else? When Cristóvão told me you were worried that I wasn't being honest with you, it seemed like a small thing, compared to what I'd been imagining. Is that all it was, that you didn't trust me?"

"I do trust you," I said. I meant it. Now that he was here, I could feel it in my bones. We were like two beings from the same planet, the only two of our kind on this earth. It sounds melodramatic, but that was how I felt.

"I thought I was the one with trust issues," he said, laughing.

I laughed too, and everything was right again, as simply as that. Life took on the happy ordinariness that is so rare to find. We walked for miles along the riverbank and had lunch at a pub. He showed me photos of the puppies. Whether Marujo, the male dog, had been involved in their creation or not, he had played his part in parenting them.

Another paternity enigma, I thought to myself. They seemed to run in our two families. This seemed like the right moment to tell him about Joaquim. How could I keep that from him now? Duarte was in the past; I was the most significant person in Marco's life from this point on. I had the right to tell him. And he had the right to know. I had been distressed by the thought that my parents kept a similar secret from me for my whole life; it felt like a colossal betrayal. Yet now I was inflicting the same deception on him. But I couldn't find the words.

Instead, we chatted about our lives and complained about winter lockdowns. I told him about the email I had received that morning, and that I might soon be working with a Portuguese charity. I hadn't been able to find a website, which concerned us both. He said he would check it out with a detective friend who worked in the fraud office in Lisbon, just to be on the safe side.

The evenings were cold, so later we lit a fire, and opened a bottle of my favourite *crémant* to celebrate. The old house took on a magic air in the firelight. You couldn't see the scuffs on the furniture or the faded patches on my oriental carpet, so unlike his perfect one. I lit candles instead of switching on the lamps.

"I know it's too soon," he said, "to talk about getting married. I mean, can we just agree we're heading that way? We are, aren't we?"

It wasn't too soon. I knew it too. "Of course we are," I replied.

Nothing more needed to be said.

The next day he headed back to Lisbon for work commitments. I drove him to the airport. It felt easier to break the news I had been suppressing while we were sitting side by side and looking ahead, rather than at each other. But I didn't do it. I still hadn't worked out where to begin. Since he walked through my door the day before, everything had been so perfect that I didn't want to risk spoiling it. We had all the time in the world ahead of us. I would do it soon.

28

LAPA, LISBON

1973

Joaquim Aurélio shrank onto his bed as the sound of shouting invaded his room. There was a crash and he wondered if it was time for him to look through the crack between the door and its frame to see if his mother needed help. Sooner or later the fighting would stop, and then he would have no choice. As the man of the house – a role his father so often failed to fulfil – he saw it as his duty to decide whether to call a doctor, or his uncle Duarte, or just to make a jug of coffee. Sometimes he froze at the sight of the injuries on her face and was unable to accomplish anything at all: those were wounds on which he could not bear to look.

Joaquim Aurélio was named after his father, Joaquim, and his mother, Aurélia. He was eight years old.

The noise stopped and a door slammed. He heard

the family's BMW roar into life and watched from his window as the car carried his father away. He padded down the stairs in bare feet, not noticing the coldness of the stone against his flesh.

Mamã sat on a chair, sobbing quietly. He ran to her, and she wrapped him up in her arms, wetting his face with her tears. He could see red, raw abrasions but thankfully no blood this time. Some crockery had smashed on the floor and a table was overturned by the door.

He pulled back and looked at her. "You want coffee *mãe*?" He loved to help her. The dual prize was the smile that appeared on her face and the knowledge that he had put it there.

He ran into the kitchen and poured water into a kettle. The family had a maid and other servants, but they were not in the house that day. He was glad, being old enough to grasp that *mamã* felt some shame over these beatings, but not yet understanding why.

She followed him into the kitchen, picking up a pair of his shoes, and he allowed her to slip them on. Her hands were soft and warm against his cold skin. Together they made coffee, she poured him a glass of milk, and they sat quietly.

"Your father's gone, Joaquinho," she said. Her gold-brown eyes, that were like his own, looked not at him but into the distance.

"*Viva!*" he replied. It was a word he had heard at the races when people wanted to celebrate a victory.

Aurélia broke into a smile and then laughed. "My funny little boy!" she said. "My clever son!"

"Is he gone for ever?" asked the boy.

"This time, yes." She paused and muttered, "Too drunk to drive but he took the car anyway."

Even at the age of eight and never having tasted alcohol, Joaquinho knew what 'drunk' meant. When 'drunk' happened, he prayed for his father to go away for good. "Will he come back *mãe*?"

"No." Her shoulders lifted slightly, as energy crept back into her body. "Not this time. It's over. I promise."

They both fell silent. He tried to imagine what the house would be like without that constant threat. It was impossible; aggression had become the backdrop to his life.

Then he dared to voice a thought that had been troubling him for some time. "I don't want his name, *mãe*. I'm not like him."

She smiled at him and then said, "What name would you like, *meu filho?*"

He stopped to think. Yesterday at school they had learned about the great explorers. He had decided that he wanted to travel the world one day and never be trapped in a bad place again. He would take *mamã* with him and they would be free.

"Marco," he said.

Aurélia thought for a moment and then nodded. "That's a beautiful name."

"I want to be Marco, like the explorer."

"Ah, the explorer. Marco Polo. Good. Then you are Marco, my son the explorer. And there was a Roman Emperor called Marco Aurélio. A wise man. He was a philosopher too."

"An Emperor, *mãe*?"

She nodded, smiling again through the tears and bruises.

"Marco Aurélio. Marco Aurélio." He tried it out several times. "*Eu sou* Marco Aurélio!"

29

SALDANHA, LISBON

2021

Lourenço sat in the waiting room scrolling his phone. He was primed to execute the next stage of his plan and impatient to get started. The Chinese hardware store had charged him only sixty-five euros for two big pans and a strainer, and though it irked him to spend that amount of time and money, Joaquim was getting impatient and needed appeasing. If the old man cooled on the plot, he would want his two thousand euros back, so Lourenço delivered the gear to the brown house to keep him quiet, and then claimed he would have to wait until after the next full moon, for the cover of darkness, to steal the oleanders. They may appear to be everywhere, he said, but in fact all sprouted from private gardens, so this operation called for the same level of care as stealing a laptop. The moon was only beginning to approach its zenith. That gave him a week or more to further his own schemes.

The door opened and he looked up. Laurinda walked in, balancing on her spiky heels, and held out her hand. "Nice to meet you, Lourenço," she said. "Would you come this way?"

He was elated to have received a reply to the email he had sent the Englishwoman, after tracking her down through her website. The idea for a connection between Portuguese charities and English ones had been a stroke of genius – she clearly enjoyed helping those she saw as less fortunate, so framing his proposal as a plea for assistance must win her support.

After exchanging a few emails which hinted at his need for funding, and her willingness to consider how she might help, she had agreed to meet him. She must be well-off if she were in line to inherit from this family. He would bet that they didn't have any poor relations, except for Joaquim of course, but that was more or less self-inflicted.

He had bought a domain name, but before going further there were some arrangements to put into place. With Joaquim's funds in his pocket, he got some nice cards printed and was setting up a website on a state-of-the-art ThinkPad stolen from a tourist villa, and not mentioned to the boss. But the site would have to look authentic to fool someone like Helen, and that was proving to be a challenge. He remembered the do-gooders who used to visit him in jail and found himself able to ape their language quite easily, but the polish required for the site was beyond him. That was when he came up with his second great idea. And here she was.

Laurinda took him into a little glass cubicle. Beyond it he could see a hall full of desks and laptops all occupied by different people. The building provided shared facilities for small businesses, and this must be all she could afford while setting up her own practice. Spending two years on Joaquim's case without billing him could not have helped her financial position, he thought, despite daddy's investment fund. She was clearly keen to acquire new clients, and even a small charity which might not pay much (like the one he was proposing) would be a step up from Joaquim who paid nothing at all.

"So how can I help?" She wore a professional smile as she shut the door and sat down opposite him. Her teeth were small, white, and even.

"I would like the free consultation you offer on your website."

"Yes, and here you are. So this is it, the free consultation. What can I do for you?"

Her manner was brisk, and he liked that. He wished she would take off her square-shouldered jacket so he could get a better view of her body.

"I'm starting a charity," he said. "I want to help prisoners. I have experience with that work (*while I was in jail*, he thought, but didn't say) and I have a contact in England where there are more charities for prisoners than here. I think they might help us. My contact is a potential backer who will put in some funds, so I need an agreement to give her."

"OK, so what are the terms?" she asked, coming

straight to the point.

He had to think quickly but had always been good at that. Guessing that throwing himself on her mercy would be the best way to get what he wanted from Laurinda, he said, "That's where I need your advice."

She reeled off half a dozen types of agreement he might reach with his English backer, interspersed with questions and suggestions. It was simple. All he had to do was follow her lead, expressing a preference for whatever would get his hands on the money the fastest, and rejecting anything that might cause complications. Once they were working together, he hoped she would help him smarten up the website too. She would know how to present it with all the right credentials and so on.

But first there were some delicate matters to be got out of the way. When he felt he had extracted all the information possible at this first free-of-charge meeting, he raised the issue of payment. "What will all this cost?" he asked. "We don't have much in the way of funds until the backing comes through."

"I charge two hundred and fifty euros an hour, so the agreement will cost about seven-fifty. I will need a deposit of half."

He stared back at her. Negotiation was something he excelled at, and not just the juggling of terms: he knew how to play on people's expectations and their fears, and was adept at recognising all of them.

"We don't have much in the way of funds until the backing comes through," he repeated. Then he waited. Silence, he often found, was effective in bringing prices down.

She looked at him and gave a little sigh. He imagined that breath on his face and almost forgot why he was here.

"OK," she said finally, "you're a charity. I will do the initial agreement for two-fifty and invoice the rest when the backer pays."

Don't give it all away, he felt like saying to her. *If you go on working for nothing you will spend the rest of your life in this glass box.*

But of course, he kept quiet. There were many ways that this venture might go, and he was enjoying the game so far.

30

OXFORD

1974

He paused at the threshold for a moment and smoothed back hair ruffled by the March winds outside. A man whom he guessed to be about his own age stood behind the bar with a cleaning cloth in his hand. The man looked tired, and with no more than a glance at his visitor said, "We're not open yet."

"I've come about the job," replied Douglas. "You advertised."

The Heron & Pike public house was the centre of what little social life existed in the village of Wychwood-under-Glyme near Oxford, where Elena and Douglas Matthews lived in a rented cottage with their daughter. However, they had never been inside it, so Douglas did not know what to expect.

The man put down his cloth and studied him. The feelings that this provoked took Douglas back to the day he had undertaken his viva exam, under the gaze of a panel of indifferent professors. That was twelve years ago, and less than the same number in miles from where they now stood.

"You're a chef?" the man asked.

Douglas nodded. At this point he was prepared to be anything that would pay a wage. In the year since their escape to England, he had rented a damp cottage, married Elena, acquired an ancient Morris Minor, and repeatedly failed to find a job. The only place in Britain that held any relevance for him was the city of Oxford, where he maintained some former friends and contacts. They had all been approached, but age and reputation worked against him: thirty-three was too old to start a new career, and the Foreign Office was closed to former diplomats who had used official funds to buy air tickets in order to abscond with a wanted criminal. So they had been forced to live in a hovel of a home that possessed neither bathroom nor inside toilet.

The man led him into a small cell lined with untidy shelves filled with files, books, tools, boxes and other paraphernalia. There was no window, and the smell of beer and cigarette smoke pervaded from the bar.

"I'm Trevor," he said, extending a hand. "I'm the owner."

Everything about Trevor looked jaded. His eyes were underscored with dark circles. His shirt, though well cut, was fraying at the cuffs, and it was some time since his shoes had seen polish. Douglas had registered all of these details by the time they sat down. This man needed help, he concluded, and his hopes began to rise. "Douglas Matthews," he said, shaking the extended hand.

"So tell me about your experience, Douglas."

It was at this point that job interviews usually foundered. At first, he had shared the details of his illustrious diplomatic career, imagining it would impress. Then he came to understand that no-one wanted a salesman, clerk, or even night porter, who had neither experience nor references, and who was over-qualified for the job. That presented him with a dilemma: he hated lying but had never done anything in his life except attend exclusive schools, graduate from an elite university, and then effortlessly take up his prestigious post at the embassy.

He thought quickly and creatively. "At home we had a cook. I loved being in her kitchen. She taught me everything she knew. She used the freshest ingredients, fine beans picked straight from our vegetable garden, prime cuts of steak from a local herd..." He stopped at the doubt that appeared on the bar-owner's face.

"I don't think we have the budget for that sort of thing," Trevor said. "It's chicken and chips they want here. Or egg and chips. We do the occasional salad, a bit of lettuce on the plate with some pickled beetroot. A nice ploughman's."

"I'm sure I can manage that," Douglas asserted confidently (puzzling over 'ploughman's' – a special for farmers perhaps, but then shouldn't it be 'ploughmen'?), because the story he had told Trevor was true. Rosa Camilleri and her husband Salvatore were Sicilians employed by the Matthews family as cook and chauffeur. They had become stranded in England during the war. Rosa could produce anything from French cuisine to a perfect English roast, but the dishes he loved the most were her native Italian ragus and pastas. She had to cook not only for the family but for all the staff on the estate: three meals a day for up to twenty hungry souls. There was no time for sifting, mixing, or complicated procedures, so by her side he had learned how to bring out flavour through the simplest of methods.

Now he happily undertook all the cooking at home. He knew how to transform sparse ingredients into feasts. So although he had never attempted chips – or ploughman's, whatever it might be – he felt confident that these dishes would present no difficulty, as long as he was not expected to eat them himself.

Trevor regarded him without enthusiasm, much as the professors had, and said, "The wages are paid weekly in cash." He named a sum that was approximately one-fifth of Douglas's salary at the Foreign Office, and which might have been high or low for a pub chef, for all Douglas knew. But it was employment.

He hadn't shared with Elena that his money was almost gone. If he didn't find a job this week, he would have to face what he saw as the shame of a visit to the dole office. He had driven past it and seen the line of men and women outside. There was something about the scene that spoke not exactly of desperation – they didn't look unhappy – but the absence of aspiration. He didn't want to become part of that indifferent mass of people who no longer had hope.

He was about to accept what he assumed to be an offer when Trevor spoke again. "So you've never actually worked in a kitchen before?"

The weight of rejection hung in the air. Was he to end up queuing for a handout in that street where he had once walked wearing cap and gown?

"Well," the man went on, "I didn't have any either when I took this on. I was a stockbroker. It never occurred to me not to follow my father into the City; everyone expected it, but I was bored stiff. After work we used to fall into an old pub, and I mean centuries old. A beautiful place. It was the only time of the day I enjoyed. One year the bonuses were bigger than usual, so I got out and put it all into this."

"That was brave of you," said Douglas. "How's it going?"

"If I'm honest, I'm struggling. I started this with my wife. She did the cooking, and I ran the bar. We were doing well with the two of us. Then she died." Trevor stopped and looked at his hands. His finger absently traced a stain on the desk.

"I'm sorry," said Douglas. It sounded inadequate. "That must have been hard."

"Here, by the bar, it was. Undiagnosed heart defect."

"What a terrible shock." Douglas shook his head in sympathy. He tried to put the thought of what life might be like without Elena out of his mind. Suddenly his prospects didn't seem so bleak. He had a wife he loved, who cheerfully tolerated living without an indoor toilet, and an enchanting daughter, now adopted and renamed Helen to distance her from dangers left behind. They were safe. They were happy. What else really mattered?

"So," Trevor said, recovering himself, "either I break even, or I employ someone and run at a loss. Six of one... But I can't do it all myself, and if I'm cooking, they don't get their drinks. The hours are killing me."

"I had an uncle who was a stockbroker." Douglas felt it would do Trevor good to chat about something other than his problems for a while.

"Really?" Trevor sat up and looked interested. "Where did you go to school?"

"Harrow."

Douglas hadn't planned on admitting this in case it put him in the over-qualified category, but his prospective employer brightened and replied, "I was at Rugby. Then Oxford, that's how I got to know this place."

A fellow alumnus. Suddenly the shabby room grew more welcoming.

Trevor got two glasses of Armagnac from the bar, and for the next hour they reminisced about student days and easier times.

"So it's been a struggle but I'm getting there," Trevor said, coming back to the subject of the pub.

Douglas nodded, looking around. He wondered what the wine cellar was like. Did pubs have wine cellars? He said nothing for fear of frightening off his potential new employer, but a vision had started to form in his mind of a place where discerning people like himself could access good food and a decent vintage. He could offer special rates to ploughmen perhaps, if that was a thing around here.

"Want to give it a try?" Trevor asked.

Douglas felt as elated as when the professors had awarded him a pass. Now he not only had a job, but would be spending most of his time in a kitchen, and a bigger one than their scullery at home. Wild garlic grew not far away on the banks of the Thames, and he had planted thyme, rosemary, and oregano in the garden of the cottage. He would bet that smallholdings nearby could supply decent produce at reasonable prices too. He would show Trevor that it was possible to make good food on a chips budget. And who knew where this might lead?

He felt a mix of excitement and relief. A new life had begun.

31

SALDANHA, LISBON

2021

Lourenço clicked on the link Helen had sent him and checked his own image on the screen. He looked professional, and the light was quite flattering, he thought.

He had set up his stolen ThinkPad in Laurinda's conference room. She would be out for the whole day at an event where she hoped to pick up some new clients, making the most of the opportunity in case the government closed everything down again. When he entered the building and sat himself at the table in the glass-walled meeting pod, no-one had challenged him. People came and went here all the time and if anyone asked, all he need say was that he worked for Laurinda.

On his previous visits to her office, he had acquainted himself with the booking system for the glass room and noted that there were no meetings listed for today. He was taking the chance that she might return unexpectedly, or that someone who actually worked there might want the space, or that they might question his presence and call her to check, but compared to some of the gambles Lourenço had played in his life this was a small one, and worth it to impress his potential English benefactor, Helen Matthews.

The website for the new charity was live now, with Laurinda's help, in Portuguese and English. It seemed to have convinced Helen. Laurinda warned him that if she asked for credentials like a registered charity number, he should just say they were in the process of setting up. These steps were time-consuming and expensive, Laurinda explained, enmeshed in bureaucracy, and there was no point in investing in that end of things until they knew there was a backer in place. Now all he had to do was reel this big fish in.

The screen flickered and Helen's face came into view. They greeted each other politely. He liked this new persona he was creating, the businessman with a heart.

"Would you like to tell me more about your work, and how you think I can help?" She smiled encouragingly.

He waffled for a few minutes in the imperfect English he had picked up while working in nightclubs and bars. While he knew how to describe various brands of gin and their prices quite fluently, he had prepared for this conversation by translating a list of technical terms recalled from the social workers who had visited him in prison. His quick brain had no problem memorising the new vernacular, and he felt that his presentation was hanging together rather well.

Occasionally she asked for more detail about one aspect or another. This made him flounder, but he recovered quickly and was confident that any hesitation might be put down to language limitations. He was surprised at how readily she accepted his answers.

After ten or fifteen minutes of this, it was time to raise the subject of costs. It was important to address that, before the conversation turned to what his charity actually wanted from her. If he could make her believe that offering funding was her own idea, she'd give more than if he asked outright. That was something he had learned about people.

The big, undecided question was at what level to pitch. It would be easier to start small and then gradually extract more money and commitment from her, but there were a number of problems with that route, the biggest being that Joaquim might kill him when he found out Helen was not being poisoned but groomed for a financial scam. To avoid that, he would have to cut Joaquim in on the proceeds, a prospect that did not appeal at all.

There was also the challenge that to keep this ruse going for any length of time, he would have to actually put some of the work he was describing into practice. Then any prison authority would check his record and discover they were dealing with someone more likely to be found on the other side of the bars.

No, this was his one chance: he had to extract as much money as possible and then disappear without a trace. The delicate question was, how much might she consider donating? Fifty thousand euros? A hundred? He really had no idea.

He also had to decide at what level it would be worth uprooting the little life he had managed to construct for himself here, and most of all sacrificing a burgeoning relationship with Laurinda, to whom he could imagine becoming quite attached. He had fancied the skinny lawyer from the first time he saw her, and this scheme had been an ideal excuse to get to know her better. He had always been successful with women – some of them classy and well-educated like her – and felt he was making good headway. It would be a pity to leave that behind, but he could see no alternative.

As she listened to his rehearsed words and phrases, Helen continued to intervene with her unnerving questions but seemed to be satisfied with his fudged answers. At first, he thought he had misheard when she suggested that she could cover some of the costs as a donation to *RedePrisão* while obtaining funding for the rest. This was almost too easy.

"In what level of moneys you think?" he asked, struggling to apply his broken English to such a sensitive matter.

"Three or four hundred thousand," she replied, looking out from the screen as coolly as if she had just offered him a cup of coffee. "I might be able to raise more. There are lots of grants for charities over here."

He knocked over a glass of water he had taken from the room's central station and placed next to his laptop, but fortunately it was off-screen and didn't flood the keyboard.

Maintaining what he hoped was a calm expression he asked, "How much time, to get these moneys?" Time was something he didn't have. "We need now. Start-up funds." Immediately he worried he had spoken too directly. His performance would have been smoother in his native Portuguese.

"Not a problem." She smiled reassuringly. "I could top up my donation with some temporary funds until the grants come through."

It was working; he must be even more clever than he had thought. A whole new realm of scams opened up in his sights, to be pursued after this one: he could change identities, use fake names – the possibilities were boundless when the world was full of people as gullible as this Englishwoman.

"So what are our next steps?" she continued, taking him straight to the place where he had not been sure she was ready to go.

"My partner she write the contracts," he said. "Then we sign. You transfer the moneys and we are in business." He added quickly, "the business of helping. The unhappy *prisioneiros*." He found himself so unnerved by the speed at which events were moving, and so unexpectedly in his favour, that his words became confused and tumbled over one another.

"That sounds fine," she said. "Send me the contracts by the end of this week if you can. I'll read them and if everything is okay, we could sign when I'm over next week."

"And you pay then?"

She looked as if she were about to laugh. The joy of helping people perhaps? He smiled back broadly.

"Yes," she said, then coughed before saying, "I'll pay then."

"*Perfeito, Senhora!*" he said, finding himself reverting to waiter-speak in his confusion. She had not just left him a tip, he reminded himself. "I'm happy for work with you. Happy for the *prisioneiros*."

The screens went blank, and relief washed through him. His mind raced to the next step, but more urgently he saw that one of the workers sitting at a desk opposite, whom he had noticed watching from time to time during his meeting, had now risen from his seat and was walking towards the glass box. The man's eyes were fixed on him and he was not smiling. Lourenço closed his laptop and quickly left.

32

REVOLUÇÃO DOS CRAVOS, LISBON
25 ABRIL 1974

Duarte sat in his study listening to the radio. The grandfather clock beside the case containing his law books chimed midnight. He would normally have been reading, or in bed, or having drinks after dinner with friends, but tonight was not a time for any of those activities. He watched the set and waited. Eventually, he got up and walked to the window; staring at the receiver would not make it play the music he waited to hear. Everything outside was quiet and dark.

Then it happened. "*Grândola, Vila Morena*" rang out in the still space. The broadcast of the protest song that had been banned for years was a signal from the rebel group, AFM, the *Movimento das Forças Armadas,* that all soldiers lying in wait should move to their designated strategic positions. The coup had begun.

He felt like running into the streets, waking up the neighbours, or calling his friends, but he had to stay by the phone in case it rang. Instead, he celebrated by opening an ebony cabinet in the corner of the room. He searched through the spirits – an eighteen-year-old Glenlivet, a half-finished Martell – and finally selected a dusty bottle of Macieira. It pooled in the glass, darkly. He raised it, to whoever and whatever was fighting out there on this night, took a sip, and lit a cigar.

Much later, he didn't know how long, an announcement was made:

"The Portuguese Armed Forces appeal to all the inhabitants of Lisbon to stay at home and to remain as calm as possible. We sincerely hope that the seriousness of the hour will not be saddened by personal injuries. We therefore appeal to the good sense of all military commanders to avoid any confrontation. It is because of our concern to spare Portuguese blood that we appeal for a civic spirit. All medical personnel, especially those in hospitals, should hold themselves ready to give help. It is hoped this will not be needed."

It was happening. Duarte lit a cigarette and then forgot to smoke it, lost in memories of other times spent waiting like this.

There was Álvaro; he had prayed all night that the boy would survive, but it did no good. That had been the worst night of his life. It had come to him then that if the God to whom he prayed were able to protect his brother, then wouldn't that same God be responsible for his death? That was when he stopped believing.

Years later, there were the hours passed at his wife's side, waiting for her to die slowly, and all the time knowing what the outcome would be.

In this same study he had awaited the arrival of a hearse for his sister, pretty Ana Belinha, killed under the wheels of a runaway car.

And then there was Joaquim. Duarte remembered him as a young savage who came into their family but would not – or could not – speak. Always the giver, *mamã* had regularly taken in the refugees who were pouring into Portugal throughout the Second World War. This child touched her heart and she kept him, vowing that he would have her protection for as long as she lived. But when that life lasted only long enough to give birth to Álvaro, Joaquim was set adrift.

Duarte knew the boy loved his adoptive brothers and sister, but there was something inside him – some unseen trigger – that shot to pieces anything good. Still, there had been love. Duarte's love for that brother had threaded itself through the years of nurturing, teaching, forgiving, and in the end, disowning. For so long, he had waited for the boy to change, always holding onto the hope that such a thing was possible. But when the boy became a man and committed his unspeakable crime, hope died. There was no way back. But the love had refused to die.

The airwaves crackled with urgent voices. The airports were closed, they said, both Lisbon and Porto! More radio stations were commandeered! The army was taking over! He became accustomed to the sound and fell into a doze punctuated by intermittent broadcasts.

A banging on his front door jolted him wide awake. Dawn was creeping up from the bottom of the sky, and by its light he identified his neighbour. Letting her in, he saw she was still in her nightgown, and shaking, whether with cold or shock he didn't know.

"What is it," she cried, "are they shooting? The radio says it's a revolution! Is it the right-wing generals? Will it be worse than Salazar?"

"Go back to your house," he reassured her. "Everything is happening as it should. It isn't the generals, but Caetano is finished. Go home and wait. Keep your radio on."

He made coffee. It landed sourly on taste buds dulled by all the cups taken during the slow passing of the night. The white sun of morning picked out full ashtrays and smeared glasses. He opened a window. Here in Lapa, there was little movement outside; the action was in the centre of town.

He showered and changed, desperate to go out but unwilling to leave the phone. The radio was playing marching music now. Appeals to the population to stay at home were regularly repeated but it seemed that no-one was complying.

In another part of town, Celeste Martins Caeiro picked her way across the tramlines, wreathed in the spicy scent of a giant bunch of carnations. She had been surprised, on arrival at the restaurant this morning, to see her workmates sitting around drinking shots of *licor* and smoking cigars. The owner had plans to celebrate the first anniversary of his business by presenting each of his customers with a carnation; there were preparations to be done and no time to waste.

But instead of giving her a task, he said, "Go home, Celeste. Stay indoors. Someone has decided to have a revolution today. They have declared a State of Catastrophe. We can't open and it's not safe on the streets."

"Who is it?" she cried, excited. "The *Comunistas*?" Celeste was a communist. Her life had been nothing but struggle so far, and they promised a better deal for workers like her.

"Who knows?" he replied, shooing her towards the door. "Communists, unions, soldiers, why did they have to choose today of all the days in the year? My carnations will die, and my customers will miss their celebration dinners."

She wondered that he could focus on his own little world at such a momentous time but said nothing. The restaurant would probably live to see another day, and she would still need a job however many dictators were deposed.

"Take these." He handed her a mass of red flowers. "They're no use to me now."

She went back the way she had come, taking the metro to *Rossio*. Her mother would like the carnations, and she would put one in her daughter's hair. They would brighten up the one room they all shared in

Chiado.

The streets were starting to fill with people. She asked who was in charge, but no-one seemed to know. One man had a newspaper that told of the first attacks by the army during the night. "They took my car," he said, "requisitioned it. For a barricade. For the revolution. They're welcome!" He laughed and so did she. There was a strange and excited sense of joy in the air.

She went on, heading for home. Tanks full of soldiers with guns lurched incongruously over the cobblestones. The vehicles looked enormous against the tree-lined avenues. The men inside were smiling, not shooting. She pushed her way through and looked up at one. "*O quê?*" she asked. "What's going on? Who's fighting?"

"We're going for the *Presidente*. He's hiding in Carmo Barracks. This time tomorrow, Portugal will be free!"

Before she could ask any more questions, and she had so many, the soldier said, "Got a cigarette, *Senhora?*"

For the first time in her life, Celeste wished that she smoked. But she did not and had none. She wanted to help them, these liberators whom she had longed for, whoever they might be, but what did she have to give? No tobacco and certainly no money. She held out her carnations.

"This is all I have. Please take them. *Viva a revolução!*"

He smiled, took one from the bunch, and placed it

in the barrel of his rifle. The other soldiers laughed, and she handed out more and more, until the bouquet was exhausted. Now each rifle held a flower. The tanks ground on.

Carnations were in season, plentiful and cheap; the market stalls were full of them, all over the city. People started to present them to other soldiers, and the flower-sellers gave them too. Soon, red-petalled blooms were everywhere – in rifles, adorning tanks – and still no bullets were fired.

Two kilometres to the west in Lapa, Duarte sat up with a start. Finally, the telephone was ringing. The sun had taken itself off to the other side of the house now, and this watershed day was in its full stride. The voice of Eugênio Ribeiro sounded down the line, hoarse and edgy. Eugênio had been part of his posse at school, alongside João de Abreu. Unlike Abreu, from whom Duarte had to keep a prudent distance to mask their clandestine activities, Eugênio remained a regular companion. No longer a callow schoolboy, he was now a Captain in the MFA, and right at the heart of the uprising. He had promised to keep his old friend informed.

"We've taken the Ministry of the Army, the City Council, the National Bank, and the Police Headquarters," Ribeiro said.

Duarte could hear many voices in the background. People were singing, celebrating victory.

Eugênio went on: "They've tried some

counterattacks, but no-one is taking orders. They told Monte Real to fly the squad over Lisbon. Cortez said it was impossible because of the fog."

"There's no fog!"

"Exactly!"

They both laughed, Ribeiro's voice cracking from strain. Duarte was exhausted after the vigil, yet had never felt more energetic than from the adrenaline that buoyed him up now.

"They ordered a frigate to fire on the crowds down at the harbour," Ribeiro continued. "It just turned the guns up into the air!"

It was exhilarating to speak like this, without fear of being overheard. Duarte couldn't remember ever having talked this freely before. At every dinner party, every meeting, there might always be a spy. But below his excitement lay apprehension; what if they failed? The *Estado Novo* would prevail more powerfully than ever.

He retuned the radio and watched the pendulum swinging on the grandfather clock. He wondered where the girl had gone, the one Álvaro was in love with. Was she alright? Did her daughter, Álvaro's child, survive? He wished he could have known them.

His housekeeper arrived and cleared up the debris. She made a sandwich of mortadella and sheep's cheese, and he realised he was hungry. She asked about the coup and he told her what he knew, and then sent her home, wreathed in smiles.

At four in the afternoon, Ribeiro rang again with the news Duarte had been waiting for. He left his house and walked quickly through streets that grew progressively more crowded as he approached the centre of town.

In Chiado there were tanks everywhere, machine guns armed and ready. But carnations too. Soldiers with carnations? He didn't understand that. It was nearly five before he reached Carmo Barracks. Slowly, he edged towards the front of the crowd until he saw Eugênio.

"He's in there," the captain said. "President Caetano. Barricaded. Thinks he'll be shot if he shows his face."

"It's a miracle he's still alive," said Duarte. "Is it true no-one has died?"

"Only five. The PIDE fired into the crowd. It was unfortunate. No weapons have been used on our side. Not one shot."

"And the carnations?"

Eugênio smiled. "I don't know what that is. Crazy kids."

It was true that the soldiers were young. Shiny hair flopped over faces still touched by the bloom of youth. Innocent eyes smiled at the crowds; some flirted with the girls. They hadn't wanted to be conscripted and they didn't want to die in Africa at the hands of other young men fighting to free their countries from Portugal's control.

The parallels struck Duarte. Wasn't his own country occupied as well, by the *Estado Novo*? And now these novice fighters would bring it all to an end. By the end of this day, Angola, Mozambique, Cape Verde – and

Portugal – would be on the road to freedom. They looked like boys playing with guns. And decorating them with flowers? People were carrying carnations too; the streets were full of them.

The crowd parted to allow a tank to rattle through. The green doors of the barracks opened to let it pass and then closed behind it. The graceful white façade of the building that had once been a nunnery belied the violence that had unfolded inside, throughout the regime's long rule. Lines of soldiers held back the crowds, but there was no aggression. Everyone waited.

"That was Spinola," said Eugênio.

"Didn't Caetano sack him?"

"Exactly. But now the old tyrant won't talk to anyone else. Spinola might be the one who takes over."

"That's good. A diplomat. He stays in with everyone."

It seemed like only minutes later that the doors opened again and the tank re-emerged. It rumbled back through the crowds and roared off. Television cameras massed outside the barracks swung round to catch sight of it.

"Caetano's gone," said Eugênio. "It's over."

Duarte grasped his friend's shoulder, smiled, and walked away. He stopped only to pick up a fallen carnation and tuck it into his jacket pocket.

In Chiado, not far from Celeste's shabby room but in what might have been another universe, Rodrigo and Alexandra Guterres sat in their opulent drawing room, transfixed in front of their television. They watched the flickering images in darkness. The day had been bewildering. As it subsided into evening, neither thought to turn on the lamps.

The small screen showed pictures of a new *Presidente* who spoke in ways that neither had expected to hear in their lifetimes. Spinola was promising democracy, prosperity, the release of political prisoners, and independence for the colonies.

"Do you think it will last?" asked Alexandra. "Can Elena come home?" Her face was haggard in the light from streetlamps that perforated the shadows.

Rodrigo was not feeling confident. His father had been a big supporter of the *Estado Novo*. He told stories of poverty in the country before the regime took over, of political chaos with parties ousting each other in quick succession. Salazar, he said, brought stability and prosperity. But that was a long time ago, before it all turned to violence and oppression. The economy had been stagnating for years. But if the regime was removed, what would replace it?

He shared none of this with his wife. "It's time for change," he said. "Let's hope they get it right. And if they do, we'll bring her home."

Tears rolled down her face. She couldn't stop; they were tears of joy. Looking out of the window, he saw people celebrating in the street outside. A waxing crescent moon was rising above them, like a sliver of hope in the night sky.

Rodrigo held her and said no more. He tried to get it all straight in his mind, to think of all the things that might change. When he had come into his inheritance, at a relatively young age, the assets were mostly held in the *Companhia de Diamantes de Angola,* which controlled the colony's lucrative diamond mines for its Portuguese masters. The returns had been exceptional. When his wife inherited, he had invested her money there too. But now, if the new regime intended to grant Angola its independence, what would happen to their wealth?

He tried to tell himself they would be compensated; they wouldn't be left destitute. But what sort of revolutionaries cared about the fortunes of the elite? Whoever took control would have other priorities.

He had spent long hours with old friends, heads of the richest families in Portugal, whose wealth depended on extracting precious minerals in Africa. In private dining rooms, snugs, and exclusive drinking holes all over Lisbon, the men had grappled with rumours of revolution and the prospect of independence for the colonies, while their women continued to party, follow fashion, and raise their children towards a future their fathers feared. They had watched with trepidation as one European nation after another relinquished its holdings. Should they move their investments into banking and insurance? The returns were tame in comparison.

Now the time had come. In the morning he would call on the broker who had served him all his life, whose father had served Rodrigo's father, and his grandfather before that. He had been trying to reach him all day, but the line was permanently busy. In any case, he knew it was too late. By now the shares would be worthless because the diamond company would surely collapse.

He looked across the darkened room toward a shadowy hulk in one corner. They could sell the piano. It was a Bechstein imported by Alexandra's mother, and worth a fortune. There were valuable paintings on every wall, and a Bentley in the garage. Would the house have to go too?

Alexandra looked up at him and smiled through her tears. She was serenely happy in the belief that her daughter and granddaughter would soon be home. She had never questioned where money came from. It had always been there.

He poured her a glass of *Madeira* wine – to celebrate, he said.

For himself, he took a strong *aguardente* to calm his nerves. Tomorrow he would see the broker.

33

MOURARIA, LISBON
2021

As he approached the bar, Lourenço could see Joaquim's bulky frame in his usual seat with his back to the wall. Lourenço no longer hid behind trees to spy on Joaquim's visitors. He had his own relationship with Laurinda now, and separate business interests too, both of which seemed to be going rather well for him. Admittedly, it was proving tricky to have hired a lawyer known not only to Joaquim but also to Helen and Marco, all three of whom he happened to be trying to deceive at that point, and while he was hoping to become involved with the lawyer in question on quite another level. But he didn't know any other *advogadas,* and especially none prepared to work for nothing because they had investment funds from their parents to fall back on.

As he sat down and signalled to Filipe for his

customary *escarchado*, he could see that Joaquim was not happy. He said nothing until his drink arrived and then, sipping the clear liquid, asked casually, 'How's things? *Tudo bem?*"

"What's going on?" asked Joaquim shortly.

"Thursday will be perfect for stealing the plants. We can't risk getting caught, *meu amigão*."

Joaquim continued to stare at him darkly.

"And I have the meeting set up for Friday," Lourenço announced proudly. "With Helen."

"Not Marco?"

Lourenço nodded firmly. "They will both be there. Marco and Helen."

"And why are they seeing you? Who do they think you are? A salesman?"

"I'm smarter than that, my friend. Why would they see a salesman? People close the door on those pests. No. I have offered them a deal. We are going to sign the contracts."

"Deal? What deal?" If there were to be a deal, it must be Joaquim's. Lourenço knew how the land lay on that score; he himself would be entitled only to commission.

"It's for charity. No money involved. She likes prisoners."

"Prisoners? What are you doing, trying to get off with her? She knows you were in jail?"

Lourenço shook his head. "I'm the charity from Portugal: *RedePrisão. S*he does the same sort of thing in England. There are contracts to sign. It is for working together, no money involved."

"You're going to work with her?"

"No, you fool." He saw Joaquim bristle and realised he might have gone too far. The old man saw himself as a mastermind, and it was important to play along with that for now. "They will offer me tea," he went on, "and then I will insist on treating them to my local brew which I will have with me in a bottle. And they will drink it, and then I will leave, taking the bottle with me. I won't touch anything. And boom, they will be dead, and we will be rich."

Joaquim continued to stare uncertainly. "What if you're seen?" he said.

"I will be clean-shaven and wear a hat." Lourenço replied. He generally nurtured a five o'clock shadow, believing it made him look sexy like a film star, and never wore hats, preferring to flaunt hair that was as thick and dark today as he edged towards fifty as it had ever been. "No-one will know me without my beard or hair. You and I will be cooking all night on Thursday, *meu amigão*, like a pair of good wives."

The more lyrical his language became, the more cynical was the look on Joaquim's face. Lourenço tried to keep his own expression blank. His meeting was actually booked for Thursday and it was with Helen alone. By Friday the bank transfer would have been made from her account to his, those hundreds of thousands that she was investing in his worthy charity, and it wouldn't matter whether Joaquim knew or not.

There remained the sticky question of what the old man or his crew of thugs might wish to do to Lourenço when he found out, but his cases were packed and by morning he would be gone, taking Helen's funds with him.

The only flaw in Lourenço's plan was that he must leave Laurinda as well. That was sad for him, very sad, because he could imagine becoming attached to her, and she had that investment fund from her parents as well. What was it worth, he wondered, and would she control it herself one day? What would she be like in bed and would he find out before he pocketed the money and ran? Of one thing he was sure: he would not wish to be on the receiving end of her anger when she discovered she had been deceived. Then again, perhaps she would miss him, although he found that hard to imagine.

He turned the options over in his mind: the magnetic Laurinda weighed against a pile of cash. As a boy, he had played at stone-balancing with friends, using rocks of all shapes and sizes that lay on beaches around Lisbon. The person whose stack stood the tallest without falling would win. Now he balanced his choices.

In one pile, the stones looked pretty much the same size and shape: they represented three hundred thousand euros, more money than he had ever seen. The rocks took on a golden hue in this heap, and then became ingots, shining like the sun.

In the other, the pattern was quite different. Toward the top lay dainty pebbles, perched impossibly and beautifully, reaching up toward the sky. Some were delicately grained marble, others pink-hued granite. The day, in his imagination, was bright. The sand was powdery and white waves frothed on the shore.

At the bottom of the sculpture-like pile sat smoothly rounded boulders, providing a solid base. There were some shiny black slates in places as well, their sharp edges sticking out of the stack. He became quite lost in the image; it was a work of art. It won the contest easily by being taller.

But the bullion weighed more. By this time tomorrow he would be rich, and in another country altogether, or lost in the villages of the South. He had better get down to planning how and where.

34

CAXIAS PRISON

1974

"I'll never complain about anything again."

Gabriela sat next to Téo in the front seat of the Mercedes, as they had so many times before, but today was different. There was no fear, no looking out for PIDE police, and no clandestine package of papers to deliver.

"Not until the next time you see Gomes," said Roberto, from the seat behind. There might have been a revolution the day before, but the law that mattered to him the most had not changed. In the eyes of the world, he was a friend of the couple Gabriela and Téo, who sat together in the front of the car.

They had spent most of the night celebrating the end of the *Estado Novo,* but found a new burst of energy when Duarte telephoned Gabriela to tell her the amazing, euphoria-inducing, unbelievable news: Luís would be released from prison today. All of the prisoners were to be freed, he said, even those who had committed real crimes. It had been argued that all criminal activity that took place under the tyranny of the *Estado Novo* was political, therefore everyone should be let go. Otherwise, individual cases might be debated for years while men and women wasted their lives behind bars. Whether that mass release would happen, Duarte said, was in question, but Luís would be out today. He could assure them.

The car sped down the highway, not ashamed to be drawing attention to itself in this new reality. They passed Leiria and its chapel without stopping this time. In every village, people were out of their houses, cautiously celebrating in the streets, or gathered around radios broadcasting in bars. Some looked wary. Was it true? Could it last? Portuguese flags were starting to be hung from windows. The new military were everywhere, relaxed and welcome.

It was a slow journey into Lisbon, through streets lined with tanks and masses of people. Rifles hung unready at soldiers' sides. Caxias prison was surrounded: there were clerks, manual workers, professors, brothers, sisters, fathers, and mothers. It seemed that half the city had come out to bring their loved ones home. Journalists threaded through the crowds, taking pictures and making notes.

Gabriela, Téo, and Roberto moved through the crowds, shifting position until they found Luís's family. They were all there: his mother, his father, and the two brothers – tall and broad, like clones of Luís.

They stood together as the afternoon darkened to evening.

Gabriela stared at the tall white walls. Through iron rungs covering stark windows, she could see some of the men inside. They were waving and shouting at the crowd. There was no sign of Luís. She was tired, not just from standing for hours, but from the weight of Luís's mother, who might have fallen without Gabriela's support.

Roberto stood beside them, and then Téo appeared, having wandered away to find someone who might know what was happening.

"Any news?" asked Gabriela.

Téo shook his head. "No-one knows anything." His eyes welled.

"Téo! What are these, happy tears?"

He didn't smile. "I betrayed you Gabi. How can you even speak to me?"

"If you had, I'd be in jail too. You were brave, as brave as anyone." She gripped his arm. "You <u>are</u> brave, my friend."

"Thank you." His voice choked as he spoke.

"It was Elena they wanted. Because of the film. They didn't need you to tell them, they knew everything."

"Do you think she escaped? With the Englishman?"

"I'm sure they did. One day we'll find out."

The soldiers looked as tired as the families, shifting from one foot to another. Then a disturbance ran through the crowd. People were shouting. Some of the military entered the building through an arched doorway. Journalists were allowed in as well, a real marker of change. The prisoners behind bars above them were going wild. None of them was Luís.

"Is he really coming out?" said his mother, her voice faint.

"*Mãe*, if they don't let him out, we'll go in and get him," said one of the brothers, belligerently. They stood ready to fight.

Their mother looked even more worried.

Gabriela glanced at Luís's father. He was staring at the towers and the tall wire fences. His jaw was set, and she doubted he heard his two elder sons at all.

And then they came; a parade of smiling young men – and women – laughing and joyful. They might have been sauntering off a pleasure boat. Mostly young, there were some older prisoners too, blinking in the light of a freedom not seen for years.

Suddenly Luís's father stepped forward, and the next moment his son was enveloped in his arms. Tears streamed down the older man's face. He wore an expression that Gabriela could only describe, when she wrote to Elena years later, as beatific. It was as if he would never let go of his son again.

Then his mother collapsed against him, and the brothers grasped his arms. Gabriela stared. This was not the Luís she had lost; he was thinner now, and although still so young, somehow haggard and haunted. That she could accept, but across one side of his face there was a scar that ran through the eyebrow and into his cheek. Physically he had survived. Now the less obvious damage would have to be healed.

He looked back at her, and the brothers stepped

away. He stretched out a hand and pulled her nearer. Not taking her eyes from his, she reached up and traced the line of the scar over his face.

He shrugged. "Got into another fight," he said, smiling. Suddenly it seemed funny. They all laughed, and cried, and laughed again. He brushed the hand that touched the scar, and then wrapped her in the familiar bear hug that had seemed to belong to another lifetime.

35

CHILTERN GRANGE, MEDMENHAM
2021

I had never expected to attend another wedding of my own. I had celebrated with my friends over the years as they married for the first time or the second, and on one occasion the third, but all I knew of marriage was the sum of a series of compromises and disappointments. Although I was generally an optimistic person, my experience of relationships had left me believing that if a couple appeared to be happy together once the rose-tinted first months were over, it must be because one was stifling their needs to accommodate those of the other.

But with Marco, I had discovered a different kind of love. It hadn't swept me away, ever, but felt deeper and calmer than anything that had gone before. The astonishing and wonderful part was that he felt the same. He described our relationship as feeling like a plane coming in to land, at last on *terra firma*, after the trauma of his marriage. He said he was learning to trust again. There hadn't been any of the doubts or torments that plagued some of my previous relationships, with one exception – the split I had foolishly initiated over that malicious email, and which I now bitterly regretted.

I sat in my study. A grey mist hovered over the river, and I couldn't see any signs of life through the haze. I was supposed to be preparing a talk I had been asked to give at the annual conference of an industrial tools corporation whose CEO was my biggest client. He asked me to speak about leadership there every year, and I had to think of something new to say.

Instead, I found myself imagining a scene in my garden unlike anything I had experienced before: our marriage, Marco and me. I pictured a marquee stretched over the upper terrace, the clink of champagne glasses and guests dressed up in their best. There were friends from the past and new ones too: Cristóvão the notary would attend, no doubt with the elegant wife I had met at a lunch in Lisbon, and in my fantasy she was dressed in pale silk. My vision went into that much detail. He might perhaps be in conversation with my neighbour, the solicitor, the one whose vehicle I had once mistaken for Marco's hire car.

Cristóvão's relationship with me had developed into a fatherly sort of friendship. I was grateful to him for risking his professional reputation, and possibly his licence, by telling me Marco was the son of Joaquim.

Breaking all his own rules on compliance and confidentiality, he had followed his sense of what was right and persuaded me to return to Lisbon, paving the way for my future with Marco.

Joaquim was also there in my wedding dream, probably talking hunting rifles with my older male friends. Surely by then he and Marco would somehow have discovered their relationship with each other. I still vacillated about telling him, and anguished over it.

The ceremony itself must be simple and not religious. While I had no need for documents to seal our relationship, Marco wanted it to be formalised, he had said during our last night together at the beach house. Though no longer a practising Catholic, the protocols were embedded in him. So there would have to be a registrar and some rigmarole, but I found myself drawn to the idea as well, if only for the public declaration of our commitment to each other and a good excuse for a party. It was a chance for our assorted friends and relatives to meet, binding the past with the future, and his life with mine.

I would wear a new dress of course. Not bridal white – I had done that once before and it had not ended well. I imagined something simple and elegant. I had a friend whose little daughters would be thrilled to act as flower girls. The youngest was only two years old and would look adorable.

I realised it was time to log on with my client and quickly clicked through the links. His smiling face appeared on the screen. Each year David Radcliffe's hair became a closer match to the grey of his eyes. He reminded me a little of my father – Douglas, that is.

"I have the plans for the conference," he said. "Could we talk about your keynote?"

We were soon exchanging ideas and planning schedules. I would arrive the night before, to attend a staff dinner and then deliver a presentation and a workshop for the directors the next day. It was the third year in a row this had happened. I knew a lot of the people quite well, and David now felt like an old friend. The two hours allotted for our meeting passed quickly.

After his image cleared, instead of going straight to review and update my notes, I opened my messages. I looked at Marco's photo in the box above his name. It had been a day and a half since he had made contact, the longest period we had gone without speaking since our reunion. The text I had sent him yesterday bore a signal showing it had been read, but he hadn't replied. I sent him another. "I hope you're having a sunny day," I said. Two grey ticks showed it was delivered but not opened. I wondered if something might be wrong. Could it be the dogs perhaps? Was Marco ill?

I tapped his number. The tone sounded but he didn't answer. Like me, he was probably seeing a client, I reassured myself, and would call later. I completed my notes, tidied my desk, and went into the garden to sweep up some twigs that had fallen during high winds last night. Then I wandered down to the river, my shoes growing wet in the grass after an earlier shower. My ancient cruiser, a relic from my parents' days, lay in the water gathering algae. Its engine had refused to start for a long time now. Marco and I had sat on it one sunny afternoon between lockdowns, before that wicked email had torn a rift between us, sipping wine and discussing what its replacement might be if I got my share of the inheritance.

I went to bed early because the following day I had to catch an early train into London, to deliver an all-day workshop for a client. I was wakeful until dawn, and then almost overslept. There was still no contact from Marco.

I checked my phone on the train, and then had to turn it off for the rest of the day. I switched on briefly at lunchtime, but there were no messages. On the home journey, I read through the emails that had accumulated since morning, and considered sending another to Marco. But I didn't.

Another day passed. I spent it in the garden, recuperating from the day before. I enjoyed leading workshops but they were exhausting, and I was not used to rush-hour travel. I felt uncomfortable now about having indulged in daydreams of a wedding. Had I jinxed the whole thing? I knew it was absurd to think that, but anxiety was beginning to gnaw at me. I couldn't concentrate on anything else. Jen was away and I had nothing planned. That evening, after a couple of glasses of wine, I sent him a text message, wondering if I would regret it when sober. "I love you," it said.

The next day I called him again. His precious face filled the screen, but it was drawn and serious. I saw the big canvas behind him and the oriental rug on the floor; he was in the city. The Tagus would be snaking outside in the sun – I could see the moving shadows it cast onto the ceiling – and I wondered if the dogs were there. Why was he not talking?

"Are you okay?" I asked softly.

He looked down. In the space of a breath, we had moved from a place where everything was right to one where nothing seemed to be. I felt awkward and frightened and didn't know what to say.

At last, he spoke. "I think it's best if we don't see each other for a while."

Then his image disappeared and I was alone.

36

COIMBRA UNIVERSITY
1974

The clock ticked in the silence, second by second. The sound echoed around the vaulted ceiling of the *Sala dos Capelas*. Forty-nine students sat facing him, their heads bowed, scribbling onto their exam papers. Not all would leave this room having earned a cap and gown, but none would have cheated, not on his watch. Gomes pulled his own gown around him. The room sweltered in the July heat, but the musty black wool gave him a sense of security in this new, tumultuous, post-revolutionary world.

No longer a Monitor, now that there was no longer a PIDE to report to, he took his remaining duties all the more seriously. His position of Invigilator brought great responsibility. He inspected his charges one by one, his eyes halting at the expanding body of Gabriela Magalhães de Quintela. Shamelessly, she made no attempt to hide her swelling belly.

He looked further back along the lines of desks to the father of her child (which appeared to be in danger of imminent arrival, right there in the exam room). Luís Rafael Coelho sat at the back, but his broad skull loomed over the others. Even from this distance, the scar running across his face was visible. It joined another over one eye. He had deserved his wounds, and Gomes wished that the prison guards who inflicted them had finished the job. Instead, this reprobate had been admitted back into law school to cram years of study into a matter of months. A radical group of professors had tutored him, one-on-one, to get him through. Now here he was, sitting his finals with a contingent from the year below, which included his immoral girlfriend, Gabriela.

The deviants were here too, placed on opposite sides of the room to each other – he had made sure of that. Teodoro Sá Nogueira de Lorena sat with his eyes on the papers in front of him, his long lashes catching the sunlight that filtered through the blinds on the windows, a summer breeze stirring his hair. Gomes shifted his gaze across the tiers of desks. Roberto dos Santos was taller, but they might have been brothers, instead of the ungodly couple that they were.

They reminded him of a pair of statues in the national museum: Heracles and his arms-bearer Hylas, the argonaut too beautiful to be left behind. He had dreamed about them. He appeared in the dream himself, wearing the black gown, but it glistened and floated like silk instead of rough wool. He wrenched his mind back to the examination room.

After the revolution upended the hierarchy that had once given his world structure, he had reported the pair of them to the *Reitor*, expecting them to be arrested for social perversion. Change of government or not, they were still committing a crime. But nothing happened. All these new leaders did was squabble with each other; the left, the communists, the new centre right. How would they ever make decisions? And the Rector himself had turned out to be a vociferous supporter of the new order. He had worn a carnation pinned to his gown for a full week after the coup.

So here they all were: an ex-convict, an unmarried mother-to-be (who by rights should be locked away in an institution for fallen women), and a pair of sexual degenerates. Two others from their circle were mercifully absent: Álvaro de Almeida and his delinquent sidekick, Elena Guterres. Gomes smiled quietly at the part he'd played in that. The boy, at least, would never trouble anyone again. And the girl had fled like a coward.

His train of thought shattered as the great doors to the *sala* crashed open. Six National Guards marched into the room. Who were they here to arrest? The perverts at last? Or was this another rebellion?

They tramped up the centre aisle and stopped in front of him. He stood and gave a slight bow. He had served the *Estado Novo* devotedly, and if the army now replaced them, he would be its servant too. Without authority there would be anarchy. Obsequious and respectful towards the *Reitor,* despite the man's regrettable disloyalty to the fallen regime, Gomes readily assumed the same attitude in the presence of these men.

"*Bom dia,*" he said. "And how may I be of assistance?"

A man stepped forward. He bore the stripes of a sergeant on his sleeve. "You are Lázaro Menezes Gomes?" he asked.

"Indeed, I am."

"*Senhor Professor.* We are here under instruction from the provisional authorities."

"The provisional authorities," Gomes repeated. He was impressed. What new rules had they come to announce?

"You are to be taken into custody for questioning regarding alleged activities during the *Estado Novo* regime."

The silence in the room suddenly seemed more intense, and as stifling as the summer heat. The ticking of the clock sounded louder and slower.

The sergeant spoke again. "Specifically, your suspected collaboration with the PIDE."

Tendrils of apprehension curled inside Gomes as the man continued. The clock chimed three times, marking a quarter to the hour. The period allowed for the paper was nearing its end.

"And the betrayal of individuals who were later executed," the man continued. His voice was tense but even.

A sudden cheer from the room broke the hush. Students were standing and applauding, behaviour completely unacceptable for the exam room.

"*Silêncio!*" Gomes shouted.

They ignored him. The feeling inside amplified into terror.

There were calls, "Take him away!" "Lock him up!" He somehow expected the guards to silence the students, but their focus remained on him.

Luís stood with his arm around the swollen figure of Gabriela. Tears streamed down her face, and through his fear, Gomes was astonished to see that Luís cried too – not such a big man after all.

A soldier dressed as a private grabbed his arm and pulled him roughly down from the dais on which he and his supervision desk were balanced. He stumbled and fell. One of them kicked him as he lay on the ground. The billowing gown foiled the man's aim, but fear stabbed him more intensely than any physical injury could.

Then Luís was standing in front of him, his face still wet, and flushed with – what? Excitement? Anger? The boy seemed like a giant, his ravaged features metres above the floor where Gomes cowered. This was the end of him, he felt certain, here in his sanctuary, in front of all the examinees.

He screamed, "Don't hurt me! Please!"

Instead of delivering the expected blow, Luís placed a hand on the arm of the guard who had kicked the fallen professor.

"There will be no violence," he said. "We're not like them. The war is won."

Tension flowed out of the room. The students fell

quiet. Luís helped Gomes to his feet.

The sergeant stepped forward. "You're coming with us."

Gomes resisted. Two men took his arms, one on either side, and propelled him forward. He tried to stand against them, but the power had left his legs. His feet dragged uselessly along the floor. Without the support of his assailants he would have fallen.

"The courts will deal with you," one said.

Another sniggered behind him. "You might even get a lawyer. If you're lucky."

A few students laughed but Luís looked stricken.

"That's more than Álvaro de Almeida had," Gabriela said. The room fell silent.

The words reached Gomes ominously through his panic.

As they hauled him through the doors, the begging started. "Please don't take me! Twenty years I've served here. I'll serve you too. Whatever you want. Let me go! Please!" The final word rose to a scream.

The voices of the students died away, leaving only the sound of his powerless feet as they scraped along the ancient corridors of Coimbra, alongside the steady tramp of the soldiers' boots. As he was dragged out of the vaulted atrium for the last time, away from the ancient halls where he had expected to spend the rest of his days, a bell in the great clock tower tolled twelve times.

37

MARQUÊS DE POMBAL, LISBON
2021

Laurinda felt tired but satisfied as she made her way through the conference centre to the bar downstairs. Despite the rules and regulations that had people talking through screens, and keeping distances marked out on the floor, she had made some contacts and had a decent collection of cards to follow up. She felt she had particularly impressed a couple who were starting a small business and must therefore be in need of a lawyer. After setting up Lourenço's charity for him, she could imagine this becoming her niche market, perhaps combined with website and promotional services as well.

She had yet to make a profit, and this was mainly down to the costs of her work with Lourenço. She could not pinpoint exactly when the dynamic had shifted, from her role as a paid lawyer to being an investor in his business. It had happened gradually. Her quote was reduced to a smaller one, and then nothing at all, and at some point, she had started to pay the fees incurred in setting up the charity on his behalf. But how else would he foot them? He had convinced her it was a promising venture and given her the opportunity of owning a share of it.

During her years as an associate at Cristóvão's firm, she had come across similar outfits where people who were undoubtedly benefiting others also pocketed reasonable returns for themselves. And there were tax breaks too. This investment looked like a smart move, and she had turned the tables in the negotiation stakes by propelling her share up to fifty per cent.

She had told him to meet her in the smallest bar downstairs. It was not serving drinks because of the restrictions, so there would be fewer people present to overhear them. She glanced around the room and saw him sitting by the window, tapping on his phone. It was the latest model, which impressed her. With his black hair, just starting to streak with grey, his muscular frame lending shape to a stylish jacket and jeans, and the trace of a beard that shadowed an angular jawline, he could have been a film star lounging there. He had a certain charm, helped rather than hindered by a faintly disreputable air, that she felt would be perfect for attracting both clients and investors.

As she approached the table from across the room, he glanced up at her. And then the strangest thing happened. It was like being hit by a little electrostatic shower, and she knew that he felt it too. This was quite unexpected and not at all welcome. Here was her first real chance at building something after the fiasco with Joaquim's inheritance, which had cost her so much effort with no return. It was not the time to mix business with pleasure, no matter how strong the attraction.

She avoided his proffered hand and sat down opposite him. A cousin had once taught her a trick: if you look at someone's mouth while they're speaking, they will think you are looking them in the eye but won't be able to read what's in yours. She had found it to be quite a useful technique over the years, and stared firmly at Lourenço's mouth as he spoke. It was quite wide but not too much so, with lips that were fleshy enough without being too fat, and pink enough without being too red. It twitched sensitively in response as he listened and shaped itself firmly into words when he spoke.

"Had a good day, my partner?" The way he said it, *partner* sounded over-familiar.

She looked away and set up her laptop on the table between them, like a barrier. She ignored his question.

"So, this is where we are," she said crisply, scrolling down the screen. "The first thing I need to know is the name of the backer."

The mouth on which she was focusing looked uncertain for a moment. She forgot the technique and looked straight into his eyes instead. What was happening there, she wondered? Could she see doubt? Or deception? Or was he simply trying to remember?

"The backer wishes to remain anonymous for now," he said after a moment's hesitation. "I can't reveal her name."

"Then how are we going to get her to sign a contract?" returned Laurinda.

"Give me the papers. I will fill them in on the day."

"What day is that?" returned Laurinda. "Have you already arranged something?"

"I have to send her the contracts to look over – we can do that by email – and then she will fix a time to sign. She's coming..." He hesitated for a moment. "She's talking about next week."

What had he been about to say, Laurinda wondered, and why had he changed it? Where was this backer coming from and why would he hide that? Her lawyer's mind, honed through years of training, picked up and questioned every detail.

Nevertheless, she opened the draft agreements on her screen and took Lourenço meticulously through the contents, checking facts with him here and making alterations there. She was a little surprised that he had no questions. If only all clients were like that, she thought, pleased to have found one who understood that his *advogada* knew best.

At the end, just before the signature page, there was a schedule which would list the payments to be made, and on what dates.

"So how much is the backer putting in?" she asked him. "Over what time scale? Have you finalised these things with her yet?" She was ready for a fair amount of vagueness and not a little over-optimism. Most of the clients she had managed at Cristóvão's believed what they wanted to hear rather than what had been said.

"She has offered three or four hundred thousand," he said. "And she might be able to get more from other backers. Leave it blank."

"Three or four HUNDRED THOUSAND!" Laurinda repeated, her voice a near-shout, and then quickly looked around the bar. No-one seemed to be paying attention. "Are you serious?"

He shrugged. He was enjoying this, she could tell. She couldn't help noticing how handsome he looked, sitting back with a little smile on that wide, firm mouth.

"That's what she said."

"Euros?"

He nodded.

"Did you suggest it or did she?"

"She did."

"Perhaps you misheard?" She felt completely unnerved.

"It's hard to confuse three or four hundred thousand with something else."

This backer must be mad, whoever she was, thought Laurinda, but didn't say it. Instead, she saved the finished document and closed down her screen. She needed to get away from him now to give her time to think, and to put a respectable business-like space between them. She got up to leave.

"Where d'you think you're going?" he asked, standing as well, and too close to her. "Let's get out of here. We have a lot to discuss."

She hesitated. If she got him drunk, she should be able to prise the backer's identity out of him. It was a technique she had used before, and she was good at it.

Twelve hours later, she watched as he lit up a cigarette.

"That's a disgusting habit," she said.

This was not meant to have happened. Last night had not gone according to her plan. Instead, here they were, lying on his bed, with her hair as tangled as his sheets.

"You taste like an ashtray," she said.

He arched his neck and blew three smoke rings straight up into the air. The shapely mouth that formed the perfect grey circles twitched and suddenly she couldn't help laughing. She was not sure what was so funny, especially at a time like this when she was mad with him for smoking and for getting her into this unwanted state of affairs. They were supposed to be business partners, and judging from her own past experience, she would say that this turn of events was extremely unwise.

Nevertheless, they laughed loudly and out of control until he extinguished the cigarette and, turning, stretched an arm towards her.

"You have work to do," she said sternly, extracting herself from the messy bed and stalking towards his bathroom in as dignified a manner as she could, knowing that he was watching her, and how they had spent the night.

She emerged from the bathroom and kept her back

to him as she dressed. She heard him get up, and turning, saw him staring. What was he, ten years older, fifteen? Tall, strong, and confident too, in fact downright insolent sometimes, she thought. He knew what he wanted and how to get it. But there were times when she glimpsed something else – there it was, and then again not – an uncertainty about him; a fear, a manchild in his eyes. Perhaps he could be saved, and she was the one to do it.

She had not so far found a life partner she could trust, or perhaps she just chose the ones who were not to be trusted, her mother said. She mulled over this from time to time, but who knew? The arrow would strike and there she would go again. But with this one, there was something about him that felt different. All the same, it was exactly the opposite of where she wanted to be at this point in time. Business and pleasure should never be mixed; that was her principle, but here they were, immersed in both.

In two hours, he was due to meet the mystery backer to sign the contracts. He made coffee, and they sat opposite each other at a table that divided a small kitchenette from the room containing the rumpled bed. In the cool morning light, she noticed that the surfaces were surprisingly clean; tidy too, like the rest of the place with its starched white linen and neatly hung clothes. It was not that dissimilar from her own flat, although she had two separate rooms and a nicer bathroom, and lived in a smarter part of town. Also, she owned hers, paid for out of the investment fund set up by her parents. That had got her through the last two years of working for Joaquim without pay.

"I'm coming with you," she said, replacing her empty cup firmly in its saucer.

The coffee was not bad, she thought, and had been made in a top-of-the-range machine. There were a number of expensive gadgets around the place, she had noticed: a Bose sound system, a couple of nice laptops, and a mobile phone that was a later model than her own. He was an enigma, this man. How could he afford such luxuries yet live in a cheap flat like this?

He shook his head. "You do the law; I do the business. Tomorrow, I will bring you the signed papers. And we will have the money."

Clearly there was no moving him. She collected her things and walked to the door. Turning, she said firmly, "Call me as soon as it's done."

He smiled. For a moment she was revisited by the electric feelings of the night before, warm and tingling, and then she resolutely stepped out of the apartment.

Across the road stood a large supermarket. Glancing up at his window to check he was not watching, she slipped through the door, found a corner behind its big glass windows where she could watch without being seen, and waited. There was no way he was taking that meeting without her.

38

OXFORD

1984

He could see Elena across the restaurant, in the window seat he had reserved. Silhouetted against the light, she looked no older than the day they had met, he thought, not the thirty-two year old mother of a teenage daughter.

He placed a pair of dishes on the counter that separated his kitchen from the dining room. One held six freshly made ravioli filled with a creamy concoction of scallops and pistachios. The pistachios were imported from the slopes of Mount Etna, and said to be the finest in Italy. It was Rosa the cook, back in the days when his parents had a team of servants, who first introduced him to the fat green seeds that she received in packages sent by her relatives back home.

Through a combination of acquaintances made on diplomatic journeys, and some new contacts in the business, Douglas had built up a network of special suppliers throughout Italy. Now his Parmesan came from Reggio Emilia, tins of sweet San Marzano tomatoes arrived from Campania, and he bought durum wheat grown in the warm and fertile plains of Foggia to make all of his pasta fresh, and by hand.

In the other dish lay a shining black swirl of *linguine al nero di seppia con gamberi,* a Venetian speciality where the pasta was suffused with squid ink and then served with garlic and giant prawns, glistening with pungent olive oil imported from Tuscany. It was a novelty and a favourite with customers.

Helen arrived. She was taller than her mother. Her hair was soft and fair, like his own. In fact, people would remark on how much she took after him; she had his grey eyes, they said. It made him smile. He had all but forgotten about Álvaro and the adoption.

There was a new trainee in the kitchen, and managing today's lunchtime sitting would be a good test for him. Douglas crossed the crowded restaurant, carrying the dishes, and sat down beside his wife and daughter. He placed the food in the centre of the table, while a waitress followed with empty plates for each of them. Elena and Helen liked to try everything, and he wanted their feedback.

He poured wine for himself and Elena, a light Rioja he imported in great quantities, and some water for Helen.

They sipped and chatted. It was a Saturday, and the place was busy with women and families, unlike the weekday crowd of business diners who were mostly men.

Helen tasted the ravioli. She was staring at him. "What are you up to, Dad?"

"Don't you like them?"

"They're gorgeous. What's this green stuff?"

"Pistachios. From Sicily. The best in the world."

"Yummy. You're excited about something, aren't you?"

He could hide nothing from this daughter, except the secret he was determined she would never know. It was one of the few things they had argued about, he and Elena, whether Helen should be told that he was not her real father. He was unshakably convinced that he was right.

"There is something I want to talk to you about," he conceded. He was always planning the next step forward. This time it would be a big one. "*Trattoria Rosa* is doing well but it's small."

The restaurant he had persuaded Trevor to set up at The Heron & Pike had become quite famous for the quality and originality of its menu and wine cellar. Douglas's ambitions had propelled them into acquiring the lease on this small café in the backstreets of Oxford, named *Trattoria Rosa* after the cook who had inspired its cuisine. Astonishingly for such a simple place, it had won a Michelin star.

"If you're cooking for twenty people, it's really no harder to cater for a hundred," he began.

"And then the profit per head would be higher," said Helen.

"Exactly," Douglas nodded. His daughter was a great analytical thinker. Perhaps one day she would be part of the business, he hoped.

"So I started looking at how to create a new restaurant in a bigger space. And I remembered places I saw in Italy. There's a building in Florence called the Medici Palace. Carved stonework, huge rooms, beautiful gardens. And I thought, what if I could make something like that here? A big main hall for the dining room; smaller rooms for private parties and special events; a cookery school maybe." He was carried away on the wings of his vision. "An orchard with heritage apples - plums, apricots, grapes even. Everything grown without pesticides. And a big industrial kitchen."

"So have you found this palace yet, Dad?"

He reached into his jacket and pulled out a leaflet which had been folded many times.

Helen took it and read every word. "It needs a lot of work," she said finally. "Where will the money come from?"

"That's what I want to talk to you about. It's a combination of factors."

She nodded through a mouthful of scallop.

"Trevor and I can sell the *Rosa* and come up with some of the funding, but it's not enough. We'd have to sell our house too."

Helen stopped chewing.

"Every time we move, we make money," he said. "Tax-free. That's how we were able to set up the trattoria."

They had renovated their way through four different homes in a soaring property market, each bigger and better than the last. Elena didn't seem to mind living on building sites, and Douglas was out working most of the time, but Helen hated the mess, the dust, and the interminable change.

"We're moving again?" she sighed.

"We've found a house we could buy without using up all the profits from our current one. Wait till you see it. We're going there after lunch. It's on a short lease. That's why it's cheap. So we can sell our place and free up money to finance the new restaurant."

"A lease?" asked Helen. "Can't we buy the freehold?"

At fourteen years old, how did she know the difference? This daughter astonished him.

"Yes, in a few years' time when the business takes off. But first, we need the equity from the current one to fund it."

She looked doubtful. "And would that give you enough to build your *Palazzo*?"

"No, there would have to be a bank loan too. We've arranged that in principle. Not a problem. They're very keen actually."

She took a mouthful of linguine and chewed it slowly. "This is gorgeous," she said. "Why's it black?"

"Cuttlefish ink."

She nodded. "Really?"

He couldn't tell whether her mind was on the food or his idea.

"We'll call it *Il Palazzo Medici Gastronomico,*" he

said, returning to his big dream. "That means 'The Gastronomic Medici Palace'."

"It's exciting," she said slowly, "but what happens if something goes wrong? If the business failed, would we lose the house as well?"

"No," he said. "The worst-case scenario is we'd be stuck with what was left on the lease. But we'd have a beautiful home. And by the time that expires you'll have your own place. We'll come and live with you!"

He laughed. Helen didn't.

"It sounds like a lot of debt, Dad. What if the cost of borrowing goes up?"

She understood interest rates too. Surely they didn't teach this at school?

"Don't worry about that. There were crazy levels in the seventies but they're stable now. It won't happen again."

They had all finished eating.

"Desserts?" Douglas asked.

Helen shook her head. "That was superb, Dad."

"Let's go and see the house," Elena said impatiently. "The agent's meeting us there at four. If we can't buy the house, he can't have his new restaurant. We have a lot of decisions to make."

She left a few coins on the table for the girl, one of a stream of students provided by a small drama school opposite, who acted the part of waitresses credibly and with little training. She had never forgotten the days when there had been no money for an inside toilet, or at times even shoes. She always tipped. It was one of the many things he loved about her.

Their car, now a second-hand Volvo big enough to carry three adults and two recently adopted Irish wolfhounds, was parked on hard-standing behind the trattoria. They drove toward the river to a building they had seen only from the water, when out in the boats of friends. Tall metal gates had partly collapsed off their hinges. A barely legible sign on the wall read 'Chiltern Grange'. The whole place had an air of mystery that had fascinated Douglas as a child. Now an estate agent stood waiting, ready to take them inside.

They dragged open the gates and picked their way over cracked flagstones, glimpsing balconies that jutted from grey stone walls. Under a pillared portico, the agent inserted an old-fashioned iron key into a heavy door. On the fourth attempt, the lock yielded. Looking relieved, he pushed with his hands and then applied a shoulder before the door groaned open. "Beautiful old fittings," he said. "Look at the wood. Oak I think."

Douglas recognised that the man was trying to put a positive slant on a defective door, but had actually been thinking the same thing himself. He looked at the dilapidated interior of the building and saw only a vision of how it might be when restored. He glanced at Elena. She was bright-eyed. Helen looked appalled.

The dark entrance hall smelled musty, and ancient patterned paper peeled off its walls. But it was a good-sized space, and would come up beautifully after a few hours with a steam stripper. A staircase with carved wooden balusters rose from the centre. Everything they saw needed renovating down to the bones. Behind the agent's back, Douglas and Elena exchanged thrilled smiles.

"This is the main lounge," the man said, pushing open a door which stubbornly refused to close when Elena tried to shut it behind her. She gave up and followed Douglas into a room with high ceilings, ornate cornicing, and a series of arched glass doors that revealed a tangle of trees and shrubs outside.

After failing to slide several rusty bolts, the agent managed to find one that opened. "I'll let you explore the garden on your own," he said. There was an air of defeat about him as he added, "I think they'll take a low offer."

When he heard that, Douglas knew the house could be theirs. And if that happened, he might just be able to build his dream *Palazzo*. They stepped into a garden whose overgrown greenery cast shadows through the interior. He could see sun filtering from above and realised the building faced south; it would be warm and light once the wilderness was cleared.

They picked their way through gloomy foliage, scratched by branches and stung by nettles. Then the vegetation cleared to reveal a broad expanse of the Thames, twinkling in the sun.

"This is incredible," Helen whispered.

She wasn't looking doubtful now, Douglas noticed happily.

"They're struggling to sell because of the state of the place, and the short lease," he said. "Forty years isn't much. But when the business grows, we can buy the freehold. Meanwhile we can do it up."

"So it's an investment,' Elena said encouragingly.

"Exactly," said Douglas.

"Could we get a mortgage?" asked Helen.

"No, but the bank loan and the sale of our house will cover it."

"What do you think, mum?" She looked at Elena.

"It's a magical place. Could you put up with more dirt and dust?"

"You won't have the money to do any renovations for a while, will you?"

"Well, that's true," said Douglas. His hopes sank. If Helen hated the idea, he really couldn't force it on her. He wasn't that kind of a man.

They looked back at the river. The water danced and sparkled in the sun. A pleasure cruiser sailed by with a laughing family on board. Old dog roses tumbled down the bank into the water.

"Dad, this is paradise," Helen said. "Let's do it."

39

SANTOS-O-VELHO, LISBON

2021

Joaquim had been watching the house since early morning. Across the street, a café provided the perfect spot for surveillance purposes: a window seat partially hidden behind a bushy fiddle-leaf fig in a stone pot. He had drunk three cups of coffee and eaten his way through an entire basket of breakfast snacks, and the idea of a *Beirão* was becoming increasingly tempting.

But then the door opposite opened and Marco stepped out. *Please God he isn't coming in here*, prayed Joaquim, and then as the subject of his stakeout walked away, *please God the Englishwoman isn't inside*. He reasoned that if she were there, she would surely have left with Marco.

It was eleven now and if Lourenço had been telling the truth (which was what Joaquim was here to find out), the appointment was booked for two in the afternoon. Lourenço had cancelled their night-time session for boiling oleander leaves, claiming to have looked after it all by himself. Joaquim didn't believe him. He had realised in retrospect that the plan was crazy and would certainly have landed him in jail for the rest of his life. Had he thought for one moment that Lourenço would go through with it, he would have ended the charade immediately.

He had been a little worried when his accomplice turned up at his house with a pile of cheap Chinese tinware, which had surely not cost anywhere near two hundred euros, and furiously regretted having parted with the two thousand. What was he thinking? Too many *Beirões*. But Lourenço was certainly up to something, and he had no intention of leaving here today until he knew what it was.

He left some notes and coins beside the debris on the table and then walked across the street, adopting a shuffling gait intended to make him inconspicuous to passers-by. It was a technique he had perfected in his criminal past.

He rang the doorbell once, and waited but there was no response, so took from his pocket a hooked metal rod that was also a relic of former times. He inserted it but hit a barrier. He applied another rod, and then a third. All the levers gave at once and the door swung silently open. He stepped inside and closed it behind him.

The place was built upside down, with a kitchen and garage on the ground floor and a living room above, a modern concept so that its occupants could look at water all the time, though why they would want to do that he couldn't imagine. He assumed that today's meeting would be upstairs. All his senses were on edge with the fear of being caught. How he had missed this feeling!

The light bouncing off the river was blinding as he stepped into the lounge. He squinted through the brightness but could see no large cupboards – damned minimalism, less to steal and nowhere to hide. There was a door off to one side, but it led only into a small cloakroom which might later be used by the visitors.

The bifold doors to the terrace slid smoothly open at first touch. Ah, what it would be to own doors like these, he thought, mentally adding them to his list of intended purchases when he finally got hold of some real money.

Outside he found what he was looking for: a slim shed, quite rustic for so modern a place, that opened to reveal a mountain bike hanging on a rack and a space large enough to stand in if he straddled a garden hose wound on a reel.

An hour later, he re-entered the empty house for a necessary toilet break in the little cloakroom – all that coffee – and then went back into hiding. If he opened the shed door further, he could sit on the hose. It was not comfortable but at least took the pressure off his back, which was no longer up to this sort of stress. Old age haunted him: it was coming. It was here.

Shortly afterwards he heard voices, doors opening, and footsteps on the stone floor inside. The heavy swish of the bifolds made him freeze, but no-one came out. Marco must have opened them, which would be all the better to hear what they were saying.

"I know what to do." It was a woman's voice, speaking English. That must be her, Helen, the niece.

He expected to hear Marco then, but instead there came another voice that he didn't recognise. "That's good. Here are the contracts. You get him to sign here... and here."

Joaquim's understanding of English, acquired mostly on travels through Europe where it seemed to act as a common language, was better than his spoken command of it. "Contracts," the man had said. That meant *contratos,* surely, it was practically the same word in Portuguese. So far everything was going to plan. Lourenço had said they would sign *contratos* and here they were.

But who was the unknown man? Was Marco there too, and would Lourenço end up poisoning all three of them? Perhaps the idiot really did intend to commit murder. He would deny all knowledge of it. Then it occurred to him that if he were found here in the shed, he would become an obvious suspect. But it was Lourenço's plan now, not his. These thoughts were confusing but he was not given to analytical thinking, so they didn't trouble him for long. All of his concentration was absorbed in hearing what was said in the room next door.

Then everything went quiet. The silence persisted for so many minutes that Joaquim gave in to the temptation to leave his sanctum and peer inside the lounge. As he did so, he brushed against the bicycle hanging on the wall. It seemed to make a colossal amount of noise, but he saved it from falling, waited, and then, certain now that they must all have left, crept out to look through the doors.

She was sitting there, the Englishwoman, on Marco's big white sofa. There were some papers spread out on a coffee table in front of her. Despite the noise he had made, she didn't look up, so Joaquim crept quietly back into the shed. So far so good.

The sound of a doorbell drifted out to him, and then the voice of Lourenço, refusing an offer from Helen of refreshments. Joaquim didn't blame him. He had tried the tasteless coffee made by English people and couldn't see the point of it, never mind their tea.

And then it occurred to him that if Lourenço was intending to kill them, this is where he should have taken out his oleander brew and persuaded them to drink it. Where was Marco? Who else was in the room? Now the young fool was apologising for being late.

"Are you ready to sign?" he heard Helen ask. "Do you have any questions?"

"No, no questions," replied Lourenço. "We sign."

A rustling of papers went on for some time, and he heard her say, "Here," and again, "Here."

Then Lourenço asked, "We make the transfer now *Senhora*?"

Relief relaxed Joaquim's aching neck. There would not be any murders today. This was about money. He stiffened again. What money?

"Here, the details of my bank," Lourenço said.

Then three things happened almost at the same

time. Joaquim burst out of his shed, falling over the hose reel and sending the bicycle crashing onto the ground. Forgetting as usual to consider his options before acting, he stormed into the room and delivered a string of swearwords to Lourenço.

Helen looked thoroughly shocked; even paler than usual. Before she could speak, Marco emerged from the cloakroom door – how lucky he had not hidden there himself, Joaquim thought, before realising that he had revealed his presence now anyway – with a man Joaquim had never seen before. He knew that look. It was a cop for sure, albeit in plain clothes. Joaquim had what he called his 'police antennae' honed from years of evading the GNR.

Marco was staring at Joaquim, looking as surprised as Helen.

Now the man was giving Lourenço a caution: "*Tudo o que disser poderá ser usado como prova...*"

Silently, a second cop had appeared as if from nowhere, standing as a witness to the words of the first one.

"You trick me!" Lourenço spat out at Helen.

Joaquim stared at her with new admiration. A bluff! She was nice-looking, this Englishwoman – tall and slim, her features fine and even. He measured her the way he used to assess horses back in Sintra. She must be clever, too, to have fooled that devious Lourenço; clever in the way that mattered.

At that point the third unexpected event occurred: Laurinda walked in. They must have left the door open downstairs, either that or she was a lockpicker too.

She stopped as abruptly as Marco had, the clack of her high heels ceasing on the floor, and a neat little laptop bag in her hand crashed to the floor.

40

SINTRA

1985

At the Almeida mansion in Lapa, the great green gates were kept closed against the heat, casual pedlars, and all criminal elements – including disgraced family members newly released from prison. Joaquim studied the metal bars and circles that turned the place into a fortress. A wall the height of two men stretched out on either side of it. A glance upwards told him nothing. All the shutters were closed behind curving balustrades. He pulled at an iron bar that was set into the stone.

A man he had never seen before opened a slatted section and stared through it without releasing the gates. He wore the livery of a steward.

"Who are you?" Joaquim said gruffly. The expression on the servant's face told him that he looked like a tramp. Last night he had slept in a charity bed courtesy of the *Santa Casa da Misericórdia*, where the nightmares and groans of homeless men allowed him little sleep. He didn't think of himself as one of them but had nowhere else to go. The washing facilities provided were minimal, so he stank, even though the nuns had given him clothing to replace the torn remnants of his own, which were still stained with the blood of his last fight before entering Caxias prison. The garments had been kept by the guards for two years and returned to him unwashed. By some miracle, his signet ring was still there, in a pocket, and he had put it on his finger before throwing the rags away. It bore the family crest.

He held out his hand to the man and showed him the engraving. "I want to see Duarte. My brother."

The servant's eyes travelled from the ring to Joaquim's face. He looked shocked. "The master is in Sintra."

"Let me in," demanded Joaquim. "I need a shower and change. Clothes. Money." What the nuns had given him didn't fit: the shirt was too big and the trousers too short. They had also provided a few coins for the bus fare to Lapa. He spent them on gin and walked there instead, and now his feet were hurting. The sisters of the Holy Houses of Mercy were not quite merciful enough to give him footwear of the right size.

The steward looked frightened. He shook his head and stepped back from the doors. Light was softening into evening and Joaquim could see his own long shadow falling across the bars and onto the wood behind. The slats began to close.

"Food!" Joaquim cried out. "At least give me some food! And shoes! Duarte's shoes. We're the same size. He's my brother," Joaquim reminded him, feeling fury rising inside. What was he doing here, being made to beg at the gates of his own family home?

The man turned back. "Wait here," he said.

He returned with a bulging plastic shopping bag, some rough walking boots, and – praise *Nossa Senhora* and all the saints – a bottle of beer. Joaquim took them through the bars. He didn't say thank you. He felt more like spitting at the insolent vassal.

He sat in the doorway of a closed shop to devour the bread, cheese, and garlic sausage in the package, and drank the beer. It was nothing special, just a *Sagres,* but in the circumstances no nectar of the gods could have surpassed it for taste.

People walked past, looking straight ahead. A woman stopped and threw two coins. She was small and round, with clouds of grey hair sprouting from a chubby, smiling face. He almost chucked the money back at her, but he needed it, so looked away instead. She frowned and moved on.

He contemplated his choices. There was another *Casa da Misericórdia* in Chiado, not half an hour's walk away, but that meant more patronising nuns and foetid bodies shouting through the night. He couldn't face it. Although the sisters might give him the bus fare to Sintra, he would only spend it on drink and have to walk anyway.

It was the shoes that got him there in the end; Duarte's walking boots fitted his feet nicely. What he had said to the steward was nonsense; he was an adopted brother who just happened to have feet the same size, but perhaps the man didn't know they weren't related by blood. After an hour of trudging, and no luck with lifts, he slept until dawn under the trees in the gardens at Calhariz de Benfica.

He awoke and breathed the air of freedom. Only two nights before he had slept in a cell at Caxias prison, that very same jail where the dissidents used to be locked up, and which now held a fair number of ex-PIDE officers among the thieves like himself.

It hadn't taken him long to recognise the wraith-like figure who kept his head down and shoulders hunched. It was Gomes: Lázaro the informer, the betrayer of Álvaro. Revenge had been sweet and brutal. Joaquim had risked his parole to call in that debt but had not been caught. Gomes was too frightened to rat on him. Eleven years, the scumbag had been there. Judging by his twisted and broken face, Joaquim had not been the first with a score to settle.

He smiled and set off for the road to Sintra. He tried to cadge lifts, but apart from a farm cart which stopped, and then quickly took off when its driver saw the state of him, no-one obliged. He walked for many kilometres.

At first his pace was brisk, then it slumped to a weary slog, and then he halted to beg food from the *Casa de Misericórdia* at Queluz, but didn't stay with them for long. A prayer or two – small payment for their hearty stew – and he was on his way.

At Mem Martins he stole a bottle of gin. After

sleeping it off in a field, he reached the family's villa in Sintra as dusk was falling, a little later than his arrival at their Lapa mansion the day before.

He didn't ring at the gates this time. Skirting the white walls of the estate, he knew exactly where the lowest point was located. As a boy he had constructed an innocent-looking pile of stones and earth on either side, just high enough to escape after sneaking out of his room at night and get him back inside before dawn. The mound was still there, covered now in little yellow flowers. The sight of them made him stop for a moment and look around, breathing the air. It was clean and it was home. As far as his tired eyes could see, the hillsides were carpeted in *estevas* and *margaridas,* all raising their innocent white blooms to the sun.

After clambering over the wall, he crept around the back of the stables, not making a sound. He had to get into the house to find Duarte before anyone saw him. Judging from the reaction of the steward in Lisbon, the servants had been warned, and after giving him the shoes, the man would surely have phoned ahead.

Winding his way through the gardens, he passed four stone cherubs who perennially drank water from a fountain. He took a gulp too. There was the tree that used to provide the passage to his room. A tall jacaranda not yet in bud, it was preparing to explode into blue glory outside his window, before covering the earth below with woody pods and dead leaves that made the gardeners complain. In its winter nakedness, the tree would be easier to climb, but would its boughs hold his adult weight? Who else might be sleeping in there? Did he even have a room here anymore?

He walked on round the building, past the turquoise waters of an elaborately tiled swimming pool that had been a pond where they swam as boys. He longed to strip off and dive in right now. A maid came out to close a shutter, saw him, and ran back inside. As he reached the raised porticos of the front entrance, the great wooden doors swung open.

"My brother!" Joaquim spoke in a voice that was half-supplicating and half-fearful.

Duarte stood there, framed by yellow-painted arches. He looked no different; just a smattering of lines on his face, and a few grey hairs.

With his words, Joaquim had tried to ignite the fraternal love that must unite brothers through any amount of misunderstandings, but inside he felt only trepidation.

"Why are you here?" said Duarte. His voice was without emotion, his face expressionless.

Joaquim could not fathom his chances. Duarte stood at the top of the steps and he at the bottom. So it had always been in their lives, he thought.

"I need help, my brother," he said. "I've done my time. I'm sorry for the past." The words sounded limp to his ears. "We can start again."

"There's nothing for you here. Get out." Duarte turned to walk inside.

"I've lost everything!" cried Joaquim, his voice searing through the birdsong and the rustle of trees in the spring breeze. "I have no-one!"

He hadn't meant to sound so pathetic, but it was true. Everyone else seemed to go about their business, spinning relationships like webs, working and earning and building a future. He had fallen outside of that human carousel and was plagued by a loneliness that was immense and self-perpetuating. It had always lurked inside him, this barren feeling, showing itself briefly at times through his cosseted boyhood, like when he was punished for hitting little Álvaro or for playing with Duarte's hunting rifle. Now it seemed to be all that was left to him.

"Our tribe!" he protested. "The brothers de Almeida!"

Duarte began to close the door.

"*Mamã* would have helped!" Joaquim pleaded, mounting the steps.

"She's dead," Duarte replied. "Like my brother."

The men faced each other.

Close up, Joaquim could see Duarte's eyes. He read agony there. Was it only for the loss of Álvaro? *But I'm your brother too.*

"I have nowhere to go," he begged again. He thought of his room from so long ago, the blue blossoms dancing outside, the pool below. He said it again. "*Mamã* would have helped me!"

Duarte called to one of the men who stood behind him, weapons in their hands. Joaquim hadn't seen them from ground level. He murmured something Joaquim couldn't hear but which made him wonder if he were about to be beaten up again. Then the servant walked away and returned with a key.

"Take this," said Duarte. It's a house in *Mouraria*. One of the drivers retired there with his wife. They're dead now. The place is empty."

Joaquim stared at an address written on a tag attached to the key. When he looked up, the door had closed, and he was alone again.

He crawled into a barn and slept as deeply as if he were back in the childhood bed of memory. When he awoke there was no food, but he drank water with the cherubs. All the doors and the windows were closed, although the sun was rising in the sky. Had they all been told to avoid him?

He discovered he had been sleeping in a cowpat so his first stop on that trek back to Lisbon was the nearest House of Mercy for some more ill-fitting clothes. There was one here in Sintra; he didn't have to go far.

The walk took only eight hours this time. He had Duarte's boots on his feet and was buoyed up by the thought of a roof over his head, and surely somewhere to wash. A farmer stopped and took him from Mem Martins to Queluz. He sat behind in the cart, next to an injured sheep.

The mellowing heat of late afternoon found him standing before a mushroom-coloured house in the Moorish Quarter of Lisbon. It was nothing fancy, squeezed on either side by its narrow neighbours, but he could see two pairs of windows, one above the other, and beneath them a low wooden door.

He turned the key. Unoiled for years, it groaned open, and he stood in a chamber that held a bench, a plain wooden table, and four wobbly chairs. He mounted the stairs. Stripping off the ill-fitting clothes, and the dust, and the grime, he stepped into the shower. A turn of the tap sent rust-coloured water cascading over his filthy limbs.

In the future he might rail against Duarte and seethe with resentment, but for now, if he had not been in such urgent need of a wash, he would have gone down on his knees and blessed him. This place would do. He and his loneliness could dwell here together until better times came around, or his brother forgave him.

41

SANTOS-O-VELHO, LISBON

2021

"Can someone please tell me what's going on here?" Helen stood up and looked at each of them in turn.

Marco held out his hands and shrugged. He looked as bewildered as everyone else. No-one spoke. None of them seemed to understand what was happening any more than Joaquim did.

Then Helen addressed the pretty lawyer. "Laurinda, why are you and Joaquim here?"

Joaquim spluttered and turned to Laurinda. Had he missed something? Why did Helen assume they were together?

Laurinda looked embarrassed. "Lourenço told you he had a partner?" she said. "It is me. I am the partner."

He struggled to understand the language. Did she just say she was Lourenço's partner? Lourenço who was now handcuffed to a radiator? She had used the English word which could be applied in two ways. Was that a *sócio* or a *namorada*? A business partner, or was he knocking her off, as Joaquim had suspected?

Having shackled Lourenço, the cop took another pair of cuffs from his pocket and headed towards Laurinda. He repeated his caution to her, the formal words bringing back echoes of occasions that Joaquim would prefer to forget. The pain in his neck merged with the one in his back. He needed to sit down.

"*O que você está fazendo?*" she cried. "*É apenas um negócio. Por caridade!* Then she looked at Helen. "It is a business deal! For charity!" she protested in English.

Then Marco stepped forward and spoke to Helen. Even Joaquim, who was better at deciphering the mechanisms on hunting rifles than human relationships, especially romantic ones, could see the awkwardness between them. In this situation, he would have expected them to touch; perhaps Marco might have hugged her for reassurance. But they stood apart.

"Are you alright?" Marco asked. His hands hung down by his sides and his face was solemn.

"I'm fine," Helen said without looking at him, though fine she obviously was not. She moved away and stood behind the cop, who then addressed the room.

"I'm *Detetive* Paulo Santos de Ferreira of the *Direção-Geral de Segurança*. I'm here to arrest this criminal." He indicated Lourenço. "And these good people have helped me." He nodded towards Marco and Helen, who were now on opposite sides of the room.

"Who might you be, sir?" he asked Joaquim and then repeated his question in Portuguese.

Joaquim had understood the English word 'criminal'. 'Arrest' he knew from his own history. Which criminals was the cop here to arrest? Joaquim himself? How much did he know?

Marco spoke up. "This man is part of my family."

Joaquim looked at him, grateful and not a little surprised. He was regarded as family? This protégé of Duarte's had protected him!

But then Marco turned to him and asked, "What are you doing here? How did you get into my house?"

Joaquim opened his mouth to speak, looked from Lourenço to the police officer, and then directed another torrent of oaths at Lourenço.

Laurinda laughed, even as Paulo locked the handcuffs among the bracelets on her little wrists. But her eyes were stretched back like a startled horse. "He is insulting your boyfriend, Helen," she said, looking not at Helen but at Marco. "He calls him a slimy little worm who infiltrated the family and stole his inheritance."

Joaquim followed enough to understand that she was translating his words – at least the repeatable ones – for Helen's benefit. Wasn't this tricky *advogada* in enough trouble already without alienating anyone further? He wondered why she seemed to find the situation funny, particularly as Paulo the cop was in the process of manacling her to a radiator. Then he saw that her hands were shaking.

Suddenly she spoke to Marco in Portuguese. Joaquim understood the words clearly enough but couldn't make sense of them. "*Ele é teu pai.*" She looked quite mean now. She turned to Joaquim. "*Ele é teu filho.*"

"*O quê?*" he said, his voice strangulated. "*Meu filho?*"

Laurinda translated for Helen, just as she had that first day at the law firm: "He says 'my son.'"

Helen glared at her. "You sent the email," she said slowly. Her face was rigid with anger.

Laurinda gave a half-hearted laugh, but there was no humour in it. She was looking worried now.

Marco stared at Joaquim and then back at Laurinda. "*Meu pai?*" he whispered.

"My father," repeated Laurinda.

"*Mas meu filho está morto!*" cried Joaquim.

"My son is dead," translated Laurinda in a flat voice, and then said to Joaquim, "He's not dead. Your son is standing over there."

She repeated it in Portuguese, and he finally understood. He stumbled and almost fell onto the nearest chair. "*Ias envenenar o meu filho?*" he shouted at Lourenço.

"You were going to poison my son," Laurinda translated mechanically and then turned to Lourenço, looking shocked. "Poison Marco?" she cried incredulously, forgetting to switch back to Portuguese.

Lourenço answered in his stilted English: "No!

Nobody poison. I here for money!"

"Ha!" barked Joaquim and then muttered something about trust and betrayal. He was relieved that there were to be no murders, just theft. Out of the corner of his eye he saw Helen sink onto one of the sofas. She had gone white. Marco was watching her from the other side of the room. They both looked distressed. Why were they so distant with each other?

Then Laurinda's words sank in. *My son*, said Joaquim to himself. *Little Joaquinho*. He walked over and sat beside the boy who was now a man, the pains in his body forgotten. Everyone else seemed to be busy being arrested or arguing with each other.

Marco turned to look at him, and Joaquim could see nothing but horror on his face, which was reasonable enough, he thought – *who would want me as their father?* But what he noticed most was the shine of those eyes, Aurélia's glorious she-wolf gold. This was indeed her son.

"Joaquinho," he said. "*Meu filho.*"

42

CHILTERN GRANGE, MEDMENHAM
1987

By two in the morning, the wind was howling. Douglas went downstairs at three, torch in hand because the electricity had failed. He found the dogs shaking on their beds and took them back up with him. He guessed that trees were falling, and some outbuildings might be damaged, but there was nothing to be done until the storm subsided. There was no sound from Helen's room. Quietly, he opened the door. She had the ability of youth to sleep through anything, so he didn't disturb her.

By first light the wind had dropped but the power remained dead. A sunless dawn revealed the jacaranda still standing, a bare skeleton that had borne autumn leaves only yesterday. It gave him hope that his precious orchard at the restaurant might have survived.

"I'm going to the *Palazzo*," Douglas said. "If I can get through."

"I'm coming with you," replied Elena.

"No, stay here, it's not safe."

"When has that ever stopped me?" she laughed, reaching for last night's clothes. "Let's go."

It was fourteen years since he had first tried to persuade her to be careful, in Lisbon, like her father before her. He knew by now it was pointless to argue; his wife could never be talked out of a challenge. Risks were few in their current lives, apart from financial ones, and she seemed to be almost enjoying the excitement of the hurricane, despite, or perhaps because of, the danger involved.

As he cleared the driveway of fallen branches, she backed out their car. The usual twenty-minute drive took forty, as they kept stopping to remove debris. At one point a tree blocked the road. There was no option but to turn around and find another route.

They entered the *Palazzo's* gates under a grey and featureless sky. The car crunched over gravel and halted outside the main portico. The sight always brought back memories of their opening night; luxury cars had disgorged passengers dressed in their best, a local rock star or two in casual black, and some minor celebrities trying to snare the cameras of lurking paparazzi.

It had been a massive success, and few of those present knew about the struggles that had gone before. Douglas's belief that interest rates would remain steady had been wrong. With the *Trattoria* sold, all of their funds invested, and no possibility of income until the building phase was complete, they had been wrung out by soaring borrowing costs, battles with local planners, and a firm of unreliable builders whose botched work had to be fixed by a team of fine, but expensive, craftsmen. Then the first set of fruit trees died during a hosepipe ban.

Nevertheless, the business had survived and thrived. Britain's economy was booming and customers poured in. In the thirteen months since its opening, the *Palazzo* had won two Michelin stars and was booked to capacity for three weeks ahead.

All those bookings would have to be cancelled now. They sat in the car and stared at the front of the building. While the stone pillars around the doorway stood firm, the porch was littered with brown leaves, broken branches, and shattered roof tiles. But what froze them in their seats was the sight of a pair of tall poplars that Douglas had loved, even designing an extension to the main restaurant to one side in order to preserve them.

That decision turned out to be a disastrous one. Where their soaring silhouettes had stood, he saw only the dull glare of the overcast sky. One had smashed through an eighteenth-century window patterned with bucolic depictions in coloured glass. Its destruction was tragic but would not affect the business.

The other had crashed directly onto the new annexe, its peak wedged into part of the original building. A restaurant couldn't open for business without a place to eat.

Elena took his hand. "Insurance," she said. "The insurance will cover it."

Douglas's throat swelled, but he was of the generation of Englishmen who were not allowed to cry. Insurance or not, would the bank recall its loan? What of their plans to repair their crumbling home? How would they pay for the freehold now?

"We've known worse," said the voice next to him. It seemed to come from a long way off. "One day this will be behind us. We'll get through it. Nobody died."

He looked at her. Sometimes he forgot that had her first lover survived, there would be no Elena for him, no daughter, and surely no Michelin stars. She knew what it was to lose everything but had rebuilt her life. So could he.

"As long as I have you," he said. "And Helen. Nothing else matters. Where would I be without you?"

She smiled encouragingly. "Probably still going to diplomatic parties and making a nuisance of yourself to younger women."

They laughed and life swung back onto its course. Somehow the business would recover. They would make it work. He turned the car around and drove home.

It was the third Friday in October. They spent the weekend assessing the damage and listening to news reports about the storm, and by Sunday he was feeling more confident about the future and his ability to rebuild it.

The next morning they woke up to Black Monday: the worst stock market crash since 1929.

43

MOURARIA

2021

"I have something to tell you."

Her voice came clipped and clear down the line, every syllable crisply enunciated, just as it always was. Joaquim could tell nothing from her tone. The shrilling of the phone had woken him. He blinked in the light and coughed. It hurt his dry throat.

"What? We won the case?"

"No, we didn't win the case."

He pushed his grey sheets to one side and sat up. He didn't sleep much anymore, and found it hard to get out of bed some mornings as well. The linen was overdue for its next trip to the wash. He would have to bag it himself and deliver it to the laundrette, where one of the girls would wash it for him; at least he wouldn't have to sit for an hour watching the tub turning. Later, he would have to remember to collect it and make up his bed. Himself. There really should be maids to do it all, and he was determined that one day soon, there would be, and not in this stinking house either. What tedious next step did Laurinda want to tell him about now?

"Listen, Miss *Advogada,* I know you're young, you don't have much experience, just a *novata* at this game. Maybe you need to call in someone who knows what he's doing. I don't want to hear any more about appeals and hearings and delays and *blá-di-blá.* Now, get out there and close this case." His voice was formidably stern, he thought; not bad before the first drink of the day.

"It is closed," she said. "The case is closed." A softness had entered her voice and it threw him. She didn't sound like herself. Why was she not putting him in his place, like she usually did?

"So we won?"

"That was not the outcome."

Grubby netting stretched across the window. He pulled it to one side and looked down. A cyclist wobbled over the cobblestones around a delivery van that was blocking the street.

"Winning is the only option." If he said it enough times, it would be true. "There is no other outcome for me."

"I'm sorry old man," she said. "You got the house. It's yours now. That's all."

The line went dead. He jabbed at the screen until her face showed again, but it was only her photograph, and there was no answer when he called.

He didn't get as far as Filipe's, and the sheets remained unwashed. There was a bar on the corner – not one he favoured – but he needed coffee and whisky, and there was none in the house. Through the second shot, and the third, and another coffee, he thought about what she had said. What was left for him now? He had a roof over his head, but that was a miserable place to live out the rest of his time. He cursed, swearing to himself that would not happen. He could sell it to a developer and lease a place, but local rents were soaring; tourists and digital nomads paid well. He could take a lodger, but who would want to live with him in that dump?

His thoughts kept returning to Lourenço. But his old friend – for that is what he had become in Joaquim's mind, now they had plotted and pilfered together for so long – was serving a sentence for half a dozen little crimes. He'd meet new accomplices in Caxias, and might never come back to see Joaquim again.

Then he remembered Marco. *Joaquinho, my son!* But now that the boy had won all the money to which his father was rightly entitled, along with the villas, and the horses, and the land, and the cars, he would probably never see Joaquim again either.

The fourth whisky went down quickly; it must have been a short measure. He turned and swore at the barman, who stood inside, looking bewildered, then tipped the table over, sending an empty cup and glass to crash into pieces on the ground.

He stormed off, stumbling over the cobbles. A

whisky, or brandy, or *Beirão* (and sometimes all three) never failed to dull his aching joints. He could move faster now. The waiter was calling after him but he barely heard.

Two blocks away, a friend of Lourenço's worked her trade in one room of a shared house. The front door was open when he got there, no doubt ready for the next client. He felt a need to talk to Lourenço, and had some vague notion that seeing her might make up for the conversation that it was now impossible for them to have. Visits to Caxias prison had to be booked in advance, and they would turn him away in any case, for being drunk.

He stormed up the stairs, ignoring the squeaking protests of a clerk behind a desk in the hall. It must be some kind of hotel, this place, he thought, as he crashed through the door into her room. He was met by a volley of swearing from the girl, and if her client had not been hindered by the removal (or possibly replacement) of his trousers, Joaquim might have been punched in the face.

He got out of the room just in time to avoid that, but as he reached the bottom of the stairs, a pair of leviathans appeared out of nowhere. One of them hit him hard in the jaw, and the other sent him crashing into the street. He lay there, tasting his own blood. One knee had collided with an uneven cobblestone, and hurt quite badly.

Filipe, he thought. Filipe always welcomed him. Filipe understood.

The day was hot and the air seemed to have been

sucked out of the city. He reeled down alleyways, and up steps that left him wheezing. Wilting jacarandas were casting brown pods onto the ground. How did that blue glory turn into this ugly mess? he thought, and then that there were surely some parallels here with his own life.

Sweating, he limped into the bar and heaved himself into his regular chair. His table was already occupied by a couple of strangers today. They rose and moved their drinks to the furthest point of the terrace. Joaquim smiled to himself. There was a hierarchy here, he thought, and somehow they knew it.

A young boy approached him, carrying a small white notebook.

"Where's Filipe?" asked Joaquim.

"He'll be here. I'm looking after the bar till he gets back. What would you like?"

It dawned on him that this was a lucky break. All he would have got from Filipe was a lecture, not a drink. Joaquim wanted the comforting presence of the man but not a sermon on his health.

"Brandy," he said. "A bottle. Old!"

To his surprise, the boy brought out a squat, brown bottle of Extra Reserve, and set it down in front of him next to a full-bellied glass. *"Algo mais, senhor?"*

Joaquim shook his head and began to drink. His thoughts were jumbled and he seemed to be having the same ones over and over again, going round like a loop in his head. Sometimes his arms felt too heavy to raise the glass, but he managed.

By the time Filipe returned, he was addressing

various people on the terrace.

"Having a good day?" he said to the couple who had moved away. "Not me. A bad day for Joaquim."

They placed some euros on the table and left.

He turned to the other side, where three women sat, eating tapas.

"I lost it all today," he said, his voice almost a growl. "*Merda toda*. The whole fucking lot."

They showed no sign of having heard. He emptied the bottle into his glass.

Filipe sat down in front of him.

"Joaquim, you need to go home."

Joaquim tried to speak but nothing came out.

"Is there anyone I can call? Who can help you?"

Joaquim shook his head and began to weep. In his head he framed the words, *I have no-one,* but he couldn't get them as far as his mouth. The world was tipping. It was the strangest binge session ever.

Sounds of shouting seemed to come from a long way away. His face was lying against the worn stone of the floor, his skin wet with tears and brandy. The moisture felt cool, and the pain in his knee had floated away.

Filipe and the barboy were turning him over. Filipe held a phone and was talking about ambulances. The last thing Joaquim saw were jacaranda pods against sunlight, fluttering above him like fat moths in the sky.

44

CHILTERN GRANGE, MEDMENHAM
1990

In all of the scenes they had imagined together as Douglas built his big dream, this was one that had not been foreseen. Elena, Douglas, and Trevor, three partners in a failing business, sat round a chipped oak table in Douglas's study. There was no admiring of nice views today; no clinking glasses, laughter, nor trips down the river. The room overlooked the front of the house and was darkened by a massive oak. A bare lightbulb glared overhead – Elena had never been able to persuade him to choose a shade for it.

Trevor handed Douglas the letter. Douglas placed it on the table in front of him and started to read.

"Statutory Demand under Section 123(1)(a) of the Insolvency Act 1986. This is an important document and should not be ignored. If you do not deal with it within twenty-one days, you could be wound up by the court."

He picked up the paper and held it closer. Elena knew he needed reading glasses, but he would never admit it.

"Part A," he went on. "Details of the creditor."

He gave up and read on silently. His whole body seemed to sink.

Elena knew the contents. After it had been delivered to Trevor, as the Company Secretary, he had called Douglas at the *Palazzo* and headed straight over to the Grange. While they waited for Douglas to arrive, she had gone through the notice so many times that she knew it virtually by heart.

"Twenty-five thousand pounds?" Douglas said, sounding incredulous.

Elena remembered when you could acquire a decent flat in London for that amount, not ten years earlier. Twenty-five thousand would not buy much now, she thought, and neither was it a great deal to owe – unless there were no customers to furnish the funds, and a long line of other creditors as well. And that seemed to be the way of it, these days.

"Can't we negotiate?" asked Douglas. "Pay part of it?"

"I've negotiated with everyone. We owe for tax, VAT, booze, butchers, tree surgeons, the lot. They're all struggling too. Don't even ask about the bank."

The interest rates that Douglas had once assured Helen would never rise again had soared to fourteen per cent. Businesses were crippled across the country.

"I rang Joe this morning. He was reasonable; he

understands. But they're up against it too. They're taking action while there's still something left in the pot. To be blunt."

Douglas's chair scraped back along the floor. He stood up and went to the window. He looked through the glass but Elena knew he was seeing his own life, not the garden outside. She didn't need to join him there. He knew. Though he had entered this marriage as the rescuer, over the years she had become his strength through all the difficulties, and had she been in another room, or even another country, he would still have been able to feel her support.

"What can we do?" she said to Trevor.

Trevor took back the letter and fiddled with it. "We're looking at voluntary insolvency."

Douglas turned slowly to face him.

"If not, it goes through the courts," Trevor went on. "That's much worse."

"How could it be any worse?" said Elena. Douglas still had not spoken.

"This way, we have some control," Trevor said.

Douglas came back to the table. He was shuffling in a way she had never seen before.

"What happens?" he said. "When?"

Trevor drew a breath. "There has to be a creditors' meeting. Within two weeks."

"Do we have to go?"

"Only one director has to attend, legally. But it looks better if we all do." He looked at Elena, relenting. "You don't need to come."

"I'll be there," she said firmly. "And then what?"

"The Official Receiver takes over. The assets are sold and distributed."

There was a silence. She knew this had to happen but somehow had not expected it.

"Can they take the house?" asked Douglas sharply.

Trevor shook his head. "There's no personal liability. The business is a limited company. We won't be out on the streets."

"Some of the people we owe money to might be," said Elena. "We could sell the house. Pay the creditors in full."

Douglas gave her a sad smile. "A thirty-two year lease won't pay many debts."

She could see he was relieved, and it was for her sake, not his own. He knew how she loved the Grange, even though the same old windows continued to let in draughts, and the plumbing made noises in the pipes. Apart from cursory splashes of paint, and an enthusiastic stripping of wallpaper, they had never been able to afford to put into practice any of their designs for their home.

The year the *Palazzo* had opened, her book, *Lisbon Flowered,* had been published. It was translated into six languages, including Portuguese, and she had done that one herself. A film was made, advances paid, and they started making plans to renovate the house and buy its freehold.

Douglas's career had thrived too. She helped him put together a book that combined his recipes with the reminiscences of life as the child of a vanishing upper-class society, mentored by an Italian servant called

Rosa. It was a short-lived bestseller and spawned a television series where he researched food all over Italy. They became quite a fashionable couple, but their excitement was dampened by the size of the tax bill that arrived the following year.

They had trusted that prosperity, now it had finally arrived, would only increase, like so many who fail to understand its fickle nature. The hurricane was the first visitor to blow it all away, followed by insurers who quibbled over rebuilds, financiers whose markets collapsed, and banks at the mercy of a fight against inflation.

A grain of hope had appeared when the insurers finally settled, and the restaurant reopened in newly repaired premises. But there were no customers in those gruelling years. The first wide-scale sackings of white-collar workers came about, along with failing businesses and repossessed homes. The *Palazzo* limped on, losing money and gaining debts, year after year, until it had come to this.

"I've been talking to an insolvency practitioner," said Trevor. "For months now. I was hoping it wouldn't go this way."

"The staff," Douglas said. The words hung in the air like a brewing storm. "We have to tell them. Give them as much time as possible to find other jobs."

"There aren't any jobs in catering," replied Trevor. "Not since the crash. People are losing their homes, never mind eating out."

"I'll speak to them this afternoon," Douglas said.

They looked at each other. The meeting was over.

The directors had agreed to cease trading, and the shareholders had passed a resolution to wind up the company. All was in order bar the paperwork and the rigmarole, and none of them would ever get over it for the rest of their lives.

45

RESIDÊNCIA QUINTA SANT'ANA, LISBON
2022

It was three in the afternoon and definitely time for a drink. A young doctor who visited regularly had told him that one glass of wine a day would 'keep his spirits up'; happiness was good for the immune system, the medic had said. In that case, his own must have the strength of an elephant, Joaquim thought, signalling to Nuno to open another bottle. Laurinda and Lourenço settled themselves onto the sofa opposite his chair, and took off their jackets – leather, and good soft quality at that.

In the fourteen months that had passed since he broke into Marco's townhouse, life had changed for Joaquim, and mostly for the better. Not entirely, though; having the stroke was a big shock.

They say that when you are dying, the life you have lived passes before your eyes. But for him, the visions that materialised in what he assumed to be his final moments, as the sights and sounds of Filipe and his bar faded from his senses, were of a different order. He saw the possessions that would never now be his to enjoy: properties unlived in, cars undriven, and all of the pleasures anticipated, during the long legal battle, that would no longer come his way.

Possibly, he had concluded, this was because he wasn't dying at all. There followed a few nasty months when he lost the power of speech, but it came back, and the power to move, which had not entirely done so. His drinking arm was unaffected, however, and he found life in his top-of-the-range wheelchair to be more than tolerable.

Having Nuno and his partner Simão, two first-class carers who actually seemed to enjoy the task, made all the difference. The boys were installed in the flat next door to his own, and catered for him around the clock. That included driving him through Lisbon to bars and the occasional card game in his classy new BMW. He often had them drop him at Filipe's, where he could resume his regular seat (at a table on which Filipe now permanently placed a 'reserved' sign), and impress cronies from his old life in the Moorish Quarter with tales of his newfound prosperity. He always paid for the drinks.

The flat had only two rooms, but they were large and enjoyed one of the best views in the development. The lounge faced south onto a sunny private terrace and the gardens beyond. A kitchen especially adapted for his disabilities, unnecessarily because it was only ever used by the carers, and a bathroom whose similar conversion was a welcome if not essential component, completed his very comfortable lifestyle in the *Residência Quinta Sant'Ana* retirement village.

He looked with satisfaction at the plump linen cushions on which his younger visitors now sat, and over their shoulders at some fine antiques chosen from brother Duarte's mansions in Lapa and Sintra. The old house in *Mouraria* had been lent to the friend of Lourenço, the one he had surprised at the start of his drunken rampage. Having given up her former profession, she had set up (with some help from Lourenço), a beauty business in the newly decorated building, offering manicures, waxing, and facials. Laurinda had no idea.

"So what's happening with you two? How's business, *malandro*?" he asked, directing his question at Lourenço.

The rascal had done his time in jail after being prosecuted for a series of offences which Joaquim regarded as innocuous, and about which he had known nothing but was not at all surprised. Joaquim had persuaded Marco to support Lourenço's application for parole, so he had served only six months of a two-year sentence. After Joaquim's immobility from the stroke, there was little more he could do to help his old partner-in-crime, but Lourenço appeared to have landed on his feet, having moved into the smart apartment provided to Laurinda by her trust fund. She seemed to be quite taken with the useless ruffian, and although Joaquim could not fathom why that should be, he was glad to see Lourenço so well settled.

"I have a job now," replied Lourenço. "I'm an executive."

"I fixed it for him," Laurinda cut in. "One of my clients needed a salesman and I knew Lourenço would be great at that. I persuaded them to overlook his criminal record."

"*Excelente*, my friend. You will do well at that. You could sell cod to a fisherman."

He can make anyone believe his lies, thought Joaquim. It was one of Lourenço's talents that he admired the most.

"I'm the manager now," added Lourenço. "I have six people under me."

"Congratulations, *meu amigão*. It's good to know you can buy a nice suit and an expensive watch like that one without having to steal them."

It was the first thing Joaquim had noticed, the Tag Heuer on Lourenço's wrist. All his years of thievery had left him with the ability to identify instantly any watch and its value.

Lourenço gave him a little frown. Surely Laurinda knew enough about her boyfriend not to be shocked? But perhaps not everything...

Since the stroke, especially in the early days when he lay in hospital unable to move, Joaquim had spent a lot of time thinking about the past. He saw something of himself in this younger man, and bitterly regretted his actions years ago in their shared cell. That had been a premeditated betrayal to save his own skin, not a mistake like the other time with Álvaro.

He was touched when Lourenço started visiting him, and then Laurinda had come too. She had been cleared of all charges after the fiasco at Marco's house; the police accepted her assertion that she knew nothing about the intended fraud. Since then, Joaquim had watched their relationship develop. It seemed that Lourenço had found someone capable of keeping him under control, which was no bad thing, especially when the controlling person had a *conta bancária* from her parents, which may in fact have paid for the nice suit, and quite likely the expensive watch as well.

He was surprised by the almost fatherly feelings he had developed towards his old cellmate. It reminded him of the time when he had his own guide and mentor in Duarte. During the long, slow months of his recovery, the memories of those adolescent years under his brother's protection kept returning to his mind. But Duarte's treatment of him after Álvaro's death was something he would never be able to understand or come to terms with. That man had been his mentor and his hero. How could he have believed that Joaquim would deliberately betray their brother?

At other times, his thoughts drifted further back, to a woman caught in a war eighty years ago who had told him to leave her and not say a word. That was as much as he could recall. Was it his mother? His feelings said yes.

He had accepted that he would die without ever knowing who he was or where he had come from, but it mattered less now because he had discovered a new identity: he was the father of Marco – or Joaquinho, as he insisted on addressing him, to Marco's great discomfort.

"Joaquinho was here this morning," he said proudly.

"You mean Marco," said Laurinda shortly.

Lourenço burst into laughter. "I will never forget the look on his face. When she told him you were his father!" He glanced at Laurinda. "Poor man! Whatever did he do to deserve that? Jesus, I got off lightly. All I had to do was six months in jail. He got a life sentence, man!"

Joaquim ignored the remark.

"I'd like to have seen his face when he got my email," said Laurinda.

"What email?" Joaquim asked, straightening up in his chair.

"Lourenço didn't tell you? I had to drive a wedge between them, Marco and Helen, little Miss English sweetheart. There's strength in numbers, and I thought they would be weaker apart."

Joaquim could see that Lourenço was staring at her, willing her to stop. What was this new deception that the pair had kept from him?

"I found a photo of her online with some rich guy. They were at a conference together. Everyone in the place had their picture taken with this man, but in hers, the way he smiled at her, he looked like her boyfriend. Maybe he was! Anyway, I sent it to Marco. Told him that's what she'd been doing in lockdown. Or that's *who*. I might have embroidered the story a little. Well, quite a lot, actually." She laughed. It was a cold, tinkling sound.

"You did what?" Joaquim said. He felt the fighting spirit of old rising inside him.

"I fixed it for you." Her eyes fluttered from side to side and avoided looking at him.

"You broke my son's heart!"

She started to rearrange the leather jacket on the back of the sofa, although it didn't need rearranging. "I did it for you, old man. While I was working for free, remember?"

"Is that why you lost the case, because you weren't being paid?"

She swore. "You'd be in prison if it wasn't for us. A murderer. If Lourenço wasn't too smart to go through with your stupid idea."

She had lost all her power to intimidate him now. He could see the defensiveness behind her attacks. There was something insecure about her, as if she had to strike before being struck.

"Oleander poison!" she rolled her eyes, her little red mouth pursed into the straight line that used to mess with his mind.

"I wasn't serious," he growled.

Lourenço put a hand on her arm and said to Joaquim in a pacifying voice, "But look how it all turned out. Here you are, living in luxury; a nice car, your carers, nothing to worry about. What would have happened to your theme park, with you in your chair?"

Joaquim had entertained the same thoughts over the last year. When he received the news of their final defeat in the courts, the drinking spree that followed had ended in the stroke. He was fortunate that it happened in Filipe's, because he might have been left for dead on the cobblestones by strangers if he had fallen in the street. That good bartender (who unexpectedly had training in First Aid – who would have thought?) had called an ambulance and saved his life.

In his wallet they found Laurinda's card, which had lain there ever since she presented it to him the first time they met, after the unfortunate reading of the will, in that very bar. Filipe rang her, and she had called Marco.

Little Joaquinho, the boy he had abandoned years ago, had stepped forward, paid all his medical bills, and set him up here, in this nice community for old people. It was not just any retirement village. This one was upmarket, and just outside Lisbon, so he could visit old haunts. It had a pool and a gym, both of which were good for his physiotherapy, and Joaquinho paid for that too.

When the probate came through, his solicitous son had invited him to pick out anything he fancied from Duarte's possessions, and had presented him with his lovely BMW, plus the carers to drive it. What a boy!

But the English girlfriend, his own niece in fact, if only in name, seemed to have disappeared off the scene. He had thought she might have taken her money and dumped Joaquinho, now that the battle was won. Perhaps she had caught him cheating on her? Was he that kind of a man; like father, like son? On the other hand, having seen the stunt she had pulled with

Lourenço, he had wondered what kind of games she might have played on Joaquinho too. The boy would never talk about it. If asked, a shadow crossed his face, and the gold eyes turned dark. Now, after all these months, he thought he knew why. The sly legal minx had messed with them, driven them apart.

"He could have been happy with his English lady. Now he's alone. You broke my son's heart!"

His voice was harsh as he repeated the accusation, but in fact Joaquim thought no worse of her for the trick; everyone behaves badly sometimes, and no-one knew that better than he. Laurinda may have lost the court case but, in a sense, she had won everything that mattered to him. If that card (in the name of her fantasy law firm, printed before it even existed), had not been in his wallet, no-one would have called her, and she would not have called Joaquinho. Without her, he and his boy might never have known they were father and son, and Joaquim would be in some grim institution for the old: childless, friendless, and alone.

As he had lain in bed recuperating, unable to fill his time with anything but thoughts (and too many of the ones he had been avoiding for years), he discovered that it was not the wrongs that had been done to him that disturbed him the most, but the pain he had inflicted on others. His betrayals of brother Álvaro, and then of Lourenço, tormented him worst of all. So in his unaccustomed financial security, and joy at reconnecting with his son, he started to consider what might be done to make amends.

It was too late for Álvaro. Although there must have

been a thousand occasions when he had wished it were possible to relive that time and retract his terrible mistake, life moved relentlessly forward in one direction only. It occurred to him that if Álvaro had never been born, his mother – Joaquim's second mother – would not have died. Álvaro had taken her life, and then he took Álvaro's. Inadvertently, both times: homicide by negligence, they called it. Was there some justice there? A diabolical balance? But he had loved them both, to the bottom of his soul. Why did either have to die? Why could he not have saved them?

Lourenço, though, had not been beyond help, and Joaquim had done what he could by arranging the man's parole.

Then, as these two people who had been his angels of fortune, and also of destruction, chattered away in front of him, Joaquim realised his chance to make things right with Joaquinho had come. Memories from years ago roamed through his mind – a little boy crying because of his father's rage, with fear and hatred in his eyes. Now that boy believed he had been betrayed again, by the woman he loved, and it was not for the first time, Joaquim knew.

The snooty old lawyer who had cut him out of Duarte's will had made him sign some papers before he was allowed any of his brother's furniture. He had taken the opportunity to grill the pompous prig for every detail he knew about Joaquinho's life since the day Joaquim had left.

He learned about the skunk of a wife who had

deceived his son, and that his trust in women had been destroyed – until he met Helen. Laurinda had hit him where it would hurt the most, but Joaquim was not going to let Joaquinho's faith in this Englishwoman be destroyed.

He liked Helen. She would be good for his son. She was his own niece! Well, sort of. His working hand gripped the side of his chair. Now was the time to atone.

46

CHILTERN GRANGE, MEDMENHAM
2010

Elena wandered through her house just breathing in its essence. It was something she loved to do when alone, imagining the changes she would make if only they had the means. She puzzled over it sometimes — how, during the brief years when their business was profitable, cash seemed to flow in from every direction, yet when money was tight, it was as if the world conspired to drain what little they had.

When the lease expires, her mind said for the umpteenth time, *I'll be seventy-two and he'll be over eighty. Where will we go?*

She opened the doors to Helen's room first, where the ceilings arched up into the attic and the windows framed the river. She had planned to install a little en-suite, but so far, her daughter had to put up with sharing the family bathroom downstairs, and that was unlikely to change.

Helen's bed was made up and her books lined the shelves. She lived in her own smart flat in Fulham now, overlooking the same river many miles downstream, and if Elena ever felt lonely, she would watch the water flow by knowing that it would pass under Helen's balcony a few days later. That clever daughter did something in banking, negotiating deals her mother didn't understand.

When Douglas took a job as a chef that required him to drive to work, Helen had bought her a brand-new Peugeot so that she wouldn't be stranded at home. Sometimes Elena wondered whether this competent and resourceful child, with one failed marriage behind her, would ever find a stable relationship. Today she was just happy that Helen would be home this weekend to celebrate her father's sixty-eighth birthday.

She made her way down a narrow staircase – this upper floor had been designed for servants – to a wider hall below. Three rooms led from it, her own study which overlooked the river, Douglas's at the front of the house, and a big bedroom that they shared. Inside it, shadows rippled on the ceiling, reflecting the movement of water under the sun outside. The walls were painted a pale aquamarine, and the furnishings a joyful miscellany of dark wood bought from local junk shops years before.

A polished walnut side table sat along one wall. Reaching underneath, she extracted a key from a hidden slot and unlocked its single drawer. It was only when President Caetano died in 1980, after years of exile in Brazil, that her friend Gabriela felt safe enough to write, having obtained the address from Duarte.

Elena now picked up the letter and read it again. The first of many that Gabriela had sent to her over the decades, it was the only one she had kept. It described in devastating detail the three days leading up to Álvaro's death. Duarte had persisted until he uncovered everything, and then shared the facts with Gabriela.

Later letters gave accounts of Luís's release from prison the day after the revolution, and of how, pregnant with her first child, Gabriela had witnessed the arrest of "*that weasel*" Gomes in front of all of the students sitting their finals. When Elena had received that one, though it was only eleven in the morning, she sat down and opened a bottle of champagne.

After destroying all the others, Elena had found herself unable to let go of the paper she now held in her hand; its contents were agonising but precious. She took it and tore it into small pieces. Helen must never know. If she did one day suspect the truth, and her parents were no longer alive to explain, she could read about it in the book.

The novel wasn't entirely faithful to reality. In the end it was Álvaro who survived and his treacherous brother who died. All of the characters were given different names, of course. The hero prospered in the newly liberated Portugal, and lived to present his wife, who became the mother of five children, with red carnations every year on the anniversary of the revolution. This part was true, though not of Álvaro and herself, but of Gabriela and Luís.

"Why don't you write another book, mum?" Helen would ask her in the cash-strapped years that followed the collapse of their business. Elena would shake her head. How could she explain to her well-meaning daughter that *Lisbon Flowered* was the story of her real father – not the Douglas they both loved, but a dreamer who gave everything for his country? Against the relatively stable backdrop of British politics, the events in pre-revolutionary Portugal seemed unreal.

Besides, Douglas was adamant that Helen should never know about her true parentage; why cloud her sky with the knowledge of the terrible fate met by her father? So Elena stayed silent, but the secrecy troubled her, so she wrote it all down in her book, a sanitised version of the truth for her daughter.

She put the torn-up pieces of the letter in her pocket and stepped down a wide staircase. It had carved balusters, much grander than the one above. At the bottom, she turned into the kitchen. Douglas had eventually built the industrial kitchen of his dreams at the *Palazzo*, and they had borrowed the workmen to create a simple one here at home. It was the only room properly refurbished so far, in spite of all their plans. After the professional kitchen had been dismantled by the developers who purchased the *Palazzo* buildings from the receivers, this was all that remained. Douglas still insisted on doing all the cooking, and would cater for his own birthday dinner on Saturday.

A pair of doors led into a lounge that stretched the

entire length of the building, filled with threadbare sofas and more junk-shop furniture. An oak cabinet held rows of books, including the ones they had written themselves. A series of graceful leaded light doors, arching up towards the ceiling, opened out onto the garden. They reminded her of the conservatory at Chiado where she had sat, with Lina before she became Helen, with her parents, and sometimes with Douglas. How ironic that her fight to free her country had led to being exiled from it forever.

Opening one of the doors, she walked down the lawn to the river. The jacaranda tree looked healthy but still had never flowered. She had planted it decades ago in the optimistic hope of seeing blossom every spring, but the climate here was too cold. She made do instead with clusters of ceanothus bushes that burst into constellations of blue all summer long, regardless of the weather, and didn't mind having their roots soaked when the river ran high.

On the bank, Douglas had built a simple wooden summerhouse, perched on stilts to escape the winter floods. Dog roses tangled over its roof, spilling a musky scent through the air. A small cabin cruiser bobbed on the water, a relic of their affluent years. It was shabby now, but still took them up to Henley or down to Marlow every summer. Life could not be better, as long as she lived in the present and managed to shut out the past and the future.

Her reflections were ended by the sight of Douglas walking on the grass down towards her. She kissed him and then drew back. His face was strained and unsmiling.

"I didn't go to work this afternoon," he said.

She waited and her breath stilled at the unnatural sound in his voice.

"I had to see a doctor."

Somehow, she knew what was about to be said, and willed time to stop so she would never have to hear it. An echo of the moment they told her of Álvaro's death hung in the air like a ghost.

"I had tests last week. I thought it would be nothing and didn't want to worry you. I'm afraid it wasn't nothing."

She waited for the world to implode.

"Pancreatic cancer. Stage Four."

"What does that mean?" Her voice sounded hollow.

"A few months."

In that moment Elena understood a truth she had known for a long time but never fully realised: she loved this man with all of her heart. Álvaro was now no more than a memory from another life, a character in the book on her shelf. That story was closed, and now she knew that this one too was reaching its end.

They put their arms around each other and cried.

47

CHILTERN GRANGE, MEDMENHAM
2022

I climbed over the stern of my boat and lowered the ladder at the back. Its beige and brown livery gave away its age; cruisers hadn't been produced in these colours for years. I recalled how Marco and I had once talked about what kind of replacement I should buy if the inheritance came through, believing that we would sail on it together.

I still hadn't decided. Even so, with a new outboard this little craft could have taken me upriver to Oxford or down to the Thames Barrier, if I had any inclination to go to either of those places, which I did not.

I slipped into the water and let go of the rungs. The summer had been unusually hot, and the Thames felt almost warm instead of its usual jarring cold. I swam to the other side and back again, my smooth strokes barely breaking the surface. I could see the swans that my neighbours and I called 'ours' in the distance, five dusky cygnets that were nearly as big as their parents this late in the year.

Walking back up the bank, I admired the restored summerhouse. The jacaranda arched gracefully behind, stubbornly gripping the damp English soil after surviving thirty-seven harsh winters, like a living monument to my mother's old life. For years it had given nothing in return, not a single blossom. "Maybe it's homesick," I remembered Marco saying. But this year, the heatwave had triggered the impossible: the first fragile flowers unfurled, not in its native blue, but a pallid mauve against the bare branches. It seemed to me a symbol that hope could grow anywhere, even in my own barren life.

Back at the house, I showered in the new bathroom that had been completed only weeks before. Once Duarte's probate was granted, I had become a wealthy woman and launched a makeover programme that was at last coming to an end.

I did some exercises, a bit of yoga, and prepared oats, nuts and seeds in a bowl. I led a healthy life. Then I took my breakfast out onto the patio through the original glass doors that had always reminded Elena of the ones at her home in Chiado. They weren't efficient but I thought them too beautiful to change. I sat in a new wrought iron chair, on new Italian stone, shaded by a custom-made electric awning, and didn't feel hungry any more.

The emptiness was disrupted by the sound of the doorbell. I had upgraded it into a complicated network of alarms and cameras, but the noise when it rang was still nerve-shattering. There were some settings, but I hadn't yet learned how to manage them.

Ever since Marco had turned up on my doorstep − over a year ago now, though it seemed like a lifetime − a little tendril of hope unfurled inside me, even when the visitor was expected. Logic told me it couldn't be him, and never would be again, but the reflex kept on happening.

On my way to the door, I stopped at a mirror in the hall. Pushed back by my fingers, my hair looked okay. I would like to have applied some makeup, but it was all upstairs. I pulled back the bolts and the door swung open, easily now, for the first time in years. It was still the original heavy panelled oak that had probably been in place since the house was built, but had been trimmed and oiled, and no longer let in draughts.

The smiling man from the local supermarket stood on the step, holding two crates, and if I had cared to look, his van stood in full sight in my driveway. I took the packages and thanked him. Although I had forgotten about the booking, I had not for a minute expected it to be Marco, I told myself.

I stacked the groceries into a new American fridge, which was surrounded by a sea of marble worksurfaces traced with pale grey veins. The floor was now heated by wires that ran underneath. In these scorching temperatures it was hard to imagine what benefit they might bring, and I was almost looking forward to winter when the house would be warm for the first time in my memory. All the windows had been repaired or replaced with faithful, expensive, and well-insulated copies.

On the top floor, my old room now boasted the little ensuite bathroom that my mother had always wanted for me but could never afford. Why I had installed it I didn't know, because there was no-one else in my life but me now, and occasional friends from London who would use the family bathroom on my floor. But it seemed to bring about some sort of closure: the last thing I could do for her.

When the news at last came through that the case was won, I had returned to Lisbon at Cristóvão's request. It was my first visit since the scene at the townhouse. After Marco's split with me, I had told his friend Paulo, the detective, that I would not now be taking part in the scheme to trap the wanted criminal Lourenço. But he was insistent; I had a duty to be there, he said. He even hinted that they could make me attend, although I doubted that.

I nurtured a tiny hope that once we were in the same room, perhaps things would change between Marco and me, or at least I might find out what had gone wrong. Would he be there with someone else, a new partner? I was dreading it, but I went and played my part as the wealthy philanthropist backer for Lourenço's charity.

All the time I was remembering the nights I had spent in that place, and the dreams we had dreamed on that terrace, watching the sun as it set over barges and fishing vessels. Marco was distant – I don't think he looked at me once. It was horrible, and I wish I had stayed at home.

So I arrived at the notary's determined that this would be my last visit to Portugal. He took me to inspect all the assets that I now co-owned with Marco so we could decide how to divide them. He dutifully pointed out some bare patches on the floors of the villa in Sintra left by furniture that Marco had given his newly discovered (if not rejoiced over) father, for the retirement flat that Marco had provided. I admired him for looking after Joaquim. It was typical of the man I thought I knew.

Why he had cut off all contact with me I still had no idea. Cristóvão seemed distant as well, if I wasn't imagining it; not the avuncular figure I had met the first time Marco and I were estranged. After Laurinda's wicked email to me, he had risked his professional integrity to heal the rift. What had changed?

While there, I called on Joaquim. I wasn't sure exactly why – perhaps guilt, curiosity, or simply the fact that he was now my only tangible link to Marco. Maybe I was just feeling kind. After all that had happened, what did it matter? He was an old man who welcomed visitors and was evidently happy to see me. His English had improved too, through socialising with some of the British retirees who lived in the village.

"You, Marco," he said abruptly in the middle of a conversation about the advantages of Lisbon over London (which he seemed unable to grasp was not where I lived). "Why you not together?"

I was taken unawares. Tears welled, but I fought

them down and replied. "I don't know. That's the way it goes sometimes."

"Life... love... death," he said dramatically, nodding between each word. This old reprobate could be frighteningly aggressive sometimes, but in quiet moments like this, there was a depth to him that I hadn't seen before.

"Your father – my brother," he began. I could see traces of ancient pain shadowing his face.

I nodded. "Álvaro."

"You want see his grave?"

This was completely unexpected.

"Here in *Prazeres*," he went on. "The *cemitério*."

"The cemetery?"

He nodded. "I take you there."

The offer hung in the air. I remembered *Prazeres*, one of those beautiful graveyards where Catholics built little houses to bury their dead. It was right in the middle of the city, and I had walked past it with Marco. He had commented on the architecture of some of the crypts without mentioning that his own family lay there – or so it seemed from what Joaquim was saying – including his guardian, Duarte, and Álvaro, my father.

"Yes," I said. "I would like to see it. But I don't have a car. Could they get us a taxi from here?" Then I added quickly, "I'll pay." There was always a discomfort in my mind that I had inherited so much of his brother's wealth.

"No need," he said triumphantly. "Nuno!"

Within a minute a slim young man appeared from

next door and stepped onto the terrace where we sat sipping *Beirão*. I had heard of the drink during my visits but had never tried it before. Joaquim had insisted, saying it would be good for my health, and I found I quite liked the taste.

"My *motorista!*" Joaquim announced. "Nuno, can you take us to *Prazeres*?"

The boy nodded cheerfully, cleared the table, and started the complicated process of organising Joaquim's transfer to the car, which turned out to be an impressive four-seater saloon with a BMW badge on the front.

"Marco gave you all this?" Because of the language difficulty and what seemed to be a fairly immense gap between our ways of thinking and living, I couldn't find a more subtle way of putting the question. With anyone else it might have seemed rude to ask, but Joaquim had a way of inviting directness, and I was beginning to like that about him.

"Joaquinho, my son!" he said proudly.

As Nuno drove, we sat behind him, and Joaquim began to talk about his family and the past.

"Is years since I go *Prazeres*. The *mausoléu*. Was my mother death last time. Yes. *Setenta* years."

I ran through the Portuguese numbers I knew, and repeated back, "Seven years?"

He shook his head and held up two sets of spread fingers seven times. One hand remained lower than the other; he was unable to raise it by much.

"Seventy years!" I counted. "She died young."

"A boy, I was. It was dark. Everything cold. And an

anjo."

"An angel?" I repeated.

"An angel. With her *cara.*" He raised his good arm and indicated his face.

"An angel with her face?" I wondered if this was an old man's rambling, or something he had misunderstood. Did he believe a supernatural being had appeared at his mother's funeral? Was he talking about a ghost?

"Yes," he said. "An... *estátua.*"

"A statue?"

"*De pedra. Uma estátua de pedra.*"

"A stone statue!"

"With face of my mother. Which mother? I not know. I not remember. One mother she give me to strangers, no speak, she say. Other mother, she die. I never leave, she say, but no difference, Joaquim *abandonado.* Two times, two mothers."

Marco had told me this story, how the little refugee had arrived near the end of the war and Duarte's parents had taken him in. He didn't speak for a whole year, Duarte said, and when he did it was in Portuguese. No-one ever knew what his own language was or where he had come from. They named him 'Joaquim' because it means 'raised by God'.

I found the tale moving and wondered what it must be like to begin life by losing everything. It seemed to me that this double loss of both mothers had merged into one big trauma in Joaquim that had shaped his whole life, and that Álvaro's death and his guilt compounded it. I had never become a mother but felt

I could understand the lengths to which people might go in order to do the best for their children. But what if that best meant sending your child away forever with strangers?

When we reached the cemetery, I walked beside Joaquim, in his motorised chair, until we found the vault that belonged to his family. One day he would join them, and eventually, Marco would too, I supposed.

On the outside was a plaque that listed all those entombed within. Duarte's name was there, freshly etched, and further up, the father I had never known: *Álvaro Tomás Aguiar de Almeida. 1951-1971*. I traced the script with my fingers. The metal was hot under the sun. I sent him a silent, godless prayer.

Then I looked up towards the carvings that arched into the sky. Gazing out into eternity over the tomb was the stone angel. It was not unlike a dozen other effigies in the cemetery, but a grieving boy had once looked at its serene features and seen the face of his dead mother, or one of them, and which one he no longer knew. In a different lifetime, or if fate had been kinder, he might not have grown up to be such a broken man.

"*Minha mamã,*" he said, and turning to me, "My mother". Then without taking his eyes off me, he continued. "Don't waste your life. Go to him. Marco. You together is... good."

I understood what he meant, and that he was searching for the right word but the only one he knew that came close was 'good'. Yes, it had been good. Very good. At least, I had thought so.

"Is *destinado*," he said.

It was a profound moment because I too had once felt as if Marco and I were destined to be together. I had never believed in fate; to me life was a series of random events which we are sometimes miraculously able to coax our way. But that time had been different.

"He doesn't want me, Joaquim," I said bleakly. "I don't know why."

He smiled. It was a cheerful grin and quite inappropriate for this discussion of my tragic life. It made me laugh and I felt better.

"You go with him," he said.

I shook my head.

"When he come to you, you go with him. He say sorry, you say all good."

That was my dream, I thought, but one that would never come true. A year had passed without a word, not even now that I was here in Lisbon. Surely Cristóvão would have told him.

"He say sorry, you say all good," he repeated. "Then he learn to trust again."

I stared past the crypts. There were rows of graves, some decked with fresh flowers. In the far corner, a quiet family stood by an open one, waiting for the person they mourned to be laid under a waiting pile of earth.

"*Promete!*" he insisted.

"You want me to promise? Okay, I promise. If he comes to me, I'll go with him. It will all be good." I said it to make him happy.

The sun had tipped from its zenith towards the

west. Tall shadows of tombs and angels darkened the cobbled walkways. It had been an emotional day, and I felt that my time here at the burial chamber was done. I said a silent goodbye to the father who had never known me, and followed Joaquim back to the car.

"What was he like, Álvaro?" I asked when the palaver of getting him into the back seat was once again accomplished by Nuno. "My father?" I felt a twinge of guilt towards Douglas at using the word, but he would have understood, I knew. He was a man with a big heart.

"*Álvaro, meu irmãozinho. Ele era corajoso. Ele era estúpido. Ele era frágil. Olhos cinzentos como os seus.*"

I took out my phone and made him say it all again to the translation app. The words played back to us in mechanical English tones. "Álvaro, my little brother. He was brave. He was stupid. He was fragile. Grey eyes like yours."

He continued in his imperfect English. "He love your mother. He die for Portugal. He die because of me. I make mistake. I not betray him."

He looked stricken. I reached over and took his hand. I didn't know which version to believe – Duarte's of betrayal, or Joaquim's of tragic error. But whatever his culpability, Joaquim appeared to have been paying the debt for the rest of his life. It must surely be settled by now.

"I know," I said.

He shook his head. "Duarte not know. Duarte never know."

We drove back in silence, each of us alone with our thoughts but somehow together in spirit.

I said goodbye before he got out of the car, and doubted I would ever see him again. I wished I could put this broken family back together, the three brothers, but death doesn't give second chances.

Since learning the truth about my own family history, I had re-read my mother's book and realised that it was not so much a novel as a memoir. I had not previously taken much notice of an inscription on the front page, which read:

"The truth is rarely pure and never simple." – *Oscar Wilde.*

Now, after all I had learned over the past few years, I wondered whether this was a message from mother to daughter, placed there in case the facts about our family surfaced one day, as they now had.

It no longer mattered. All the people involved were gone, and my last connection with them – Marco, my cousin-by-adoption, my lover, the one who had felt like my soulmate (and I was cynical about that again now) – was broken.

When feelings of melancholy got to me during that bleak period, my remedy was to keep busy. I had thought of taking up riding, now I could afford it, and decided to visit the local stables to find out more. But the memory of that Almeida tomb sent me in another direction. A ten-minute car ride saw me walking through a different kind of graveyard, an English one where crumbling, illegible stones mingled with new monuments, freshly adorned with flowers.

Two sets of ashes lay here, with a plaque above: *Douglas Matthews 1942-2011; Elena Matthews 1952-2016.*

Losing Douglas had changed both of us. I found that for the whole of the following year I lost all appetite for work or pleasure. Eventually, I was somehow able to knit the grief into my being in a way that allowed me to move on; that was when I had re-evaluated my life, left my job, and started my business.

But for my mother the blow seemed mortal. Although I visited regularly, for at that time I was living in London, her spirit seemed to have died along with her husband. The approaching loss of her home dragged her down. She was afraid. She took to drinking in the morning, not getting drunk, ever, but just quietly tippling through the day. It was like Valium to her, I thought at the time, and who was to say that this was any worse?

What really concerned me was that on car journeys she would carry wine in her bag to sip as she drove. I tried to persuade her to give up this habit, but it did no good. One day when she was out alone, her car somehow left the road and careered down a steep verge, somersaulting as it fell. The cause of death was identified as a stroke, but no-one could say whether that was the trigger or the result of the crash.

Doesn't everything die at last, and too soon? The words of the poem came to me. Here lay two people who had lived their wild and precious lives to the utmost, fighting for their dreams and taking failure in their stride. Yet, despite my business and charity work, my own existence seemed to stretch ahead of me, empty and without direction.

I remembered the sense of inevitability I had felt when Marco and I first fell in love. How could I have been so wrong about something that felt so right? What had I said or done that changed everything? What was it in me that was not enough for him, and where was I lacking?

I had spent too many hours tormenting myself like this. I turned and walked purposefully back through the grass, determined not to waste another day wallowing in self-recrimination.

I looked towards my car and stopped. There was a man standing beside it and for a moment I thought it was Marco. I cursed myself again. I was seeing him everywhere: in the city, on a train, in the turn of a head or a half-seen profile. It would have to stop. I must get over him.

During our last hours together, we had started to plan a big party to celebrate the fiftieth anniversary of the Carnation Revolution two years hence. He was probably still organising it without me, and perhaps with a new lover. I had resolved to be on a luxury cruise at the other side of the world when it happened, as far away from Lisbon as I could get.

As I neared the car I looked again. The man was still there. Surely it was Marco.

I was conscious of the August sun warming my back. The amber in his eyes matched the summer tan on his skin. I felt a little spark of joy.

He stood with his hands clasped in front of him and then opened them out as I reached him.

"I'm sorry," was the first thing he said.

EPILOGUE

2025

Reader, they married.

Dividing their time between Portugal and England, Marco continued his architectural practice and Helen devoted herself entirely to charity work with prisons.

Elena's book 'Lisbon Flowered' was reissued to coincide with the fiftieth anniversary celebrations of the Carnation Revolution in April 2024. Marco and Helen gave a big party in honour of 'Celeste of the Carnations'. She attended it in person before her death later that year.

Luís, now a successful lawyer, and Gabriela, a grandmother of nine, made contact and were able to answer most of Helen's remaining questions about her mother and Álvaro de Almeida.

Lázaro Gomes hanged himself in Caxias prison in 1987.

Téo and Roberto were the first gay couple to marry in Portugal, at the age of fifty-eight, as soon as such unions became legal. They have enjoyed long careers as a psychiatrist and surgeon respectively.

In 2027, Elena's book will be remade as a primetime television series that will catapult her novel *Lisbon Flowered* into the bestseller list.

In 2040 Helen and Marco will both retire to the

yellow-walled villa in Sintra, to spend their days reading, writing, swimming in the turquoise pool, and riding in the flower-speckled hills. They will never attempt to shoot wild boar. Helen will give up the use of her house in Medmenham to a prison charity for their rehabilitation programmes. Her jacaranda will never flower again, but the one in Sintra will blossom without fail every year.

Laurinda and Lourenço will marry and later divorce after having two children together. They will remain friends for life. Helen and Marco will be godparents to their son and daughter. Laurinda will become a lawyer to celebrities, and Lourenço a trader in commodities. He will never relapse into crime but will develop a reputation for sharp-edged business practices.

After a few years of luxury living in his retirement village, Joaquim will be laid to rest in the family crypt, guarded by the stone angel with the face of his mother. His funeral will be attended by Helen, Marco, Laurinda, Lourenço, Cristóvão Teixeira do Nascimento, and Filipe the bar-owner, who once saved his life.

~ The End ~

HISTORICAL AFTERWORD
Facts

The Carnation Revolution (*Revolução dos Cravos*) took place as described on 25 April 1974. It is widely celebrated in Portugal today. Almost every town and village has a *Rua 25 de Abril* (25 April Street) in its honour.

The authoritarian regime known as the *Estado Novo* was founded by *António de Oliveira Salazar* in 1933. It was one of the longest-standing dictatorships in Europe. In 1968, *Marcelo Caetano* succeeded *Salazar* and maintained the autocracy until ousted by the 1974 coup.

Celeste Martins Caeiro (Celeste dos Cravos) was a real woman who participated in the events of the revolution as described. Her simple gesture of giving a soldier a carnation is regarded as pivotal to its bloodless outcome. She took part in the fiftieth anniversary celebrations in Lisbon, in 2024, before her death at the age of ninety-one later that year.

The Three Marias (As Três Marias) – *Maria Isabel Barreno, Maria Teresa Horta,* and *Maria Velho da Costa* – were prominent feminist writers and activists. Their book, *New Portuguese Letters*, challenged censorship and patriarchy and led to their imprisonment in a men's jail. They are regarded as icons of the Portuguese feminist and democratic movements. Many cafés, restaurants, and public spaces in Portugal today bear the name *"3 Marias"* in their honour.

The *Aljube Museum of Resistance and Freedom* is housed in a former political prison in Lisbon used by the *Estado Novo* regime, including the PIDE (secret police). Today, it serves as a memorial to those who resisted the dictatorship. I took some artistic licence in naming it as the place where Álvaro was incarcerated. It was in fact closed as a prison in 1965, because of complaints from the local people about the screams of those being tortured within. The inmates were moved to *Caxias*, where the fictional Luís was imprisoned.

The scene of Luís's release was inspired by existing film footage of the liberation of all the *Estado Novo's* political prisoners from *Caxias* in 1974.

The resistance that ultimately brought down the dictatorship arose from a coalition of students, workers, communists, and soldiers. While the rest of the Western world was granting independence to colonies during that period, the *Estado Novo* in Portugal refused to let go of its holdings in Africa. Conscription was sending young men to injury or death. The coup was staged by the *Armed Forces Movement (MFA),* the *Movimento das Forças Armadas,* formed from the lower ranks of the army, and led by non-commissioned officers.

Fiction

The attack on the law school in *Coimbra* is fictional but draws on real accounts of state violence against student protestors.

All the other characters and events portrayed in this novel are entirely fictional. Any resemblance to actual persons, living or dead, is purely coincidental.

A NOTE FROM THE AUTHOR

If you enjoyed this book, I'd be really grateful if you could take just one minute to share a quick review online on Amazon, Goodreads, or similar online platforms. Your feedback will help other readers to discover this book.

Thank you,

C. A. Wilson.

FOR READING CLUBS AND BOOK CLUBS

If you've read Carnations in Lisbon with a group, or are planning to, a Book Club Guide is available including discussion questions, character notes, and a historical timeline.

You can request a copy via this email address:

bookclubs@bishambooks.com

or download it from the website:

www.bishambooks.com/bookclubs

Printed in Dunstable, United Kingdom